Cover Design: Megan Parker-Squiers @ EmCat Designs
Editing by: PWA & IDIM Editorial
Shander, H.M., 1975—Serving Up Devotion

To my family and friends
Who I am hopelessly devoted to —
Thanks for being you.

Table of Contents

—Chapter One

I slammed my empty tray on the table beside the computer a little louder than I'd intended. Customers didn't notice, but it sure made my manager startle. "When are you getting new help, Niall?"

He looked me over as I waited expectantly for answer I knew I wouldn't get. At least not one I wanted to hear.

Niall looked like crap. He slumped more than usual, and his eyes wore tired like a neon sign. He wasn't used to waiting tables, but for the last few weeks we'd been short staffed, and he came out onto the floor to help us out. Well, good for him. If he'd hired staff by now, I wouldn't be so irritable and overworked, and he could go back to doing whatever it was I kept pulling him away from.

I tapped my foot, and Niall looked back to the screen.

"Damn, that supper rush was crazy. I forgot how demanding being on the front end was, especially trying to keep the floor running smoothly. I'll punch in L7's order, and you can finish it up for me." When I didn't move, his shoulders rolled inward, followed by a sigh. "I'm sorry, but the applications just aren't coming in."

"Any help is better than no help, right? I can't keep going

1

on like this." I stuck the notepad into my apron and marched around the wall that separated the front end from the tiny server station, calling over my shoulder. "As of next week, I'm back to working a max of six shifts a week. Double shifts on the weekend are a no-go."

"Evanora, we discussed this already." Like a gust of wind, he followed me into the station and stopped in front of the pop machine.

"No, you said, and I disagreed. There was no discussion. But I'm telling you, Niall, as of Monday, I'm back to working a regular schedule. Either that, or you start paying me double time and a half." With that kind of money, I'd be tempted to work more, but I knew better. "I have no issues with taking my employment elsewhere."

Niall stepped exceeding close to me. "Is that an ultimatum?"

I snorted as he called my bluff. It was Edmonton, in the middle of a recession. Jobs were scarce.

"Only if you don't hire help. You won't work me to the bone. I refuse."

"And what about Michael?"

I froze in my tracks. The whole point of working my ass off was because of Michael, well, more for him. He deserved a home that worked with his disabilities, not against it, and those never came cheap. Nor did his fabulous caregiver who spent more time with him lately than I was.

I softened my tone but firmed my words. "He'll be just fine regardless of where I work. Him I'll go the extra mile for, but not you, Niall. Not anymore."

Filling three glasses with Heineken beer, I stormed by.

However, Niall wasn't done with me yet. It sucked having a former boyfriend as your boss even though it had been a long time since we were together. Although he tried, and it probably pained him, he kept the personal stuff out of the restaurant, better than I was. But not always.

He cornered me and Joy as she danced her way into the station. Seriously the girl leaked happiness out of her with every step and I for one, tried to avoid walking through it. No one should be that happy, all the time. It was weird. That's why her nametag read Joy.

"Joy, can you hold the fort down for a few minutes, I need to speak to Evanora in my office."

"Sure thing," she said, her voice pitching in a childlike voice. "Anything I need to take care of?"

I rolled my eyes. "Nope. I'll drop this off. Otherwise, I'm just waiting on two steak bowls, but I won't be that long, will I, Niall?"

He gave me a compassionate half-smile which always had the power to defuse my anger, along with a gentle pat on the shoulder. "Not really."

A quick turn, and he headed to the office at the back of the restaurant, while I dropped off the drinks.

The building Westside occupied was built in the 1970s as an old pizza joint, complete with a takeout area. Aside from the spacious dining area, the rest of the interior was tightly squeezed together, but it was an efficient layout. Our server station was smaller than the average sized apartment kitchen, but held a pop machine, a coffee machine, two taps of draft, a small beer fridge that even held two varieties of cheesecake we offered as dessert, and a small sink. The shelving space around it was packed with supplies.

As I walked through the server station, where I dropped off my tray, I passed the cash register, a definite relic from the 80s, and the takeout area, nestled off to the side of the main entrance. A stainless-steel half wall on my left divided the cash area from the kitchen where the cooks whipped up the dishes we'd become famous for—our steak bowls. And the aromatic spices floating in the air smelled delicious.

"What's up?" I folded my arms across my chest. As much as I didn't like being on the floor, I didn't like wasting my time in limbo either.

I stood at the door of the office, or a closet if you really wanted to know. Designed as an after thought because the office door opened out. There was barely room for an office chair, and the built-in desk was just big enough for a computer, a few file stands, and a cup of coffee with a ring around the inside.

He rifled through a file on the desk and handed me a stack of papers, as he cleared his throat. "Take a look and tell me if any seem suitable to you."

The lone office chair creaked as he leaned back into it, putting his left ankle atop his right knee.

I hopped onto the desk as there wasn't another chair and crossed my legs. My skirt shifted up a little, but whatever. I was no longer his for the taking, and he could stare all he wanted. It didn't bother me. "Why are you showing me these?"

"You're the senior server. I figured you'd maybe be able to help me out."

"What does Meghan say?"

Meghan was the daytime manager and owner, bitchier than me, and not someone I got along with. A huge reason I never worked the day shift.

"She said none will work."

I raised an eyebrow and yanked the file. There wasn't much I enjoyed doing more than proving people wrong.

Inside were seven applications, and none listed serving in their previous experience. Each of them as green as the last hire had been, although I hated to admit it, Jade worked out okay. Minor

4

spillage and tray dumping, but that was expected. One application caught my eye though, and I pulled it free of the stack.

Pushing it into Niall's hands, I said, "He could work."

He read over the application. "He's got no restaurant experience."

"A minor detail. He's trainable and he's willing to work evenings and weekends." I closed the file and handed it to him. "A huge plus, since that's where we're short staffed."

Daytime shifts were easy to fill, no shortages there. But no one wanted to work late during the week and on the weekends. Except for the romantic duo. Suddenly, I started to miss Jasper and Jade being around.

"Fine. Interview him with me," he said as a plea with hope in his voice. Niall put both his feet on the floor and scooted his chair closer.

"Why? I'm no manager."

"Because someday you're going to be."

I laughed softly in his face and shook my head. "Not here, I won't."

"Please. I trust your judgement."

"Do you really? That's a first." Even I recoiled as my snark flew out. Well, I didn't mean it like *that*, but it was too late to take it back.

Niall's blue-green eyes were already wide, the hurt shining through painfully stabbed what bit of compassion I had left for the guy.

The Adam's Apple bobbed up and down in his throat and he rose, bridging the distance between us, which was already constricting and made me feel like I was being smothered. Way too close for my preference. "You're painfully honest. I think we need the applicants to know what they're getting into."

"So, you want me to drive them away? Because telling them

like it is will not work out to Westside's benefit, I can tell you that."

"I need your help."

"Then you're a shittier manager than I expected."

He sighed; a big, heavy weight of the world on his shoulders sigh. "Meghan has threatened to become night manager."

Deep down, something in my gut twisted and churned. Her joining the night squad would be a disaster of epic proportions. The limited amount of fun the staff enjoyed now would all be gone. She was a drill sergeant of the highest order. If she switched to nights, I may as well turn in my apron. No way was I going to work under her, and there weren't enough dayside tips to keep it interesting. Niall, I could easily handle. Her? Nightmare.

I tugged down the hem of my skirt but kept my focus on him. "Tomorrow night, after the rush. Joy can hold the floor for a few minutes."

"Thank you, I'll set up the interview."

"Anything else I can do for you?"

He rose and closed the door, trapping me. "Audrina…" He switched from manager to former boyfriend in a heartbeat. Using my real name at work was a no-no. "I know you're overworked, and the shortage is hard on all of us, but something else is bothering you. You're not usually this short."

I cocked an eyebrow.

His hand twitched, as if he wanted to comfort me, even though I wasn't a touchy-feely person. "Is everything okay with Michael?"

I jumped off the desk and fanned myself with the heavy, green polo we were forced to wear. "We're going to be fine." A lump suddenly formed in the back of my throat. "We have to be."

Like a flame blown out, so was my anger. Michael was my heart and soul, and there was nothing I wouldn't do for him. Niall either.

He grabbed my wrist gently as I headed for the kitchen. "Tell me what I can do to help."

My expression hardened and my focus drifted to the front of the restaurant. "I need a miracle. Do you have any of those?"

Niall fell back into his chair. "Don't I wish."

Chapter Two

*J*t was a solid hour before I made it home as my last table camped too long. It never failed—when you want to go home, something always prevented it. Exhausted, I parked in the back lot of my house, and stared at the freaking blinds left wide open into the kitchen. I could see clearly inside, and this was not the kind of neighbourhood I wanted to showcase my life to, not even with the roaming police cars that alluded to false sense of safety. If I've said it once, I've said it a million times - once the sun sets, the blinds close. Geezus, it wasn't rocket science.

Cracking my neck and shaking out my limbs, I breathed out work and inhaled home. My sanctuary. My peace.

My place was an older style home in a rundown part of the city; a place where sidewalk cracks were the norm, instead of the exception, and cost less to attempt a fill rather than replace. The trees lining the road were old and ancient. Their giant limbs covered the narrow roadway and provided an idyllic look — if you looked past the weedy, unkempt lawn beside my house, and ignored the dilapidated house facing mine. However, once you stepped onto my front porch and through the door, you'd never know it was in the ghetto.

The house came with hardwood flooring throughout the main level, and wall to wall carpet in the basement which was fine as it took away some of the chill. The walls on the main floor had a light taupe colour brushed across them, and the south-facing windows were huge, making the tiny space bright and airy. The bungalow's main floor contained the living room, the kitchen, a full bathroom and two tiny bedrooms barely big enough for a bed and dresser.

But the best part of coming home were the voices I heard as I walked up the back stairs into my kitchen, twisting the blinds closed as I went. Two voices chatted in the living room, and I leaned against the wall separating the back of the fridge from the living room, listening for a moment.

"My pick. I've had enough Ninja Warrior," the short brunette said, and pinched the remote out of Michael's hand.

"No, m-m-more." His speech slurred a bit, but nothing I couldn't understand.

It would never get better, nor crisper. Sadly, it was also an indicator of the pain he was in. The more the slur, the higher the pain. The more the stutter, the more tired he was.

I silently stood there watching my brother and his caregiver play and have fun. Such a change from a few months ago when I pulled him out of the hell-hole home he was in. The aides there abused him, mentally and physically, and to a small degree, financially as well. My mother never saw it though and as much as I begged her daily to move him, she never did. When she passed away seven months ago, the best thing about that whole situation was becoming Michael's legal guardian.

I got him the hell out of *Billingsgate Manor* and moved him into the empty bedroom in my house. It took a bit of time, but he lightened up and became the boy with the happy smile and positive outlook on life. Something I envied and tried to be in his presence.

9

"H-hey, look." He pointed in my direction.

"Hey, Michael, Melody." I padded around the couch and took the oversized chair in front of them.

"She w-w-won't let me w-w-watch anymore N-N-Ninja W-W-Warrior."

"Because you're tired. It's nearly ten."

"I w-w-wanted you t-t-to t-t-tuck m-m-me in."

His hair was dishevelled, the dark brown waves standing out. Michael reminded me of Flint Lockwood from *Cloudy with a Chance of Meatballs*, but he only had a tenth of the IQ. A ten-year-old boy trapped in the body of a twenty-two-year-old man.

"Are your teeth brushed?"

He shook his head.

"Say goodnight to Melody and brush your teeth." I smiled at the goofy grin plastered on his face. "I'll be there in five minutes."

He pushed himself to a stand, taking close to a minute to do so. I wanted to jump up and help him, not because I was impatient, but for the pinched expression he held. Melody, bless her heart, had told me to only help if he asked for it, or truly needed it, or was in any danger. He was in none of those situations, so I sat helplessly and waited. Standing on his own two feet, he walked to the bathroom, slapping his bare feet against the hardwood as he limped his awkward gait across the floor.

The door clicked close.

"How was he tonight?" A standard question to ask. If anything had arisen, she would've texted me at some point, so nothing major had occurred. Still, as the big sister, and mother figure, I needed to know.

"Good. A little stiff in the joints, but I think the approaching weather change is the catalyst for that." She was a perky little thing, but oh so good to Michael.

From the very first time I met her, I knew she had to be

Michael's aide. Kind and compassionate, I never had a reason to worry when she was around.

I removed my Evanora nametag from my shirt and tossed it onto the side table.

Melody laughed as it skittered onto the floor. She bent over and quickly picked it up. "I always find it amusing how they call you Evanora at work."

I countered her laugh with one of my own. "You should see me there, I'm a complete witch. If they're going to give me that name, I may as well live up the reputation."

A few years back, a safety issue arose with the use of our real names on the bills, and someone suggested fake names based on personality. When it came to mine, I joked about being a witch but hated the name Glenda as I wasn't pure and good, so some dingbat suggested Evanora, the wicked witch of the east. It stuck.

"I hardly believe you're that bad, Audrina, when you're so sweet with Michael."

"Thanks. I try to keep work and home very separated."

"Oh, you should check out the book."

She retrieved a logbook from the table and tossed it in my direction. It had been her idea to give me a run down of what they did during their time together. I enjoyed the peek into how he spent his evenings while I worked my ass off. Inside was a very detailed running list of the timing and dosage of his medications, and any rare trips they made into the backyard.

"You took him outside?" I was stunned as I hadn't seen an entry for that in days. It caused a smile to bubble up out of me.

"Yeah, it took a while to descend the front stairs, but he wanted out. Wanted to see the woodpecker he heard in the tree up close."

"That's great."

But my heart stung a little. I'd tried earlier to encourage

some fresh air, but he said no, and I didn't push it. It took way too long to get in and out of the house, and I always worried about him falling and getting hurt. My house was older, with tight narrow stairwells and most certainly not adequate for someone with disabilities. It was the main reason I worked myself to the bone, so I could pay for a new deck with a ramp.

"Should be easier to get in and out soon. The new carpenter's supposed to start around nine tomorrow."

My original guy cancelled late last month, and after I gave him a piece of my mind, he refused to answer my calls. Dammit. I did more research on my number two selection and interviewed Chad, who allegedly should arrive by nine. I rolled my eyes and hedged my bets. Trade workers were never punctual in my experience, yet if you were one day late in paying, they threatened to take you to small claims court. The lunacy was ridiculous.

Melody stood and stretched out her petite framed body. Shorter than Michael by a full head, nevertheless she was a powerhouse, her strength hidden under her clothes. Someone better and more qualified than a babysitter. Someone who could help him with any kind of issue. Someone who could love him better on his worst day than our mother ever did on his best.

"Alright, I'm going. I'll be back at four tomorrow." She ran her hands through her short hair.

"That would be great, thanks."

She walked over to the bathroom and rapped her knuckles against the door. "Night, Mikey."

"N-N-Night, M-M-Mel."

I tucked Michael into bed and rubbed my fingers over his forehead in slow soothing ovals. My knees creaked and groaned from kneeling beside him on the floor, but I wasn't ready to leave. Instead, I watched as sleep overtook my little brother in a matter of minutes. The sweet relaxation wrapped him like a blanket.

Confident Mr. Sandman was sprinkling sweet dreams over him, I kissed his forehead and ventured the ten steps into my own closet-sized bedroom.

I sat on my bed and opened the white envelope containing my nightly tip out. It had been a good night, and for a family place like Westside the tips were decent. Sure, I wasn't making the tips like I could at a fancier place, but I was reasonably content with my earnings.

Hidden in the wall, behind a picture, was my wall safe. Opening it, I added today's cash to the stack nestled deep inside. Things like making a ramp off the front porch didn't come cheap, and the tip money helped greatly. There was no way I was dipping into Michael's government cheques like mother had; those meagre amounts aided in paying for Melody, who he needed while I worked. Besides, I preferred cash over credit cards and certainly over cheques. Some people took forever to deposit those and waiting... grr.

As a bonus, in my negotiations with contractors, paying cash netted a small discount. It was win-win for us both. He was paid ASAP, and I didn't have a bill hanging over my head. It had taken me a few months of saving every tip dollar, but it was so worth it. Michael was worth it, and he deserved a home he could function in and out of. Locking the safe, I twisted the dial and closed the picture back over it.

The large 16x20 picture looked right at home; the bright greens and tree bark browns matched my bedding. It was one of my favourite pictures in the whole world, and I adored the story within the frame. We were innocent back then, our youthfulness stretched out before us; I was eight and he was just four. In search of fairies and ghosts, we left the safety of our back yard with our digital camera in hand. We were going to capture one and prove to the world the existence of all things magical. How he giggled as he tromped through chest-high wild grass, hunting and whispering and begging the green fairy to show herself. It was so sweet, I took his picture.

Later when I showed our mother, she claimed the picture as her own, to show off to her friends that she was a good mother, because look, she went fairy hunting in the forest with her children, see? She lied to her friends to make herself look better, but I knew the truth. Despite my begging, she denied me a copy and it was only years later when we moved Michael into Billingsgate Manor that I found the camera card and made myself a giant copy. Housed in a simple Ikea black frame, it reminded me of everything he still was, and how the simple pleasures in life are there if you truly believed.

Chapter Three

The fresh scent of August rain as it wafted in through the three-inch opening of the bedroom window, was a perfect way to rise. A cut-up broom stick prevented it from being all the way open. I loved fresh air, but not at the expense of safety. According to the neighbourhood watch page, three nights ago a neighbour's house two streets over was broken into. Not something I wanted to go through.

I tiptoed into Michael's room to check on him. Sound asleep and breathing fine. Thank goodness.

Once not long ago when Michael came to live with me, I was heading to bed when I heard this god-awful gasp of air, almost like he was holding his breath. I freaked out and rushed my dozy brother into the emergency room. The ER doctor confirmed he was okay, said he may have sleep apnea, and to follow up with his doctor. Of course, I did, but without further testing, he wouldn't deny nor confirm so I kept a tight watch over him. Sometimes, I'd even check on him in the middle of the night if I was up for a bathroom break or a sip of water. But there hadn't been too many issues, and his doctor said as his disease progressed, any apnea that showed itself will be the least of his worries.

Still, I checked.

Michael was sprawled over his covers, a trickle of drool hanging off his mouth. His chest rose and fell like normal, but otherwise, he was sound asleep. No hand twitches and no fluttering of his eyelids, it was like he didn't notice I was there.

Michael should be asleep for another hour or so, which meant I had time for a quick run. Time to shake out the energy and let go of the stress from Westside, and the staffing problems. When I ran, it was just for me. And I only went out when he was still fast asleep.

I pushed myself harder than normal, and forty-five minutes later, rounded the far end of the block drenched in a heavy sweat. My cheeks were hot, and loose hair strands plastered themselves to my forehead. But I felt good, dammit, really good. I slowed my pace to a brisk walk and headed home.

As I approached, a clean navy-blue truck with white and yellow lettering reading *Lewandowski Construction* was parked in front of my house.

Shit, he's early.

Giving my face a wipe with the sleeve of my hoodie, I ran the length of sidewalk to where a man stood in blue jeans and a white tee, knocking on my door.

"Don't! He's still sleeping," I snapped and waved my hands frantically as I bolted up the seven steps.

He turned around, and a voice deep and throaty spoke. "Are you Audrina?"

I nodded, but really, it took all my will power to keep a neutral, unimpressed exterior. The guy was way better looking than what I remembered from the social media I'd creeped. And I'd creeped a lot. But my already racing heart from my run pounded a little more when I took a quick glance at his sun-kissed, freshly shaved face.

16

What was I doing?! I mean, I can look right? But the way my cheeks were burning, I was glad I'd pushed myself during that run to cover the blushing I hoped wasn't evident.

I was supposed to be mad. He could've woken up Michael, who needed his rest. I was about to snap further when he extended his hand.

"Chad Lewandowski. I thought I'd been stood up." His strong grip was rough and calloused yet sent a shot of electricity through me.

For the briefest of moments, I imagined how his hands would feel running over my skin... but I trampled the thought out. There was no time for any kind of romantic encounters. Everything was about Michael right now. I blinked hard and refocused. I didn't need a man. I didn't need the distraction. He's here to build me a ramp, even though he was sizing me up as well and that was where it was going to end.

I fought the urge to unwrap the hoodie tied around my waist and pull it back on. My running outfit was pretty minimal; a pair of capri-length leggings and a sports bra that was none too sexy, even though it was low-cut. Feeling super self-conscious as a bead a wet dripped off my forehead, I did unwrap my hoodie and held it against my body, using the sleeve to wipe dry my face.

My will was stronger than some hunk with a hammer. I cleared my throat and looked at my phone I'd retrieved from the armband and glanced at the time to divert myself from staring at him further. Handsome or not, there was such a thing as punctuality and this guy didn't have it.

"It's barely eight-thirty." I showed him for good measure. "You're supposed to be here at nine."

"I know what time it is. I like to be early. Besides, it's going to be a scorcher today, and I'd like to get a head start if that's okay with you." Those light blue eyes pierced my soul with his honesty.

17

It made my knees a little weak.

I straightened up and pushed back my shoulders. "Yeah, well, maybe you should have mentioned you have a punctuality problem. There was nothing on your ad, Linkedin, Facebook or Twitter pages to indicate that."

He stepped back, a smug smile inching from the corners of his lips. "Wow, you're pretty thorough."

"Damn right. I also read all your reviews."

And of every review on every page or hit I found only two mentioned how he'd been early, but not thirty minutes kind of early.

He held his breath.

I shrugged it off. Better to be early I suppose than ridiculously late. "But your reviews were great, that's why I contacted you."

Based on the scrutiny I was under, which really should've been the other way around, he didn't speak for a breath or two. Finally, his lips moved again, kindness laced into his words. "So, is it okay if we get started?"

"That's fine."

I stood there like a dumbass, words escaping me. It always threw me when someone was nice to me as I kept waiting for the other shoe to fall. Here this guy I was about to hire showed up early to a job, and I was biting his head off. Yeah, bitch would be a good word to describe me I suppose.

"Actually, can you give me a minute? I just need to check on my brother." I pointed toward the inside of the house.

"Yeah, sure, go ahead." He shifted the metal case in his hand.

Relief blanketed me as I closed the front door and peeked my head into Michael's room. His breathing pattern had changed as if he were starting to wake up, but since he hadn't blinked or twitched with my steps on the floor, he was still out.

18

I pulled the hoodie on and went back to the front door.

Chad pulled his gaze up from his grey clipboard and shook his head. "I was thinking about the design you emailed me." He opened the book and pointed to the picture I had roughly sketched out and scanned over. "Now, I can do this exactly like what you've envisioned, and it would come under the budget you've requested. Or..." The page flipped. "I can do something like this, and I would make it work for your price."

The way my front porch was designed, the stairs came right out in the middle of the deck, ten feet off the front door. Based on the research, and the info the original contractor told me, putting a ramp from there at the proper incline would mean it extended over my property line and onto the edge of the city sidewalk. City planners would have a field day and have me tear it down, but I wasn't sure what else to do. Michael needed a ramp, and the incline was quite specific, especially if he ever needed a wheelchair.

Chad's idea was to close off the stairs and have the ramp criss-cross the front of the house, with the stairs at the far end. His drawing looked beautiful. And expensive.

I tapped the design. "I'm pretty sure that won't fall within my budget."

"It would be close."

"I don't do close. I do exact."

I had earmarked a few thousand for this project, and even with the first contractor bailing, I'd continued to save up more, for any surprise incidentals. However, I wasn't thrilled I may need more over and above what contractor A had quoted.

Chad shifted on his feet, the front porch creaking with each movement. A cock of his head and he paced the length of the deck. "How old did you say this porch was?"

I thought back to the email I'd sent him and our one phone call. "I didn't."

"How old is the house?"

My hand planted itself on my hip as I shifted on my feet. "Gosh, I can't remember specifically. Maybe seventy-five years old? This is a very old neighbourhood."

I'd bought it just before the housing market took off and therefore, got a helluva deal on it. The houses currently being listed were easily going for twice what I paid and were being bulldozed to make a new one. It was some kind of neighbourhood revitalization project.

He rocked back and forth. "Well, I doubt the deck is that old, but it's very creaky."

"It adds character."

"Not if it's so old the beams are rotten."

Well, shit. Last thing I needed, or Michael for that matter, was to have it break while someone walked across it.

"You going to be here a while?" he asked and set his clipboard down on the edge of the railing.

"Yeah?" I drawled out my response.

"I'd like to do some sleuthing under the deck before I go ahead with any plans. If there's rotting beams, your whole idea could be for naught."

Fabulous. "Fine. I'll leave the door open. Just holler when you're ready." When I was through the door, I latched the screen door and left the inside door ajar.

A soft grunt came out of Michael's room, so I headed in to investigate. He sat on the edge of his bed, feet on the floor but it was the pained expression capturing my interest.

"You okay?" I stepped closer, the smell of sweat smacking me in the face.

"I c-c-can't stand up."

"Would you like some help?"

His grown-up features morphed into childlike ones, and he

sighed, slumping further as he inhaled sharply. "P-p-p-lease."

My arms wrapped around his thinning torso. I was afraid to squeeze too hard and crack a rib or something. "On three."

There was little strength in his grip around my neck. My heart broke a little in how fast he weakened. The last time I'd helped him up there had been more assistance on his part.

"One. Two. Three." I hoisted him up easily enough but tried to go slowly so his joints wouldn't snap with the sudden shift. Until I felt he could steady himself, I wasn't letting go.

He nuzzled his nose against my neck, and a soft sob touched my ears. "I s-s-scared."

My grip around his torso tightened as I knew what he referred to. The last doctor's appointment had been less than promising, but I wanted to play dumb. "I promise I'll never let you go."

He cried more. A hot tear fell off his cheek and rolled down my neck.

My hand ran over the back of his head in a gentle motion. "What's troubling you, baby bird?"

"I h-h-hurt s-s-s-so m-m-m-much."

"Okay." Well, damn. For him to actually vocalize his pain meant it was pretty severe. However, I could handle it - pain management was within my control. "Let me help you into the living room, and I'll get your meds, okay?"

He pulled back a little and looked into my eyes. His mossy green irises were brighter because of his tears. I've never understood how they changed so much with crying.

"K-k-kay."

Letting him use his own power, but never removing my arms from around him, I allowed him to lead us into the living room. He got himself settled with the full array of couch cushions surrounding him.

After I gave him his cocktail of pills, I prepared a tray for him, complete with a good protein-based meal. I set up the tv tray, so he could pick as he wanted. As much as I would've constantly prodded him to eat, his doctor advised against it, as we never knew until it was too late if it would make him sick. And when your joints are already stiff and sore, the jerking motions from vomiting never helped.

Still, I loaded up a fork and raised it to his lips. "Want a bite?"

He shook his head no and closed his eyes.

My heart ached. Today was going to be a bad day as it so rarely improved when he woke up feeling like he did. I gave his knee a rub, the bones prominent against my skin.

My little brother, four years younger than me, shuddered and winced, a lone tear escaping out his left eye. I wiped it away being careful to not apply too much pressure. Sometimes being touched too much sent him into sensory overload, and when he's already in pain...

A knock on the screen door, and I shot my gaze over there. Chad, whom I'd long forgotten about, stood on the other side.

I focused back on Michael. "You be okay for a minute while I talk to the carpenter?"

His lips vibrated a yes.

Rising, I walked over to the door, furtively checking on him as I moved away. I unlatched the screen door and stepped onto the front porch. "Yes?"

"I did some checking underneath." He grabbed the clipboard off the ledge. "It's not good. A lot of the beams are rotten."

"Well, fuck!" I tore my gaze away from Chad to Michael.

It was rare I let a swear word out in his presence. He seemed to ignore it. I turned back to Chad, who wore a sympathetic smile.

"I was hoping I'd have better news too."

"Yeah, you and me both." I stared into the distance wondering what else could go wrong today. It wasn't even nine-thirty and my day was off to a terrible start.

"Now..." He opened the clipboard and referenced the drawing he'd made originally. "If I were to go ahead with this, it would change your cost."

"No shit." I glanced up into his eyes.

They were kind and calm, and genuinely sorry for the news he was giving me. It bit off part of the edginess I felt since I knew it wasn't his fault the beams deteriorated.

"They should be replaced, and that's my professional spiel. You can get a second opinion, which I strongly encourage you to do, and we can move forward after that." He closed the clipboard and dropped it onto the ledge.

"And if I were to say screw it, just go with what I wanted?"

He shuffled his feet. "As much as I'd like the money, I'd have to walk away. I couldn't do it knowing it would probably wreck completely by next summer if not before, and all the money you'd put into it would be for naught."

A whimper drew my attention back into the living room, and I stared in through the screen, cupping my hands around the side of my cheeks and eyes. Michael hadn't moved.

Opening the screen door, I stuck my head in. "You okay?" When he nodded, I looked back at Chad. "And a second opinion would take what? A good couple of weeks at least before I'd get another estimate."

"I honestly couldn't tell you. I can give you a list of others I'd recommend, but I can't say what their schedules are like."

"Damn, I wanted this done like last month."

We're already behind the schedule I'd planned for this – this was supposed to be finished in July. A second opinion at this stage would push a completion date well into September. I leaned against the frame of the door and surveyed the floor, a shudder rippling through me at the thought of someone falling or getting hurt because of rotten foundation.

"And if I went ahead and told you to just fix it properly? What would the cost be, and how long extra would that take?"

He reached for the clipboard again and opened it. Lips in dire need of lip balm mumbled as he went over the figures he'd written down. "On the high end, I'd say an increase of 50%, but would likely be in the twenty-five to thirty range."

I struggled to hold back my gasp. Fifty percent was a huge increase, but with the first contractor's bail out and the subsequent delay in getting Chad here, I was close to making up that difference. But still, it was a lot of money. Damn rotten beams.

Safety first though. And as the numbers swirled in my head, it *could* work. Worse case scenario, it meant I'd have to put off the weekend getaway I'd hoped to take with Michael in October – a surprise birthday present for him. I'd maybe even have to continue with the double shifts. Niall would be thrilled about that, even if I wasn't.

I glanced into the living room.

Michael had tipped to the side.

"Give me a sec," I said to Chad as I bolted inside.

The laboured breaths flew in and out of Michael, his chest rising and falling. My panic subsided a bit, and I lifted his legs onto the couch, moving slow enough to make my own back ache with the gradual pace. I ran my fingers through his hair, the heat seeping into mine. I didn't like the heat rolling off him. Content that he was comfortable, as least as comfortable as he appeared, I moved back to the front porch.

"Okay," I said, regaining my composure and throwing my shoulders back.

Michael needed this, needed to be able to be free to move outside and not have the hazards of the stairs. This should've been done when he moved in, but I hadn't any money set aside for incidentals like this. The medical bills pretty much ate that all up. I nodded at Chad, but words failed to come from me.

His arms hung by his side and he shifted his weight to his left foot. "I'm sorry, I don't know what your head bobbing means."

"Fix it. Fix it properly. Whatever it takes to make it sturdy and safe." I mentally tallied the cash sitting locked in my safe. There should be enough. "I can pay you what you had originally quoted me at right now, but I'll need more time for the extra."

The tall, sandy haired carpenter tapped his pencil against the edge of the clipboard. "Make you a deal. You help me out on occasion, which will reduce the number of man hours I'll need, and I'll be able to knock the price down."

"How much?"

"Time or price?" He focused on my face.

"Both."

Lowering his gaze to his clipboard, he stared at the mess of numbers written down. Arrows were drawn all over, and some numbers had been circled where others were crossed out with angry scratches. I had no clue what was written or even how to follow it. It was like carpenter code or something.

"If you helped me out a few hours each day... working on the upgraded design... I could reduce it to..." He tapped the pencil against the clipboard again and scribbled down more numbers.

My math skills were pretty decent, but I didn't follow his multiplication and subtraction and addition. It was all over the map.

A soft expression with a weak smile greeted me as he raised his head. "Ten percent over the original quote for your ramp quote."

Wow. I blinked rapidly and took that in. Only ten percent over as long as I helped, and I'd get a nicer looking deck in the end.

I tossed more numbers around in my head. Helping out hadn't equated into my plans. Michael could go for periods of time without me hanging over his shoulder, so to speak, but as the big sister it was important that me or Melody be around. So, I'd likely need to hire her more to watch over Michael while I assisted Chad in carrying lumber or something. That would account for an increase, and the extra I'd banked in the month-long delay would really help with covering her additional cost. *And* it would also get the deck built quicker which I needed like a month ago. I wavered back and forth on my feet as I weighed my potions. In the end, it would work, it had to.

"Sure. Let's do that. What do you need from me?"

He produced a fresh piece of paper, a contract by the looks of it. "A deposit of 50% now, the rest due upon completion, and to your satisfaction." He produced a pen from his shirt pocket and scratched down the date on the contract.

"Aren't you afraid that people might not pay the rest off if you run things like that?"

"Yes, but I stand by my work. You signed a contract so if you decide to shirk me, I have something to take to small claims court." He eyed me hard and shifted his weight to the other foot. "Are you planning on not paying?" His baseball cap had lowered, and he flicked it back.

I nearly spit out my disgust. "It never crossed my mind. I don't operate that way."

He took a small step back. "Good. I promise you I'll do a great job."

His design was beautiful, and instead of a long ramp jutting straight out, it made it look part of the house and not such a blatant add on. His numbers had to be wrong. There was no way even with my help this design would only be a 10% increase. No way.

"How much will the extra set you back?" I asked and

gauged his response.

Without skipping a beat, he replied, "Your help reduces any overages."

I glared but breathed in a fresh breath to calm myself. "You'll put that in the contract?"

"You will get a full breakdown of supplies and labour."

"Fine." I crossed my arms over my chest. "Let's get started."

"You won't be disappointed." He grabbed his clipboard and hopped down the steps.

I whispered under my breath. "Disappointment is the story of my life."

Chapter Four

ichael slept on and off on the couch all day. Between making sure he was still breathing, and he was at least moderately comfortable, I fanned myself, as sweat build in unladylike places.

The heat had become unbearable as the temperature rose, pushing the mercury to sit in the low 30 degrees Celsius. To combat the stifling air, I opened all the windows and prayed for a breeze to stir while grabbing the couple of fans I had and sending a current of moving air in Michael's direction. I placed his favourite blanket, the one with the Minky Dots, beside his cheeks while putting the inside of my wrist against his forehead on occasion. It was warm, but not a heat warm. Almost a feverish warmth. But I wasn't sure.

The one I trusted impeccably to know was on the receiving end of the call.

She was an MD, a former friend, and although we had a huge falling out back in January, she'd said because Michael wasn't involved she'd always be able to help. She'd made several amazing recommendations for his care, since in my mother's death I'd essentially fired the jokers he had been under. Katrina was a Pediatric Respirologist, and not that Michael was a child, but he did have some minor pulmonary issues. Undoubtedly, she was trustworthy about her knowledge.

The phone rang twice.

"Dr. Patches' office."

"Katrina Patches please." I ran my thumb over the edge of my ring finger's nail as the terrible hold music played in the background. It was time for a trim my nails, turning my hand over to see them in their length.

"She's with a patient," the chipper voice said. "Can I get her to call you back?"

"I'll hold."

A deep, irritated sigh. "And who's calling?"

"Michael Finlayson. She'll take my call."

I could only imagine the daggers the receptionist shot into the phone. No, I wasn't Michael, but if that name were relayed to Katrina, she'd hopefully see it as a concerning call, and not the *can't we just be* friends type of call. Those had ceased a few months back.

As the horrible classical music chimed away, I stole glances at Chad.

He was sitting on the end gate of his truck having lunch. A thermos of what I hoped was a cool drink rose up to meet his lips. Remembering I still had coffee frozen in cubes, I walked into the kitchen tossing my phone into speakerphone mode and setting it on the counter.

The blender filled with milk, and I added a spoonful of sugar and a squeeze of chocolate syrup. I dropped the coffee cubes in and grinded it all together. A frothy concoction formed, and I poured it into a thermal mug. I was just on my way to give it to him when a voice spoke up from my phone.

"Ms. Finlayson?"

"Yes," I said, not eager to recognise the receptionist. I'd been hoping for Katrina.

29

"Dr. Patches has a full schedule today, but said she'll call you back as soon as she can."

It was the best I was going to get. "Fine. Please make sure she does." I rattled off my cell number for good measure.

I pocketed my phone and after a quick check on Michael, went to deliver the drink to Chad.

He looked up my way as I came into view and hopped off the end gate. "I was just having lunch."

"It's all good, you're allowed a break," I said, the penetrating heat pushing on me. Holy smokes. Going into work tonight would be a blessing, I only hoped the AC was on full blast. I thrust the drink into his hand. "I hope you like coffee flavoured drinks."

"If it's cold, I'll drink anything." He motioned to the front porch. "It'll be nice when the sun crests the top of your house. Then I'll be in the shade."

My beautiful porch was a nice sanctuary on the evenings I didn't work. Michael and I would sit out there on camping chairs and listen to the birds sing. And the neighbours fight.

"That's why I like the porch. It's nice in the evenings."

"It'll be even better when I finish, you'll see." He pulled the cap from his head and ran his hand through his sandy-brown hair, the sweat slicking it back. A smile sprung onto his face, the left corner rising higher than the right. "I hate to impose, but could I use your bathroom?"

"Ah…" I hesitated. "Sure."

There was a slight narrow to his eyes that disappeared as quickly as it came. "Hey look, it's okay. I get it, you don't know me. Just point me in the direction of the nearest gas station." He closed the end gate with a solid slam.

I wanted to laugh, but it felt misplaced. "It's okay." I glanced to the door. "Just my brother's sleeping on the couch, and

I don't want him disturbed."

"Not a problem. My older sister has twins and let me tell you when they're sleeping, I'm barely allowed to breathe. I promise to be quiet."

I nodded, fighting the odds and failing miserably of being able to suppress the building laughter. It was funny as hell to watch him as he covered his lips with a finger and mocked tiptoeing across the grass. I managed my way up the front steps and creaked open the door.

Chad followed me up and in.

"The bathroom's right there," I said, pointing to the door behind the wall leading to my bedroom. The bathroom entrance was closer to my room than Michael's.

"Thank you." He disappeared as the door clicked shut.

As I walked over to check on my baby brother, my phone buzzed from my back pocket. Katrina's name on the screen.

"Hey, Katrina."

She cut right through the pleasantries. "What's up with Michael?"

"He's off. I had to help him up this morning, and he's been super dozy since his meds this morning."

The silence between us wandered on and on, until finally a lightbulb went off in my head. *Since his meds.* Oh, shit, did I mix something up? I jetted into the kitchen and stared at the multiple containers littered across the counter.

"Audrina?" Her irritated voice squawked in my ear.

"I think I mixed up his meds." Lifting the one orange container I stared at the warning label – *may cause drowsiness*. It was a night-time pain relief pill, not a morning one. Shit! What the hell was I thinking this morning? Dammit.

"Audrina?"

Like an idiot, I shook my head. "I figured it out."

Her sarcasm rolled out of her too easily, and shot in my direction. "Glad I was pulled away from actual patients for this."

"Hey," I barked back, "you told me whenever I had an issue with Michael's health to call you, so I did."

She sighed. "You're right, I'm sorry. What did you give him this morning?"

I listed the medications, sorting them as I called them out. Day pills on the left, evening ones on the right.

Her voice softened to a doctor's version of kind, not to the *you used to be my best friend until you screwed around with my boyfriend and now I hate you* tone I usually got. "He'll be fine, Audrina. It should wear off soon, and if not, take him into the hospital and have him checked out."

"He'll be okay." I barely breathed out the statement.

That's all it was. The wrong pain pill. Not a toxic mix up, just an innocent mistake. He'll be awake soon. However, I was still a major idiot, and I slammed the heel of my hand into my forehead for effect.

"Anything else?"

"No. But thank you for calling me back."

"Anything for Michael, you know that." And the phone call ended. No goodbyes. Nothing. It was over. Like our friendship.

I pocketed the phone and went back into the living room. Chad was just closing the front screen and doing his mock tiptoe thing off the deck. It caused a small smile to bubble to my lips. What a funny guy.

I ran my hands tenderly over Michael's face, and through the wayward strands of his hair. The fans had cooled him a little. Brushing the hair from his forehead, I gave him a quick kiss.

"Rest my baby bird. I'm so sorry I mixed up your pills. I swear it won't happen again."

And no way in hell would it. Laptop in hand, I sat at the

32

kitchen table, Michael in eyesight, and drafted a list of what meds he took at and at what time of the day. For extra effect, I colour coded the lids with a dot and placed a similar dot on the printed list, taping it above the array of seventeen different-sized containers. Lesson learned, and thankfully, aside from a little extra sleep, Michael probably wouldn't be harmed.

I arranged the pills in five straight lines; morning, lunch, supper, additional support which included his pain pills for anytime up until supper, and the pills that caused drowsiness—his evening meds. Content the list would help remind me, I walked back into the living room.

Michael's eyelids fluttered, and he struggled to push up into a sitting position. A heartbeat or two later, he was upright.

"D-D-Drina."

His colour had returned a little, although he still bore the remnants of those sweet pink cheeks he got when he first woke up. It made him appear more like a child than anything else. Moving slowly, he rubbed his eyes and reached for the drink I'd made earlier for him. It was in a thermal container, so I wasn't worried about it having spoiled. He took a long sip.

The Price is Right played on the tv across from him, and the host called out a contestant's name.

I tousled his hair and sat across beside him. "You're okay?"

Michael smiled, bits of pink-tinged drool sliding out of his mouth. A strong laugh came out. "Sh-sh-sh-she f-f-f-f-ell."

I grabbed the remote and rewound, watching as the lady jumped out of her seat and over to the aisle. In her rush, she tripped over her own foot and fell chest down onto the floor. Seeing it again had Michael laughing harder, and it warmed my heart. He *was* going to be okay.

I gave his bony leg a rub. "I'm sorry. It's my fault you were so sleepy."

33

I choked back the tears, a solid lump of shame clogging my throat.

"S'okay." His vision locked on me. "I s-s-still love you."

"And I you."

Michael was such an easy going soul, and yet he always managed to dust away the bad, forgiveness coming from him like rays of sunshine. He never stayed angry. He never blamed anyone for what happened, when maybe he should. I didn't know how he did it.

I guess I was perpetually mad for both of us. The attending doctor at his birth somehow caused his cerebral palsy, at least according to mother. That resulted in a lack of oxygen getting to his brain because of a pinched cord or something. No one noticed his slower than normal speech or his lack of co-ordination, and if they did, didn't feel it was worth mentioning. When he wasn't hitting age-related milestones in early childhood, my saint of a mother blamed his lack of development on me because I was the big sister who carried him everywhere and spoke for him and 'babied' him. But he was my baby bird, what else was I supposed to have done?

He did eventually meet those milestones, but of course it was much, *much* later than average. My mother didn't truly care though, too busy wrapped up in her professional life to give a shit. As Michael entered the school system, a variety of tests were administered, and it turned out his IQ was barely above 70. After that, he was coded and given an aide. But he didn't do much educationally, and Michael went to a special home. A place where my mother could forget all about her problem child and continue living her life.

Yeah, I hated her, even in her death that anger never faded.

But the cerebral palsy wasn't enough for my little ray of sunshine. A few years back, Michael started falling. A lot. It was a visitor of another special needs person at the home who noticed it, and quietly took me aside telling me what he'd observed. Michael went in for some new testing and the result was muscular dystrophy. Because he wasn't suffering enough, right?

Oh, I was so angry at the home for failing to care for him, but there wasn't much I could do. Mother was his legal guardian. Until she died. Before her funeral, Michael was out of that home and living with me.

I sat and continued encouraging him to keep drinking his shake. Finished and after a quick bathroom break, I settled him back in. "I'm going to go and help Chad for a bit, okay?"

He nodded, his focus on the game show.

"I'll be back to check on you in a few minutes."

Knowing he'd be okay if I stepped outside for a while, I left him with another high protein shake and an improv show. The more adult-natured jokes would go over his head, but the physical comedy part would entertain him.

The front door had been barricaded in preparation for the deck reconstruction, so I exited through the back door and made my way along the side of the house. Even in the shade it was monstrously hot. Yuck.

Chad disassembled the front stairs, prying them off with the crowbar held tightly in his hands. The muscles in his back and arms contracted making them hard and corded. Very manly. His white tee did nothing to hide it either. He grunted and with a solid thrust, the stairs fell away, a piece of plywood flying in my direction.

I picked it up and walked over to him, adding it to the pile near his feet.

"Oh sorry, didn't know anyone was there." He didn't look at me though and hoisted the stairs over to his truck.

They looked heavy and awkward, so I reached out and gave him a hand to load it into the box.

"Thanks," he said, dusting his gloves off.

35

I spotted another pair sitting on top of a toolbox and slipped my hands inside. "What can I help you with?"

He blew out a sigh. "Umm… nothing at the moment."

My eyes couldn't help but search out his body. So tan, so strong, so amazing.

"Hey, my eyes are up here." He wiggled his hand near his hips and drew it up.

Busted, and I felt like such a jerk. "Sorry."

"Are you good with swinging a hammer?" He dug into the toolbox attached to the truck, pulled out a sizeable hammer, and passed it to me.

"Yeah, who isn't?"

"Great, let's go break your deck apart."

"Really?"

Didn't think I'd get to break anything. That would be a lot of fun.

Yeah, it wasn't so much fun when a couple of hours later, I needed to stop because my back ached, and my forearms hurt in indescribable ways. Plus, the radio DJ announced it was after three.

"Thanks for your help, Audrina." My name had never sounded so nice rolling out of someone's mouth.

"You're welcome." I gave my lower back a quick rub. "I'd stay and help, but I've got to head into work and pay for this renovation."

I could almost see his vision for the front. Almost. Had to look beyond the two by fours blocking the entrance, and the ripped open flooring. And the deck missing the railings. But yeah, I could almost see it.

"I'll be back tomorrow around eight or so. Does that work for you?"

"As in truly eight am, or more like seven-thirty?" I cocked

my eyebrow and wiped away a bead of sweat trickling down my chest.

"I'll aim for closer to eight. It is a Saturday morning."

"Yes, it is."

The day of the week made no difference to me, but my neighbours would get bent out of shape with any pounding prior to nine am. Oh well, they can kiss my ass. That lost hour wouldn't affect any of their lives, but if Chad started an extra hour earlier, this project could be done much quicker, and Michael would be able to enjoy the great outdoors more often. I waved and headed around back, very uneager to shower and change into the horribly uncomfortable Westside clothing.

# # #

The rush had subsided, and Niall and I sat the staff booth, going over the recent interviewee. We'd argued back and forth about whether Jacob would actually show up. I lost. He did.

"So, what did you think?"

"Overall, meh, I think he's teachable. Seems eager enough," I said. "As a manager, I'd feel the need to dig into his previous job and do some sleuthing there, see if his reasons for leaving match up with what the former employers say. I'd definitely do my due diligence before I'd offer him a job."

Niall shook his head. "This isn't someone who'll be caring for your brother, it's just a serving job."

My palm smacked the table. "That's awesome. Thanks for thinking so highly of us lowly wait staff." I slid out of the booth.

"Jesus, Audrina."

I froze in my angry walk. Niall rarely called me by my real name within the four inner walls of Westside, and never in the open restaurant where customers sat.

"That's not what I meant. Now sit back down." His voice was firm, and it sent chills through my body.

I complied and scooted back in, staying close to the edge though. I was more interested in getting home than I was in continuing a conversation.

"As I was saying..." He ran his long fingers through his short blond hair. "Being a server is hard work. I simply meant that this isn't a position that requires a lot of responsibility. You interviewed how many aides before you settled on Melody? Twenty? Or was it more?"

There was no way I was going to answer that without some sass in my voice. "Whoever I hired needed to be put through the ringer. My brother's health, both physical and mental, was at stake."

"Exactly my point." He stared deeply into my eyes, a depth he had not penetrated in a very long time. "This job, really, in the grand scheme of things, won't make the difference in anyone's life."

"Oh yeah? One of our former servers would've argued that with you."

He chuckled. "Yes, Jasper probably would've. But that's neither here nor there. I'll investigate Jacob's past employment, that was never in question. If a police record shows any criminal activity, then he won't be working here. But I won't not give him a job because he said he quit Loblaws because they wouldn't give him nights when in truth it was because he demanded more money. You said so yourself, we're under-staffed and bad help is better than no help at all."

I wanted to scowl and shoot daggers his way, but I held back, not understanding the overwhelming need to lash out at him. My problem wasn't Niall.

The restaurant around us was quiet, aside from Joy's singing of a merry tune and Robin's hands smacking against an empty tray like a bongo drum. He was a skinny dude who ate like a bird and was called in from the weekdays to pitch in. The two interacted with each other, playful yet still getting the job done.

I sighed, pushing my hot mess of an attitude into the pit of my gut.

"So, what did you think of Jacob? Honestly."

"Truth be told, I think he's bad news. He's a little shifty and will need to be watched. He rarely made eye contact."

"He could've been nervous."

My head twisted from side to side. "Nope, because his body language would've said as much. There was nothing to indicate that he was. He wiggled in his seat."

"He was getting comfortable."

"If that's what you want to believe, then sure. He was just trying to get comfortable." I rested my chin on my hands and stared at his application form. "Did you notice when he spoke about Loblaws the hint of anger in his voice?"

"Really?"

"It was subtle, but it was there. Do some digging on him and talk to his previous manager."

"You don't think he'll work out here?"

"On paper, he looked teachable, and I said someone less than perfect was better than no one. But I don't trust him as far as I can throw him. There's something he's hiding with regards to his previous employment."

Niall gathered the application and tucked it into a file folder. "Have you ever been wrong about someone?"

"Just once." I pulled myself out of the booth and stood.

Niall's face morphed into eager curiosity. "Oh, yeah? Who?"

"You."

Chapter Five

Saturday morning, Michael was more like himself; the smile was back on his face and there was a bit of a hop to his walk, if you could call it that. I certainly noticed but that's not to say anyone else would. He even managed to get dressed by himself, so perhaps a solid day of sleeping and rest was just what he needed but that's what I kept telling myself to dissipate the raging guilt I carried. Try as I did, it didn't go away.

Chad arrived just before eight, his pickup truck towing a lengthy trailer.

I couldn't help but peek from between the blinds like a stalker. Looking good in a fresh white tee, blue jeans, with a face a little darker with stubble. Sigh, as much eye candy as he was, that was *all* he was. Still … it was nice to have something pleasant to look at.

I froze a few more coffee cubes to make him a cool drink at lunch since it was forecasted to be another scorcher, with the threat of an afternoon storm. Those were never fun. Michael was terrified of them and always snuggled into me and covered his eyes while I covered his ears.

I opened the screen door.

Chad yelled out, "Don't!"

"I know. I can't go anywhere."

The door was barricaded with two by fours nailed about two feet apart roughly parallel to each other. Where did he think I was going to go?

"I wanted to ask how I can help you today?"

Was he doing it on purpose, sporting a pair of thick gloves as he leaned against his sledgehammer, and giving me a sexy smirk, or was it natural? Because it was as if he were posing for Carpenters Weekly or something.

"We're going to pull apart the rest of the deck." A chipper voice greeted my ears, and it flickered a spark of desire.

He does this with all his clients, you're nothing special. He's just being friendly.

I swallowed. "Give me a few minutes, and I'll be right out."

He tugged on his ball cap and nodded.

"Hey, Michael." I walked into the living room where he was finishing his breakfast. It was so nice to see him eating again. "Do you want to come outside with me and get some fresh air? Watch me swing a hammer and wreck the deck?"

"Y-y-you g-g-going to w-w-eck the d-d-deck?"

"Yep. Want to watch?"

His whole face lit up in anticipation.

"Let's go."

He shuffled to the back stairs, and I went down first, going backwards and bracing myself that in case he fell, he wouldn't knock us both down. Thank goodness it was only three stairs to the first landing.

A few minutes later, he struggled to put his shoes on but managed.

"Okay, worst set is ahead."

Indeed. The four concrete stairs leading off the back of the house had no rails and to get him down from them always gave my heart a workout. Perhaps I should stick to getting him in and out of the house as my main cardio, rather than my daily runs. I laughed internally while I steadied myself, balancing properly on the stairs.

He made the first step down okay, but stumbled on the second, and I caught him before he fell further. Oh, my beating heart.

Finally, both feet were on the sidewalk. Navigating to the front of the house would be hard, as it was cracked and uneven, but it would be easier on both of us than the friggin' stairs. The new ramp would be a godsend in more ways than one.

"You head to the front, and I'll grab you a chair, okay?"

He turned and limped off, his head bobbing left and right as he took in the different sights. A light breeze filtered through the trees and he stopped, staring up into it.

"B-b-birds," he said, his voice chipper with enthusiasm.

I grabbed a folding chair stashed beside the fence, under the shade of the backyard trees. It was too firm for my liking, but it would be easier for Michael to get in and out of. Standing with the chair in my hand, I too looked up into the trees. There on the branches were a small handful of little birds. Tiny enough they'd easily fit into the cup of my hand.

"M-m-more b-birds." A spray of spit came out with his eager announcement.

"Maybe we should get a bird feeder?"

Where would be the best place to hang it? Obviously, somewhere he could easily watch the birds zoom in and out as if it were air traffic control.

"Y-yes." He clapped his hands.

"Come on, maybe there are more in the front yard?"

Our front yard had two tall trees. A type of elm, which hung lazily over the road, and a big and beautiful willow, which covered part of the front in a filtered shade. Both dropped a tonne of leaves in the fall but were stunning in their full glory. If one was able to climb, the elm would be perfect with its many thick branches spreading out.

We slowly made our way to a safe and shaded spot under the willow, and I opened the folding chair.

Michael sat down immediately and pointed to Chad. "H-h-who's th-th-that?"

"That's Chad. He's going to build you a proper front deck."

At the sound of his name, Chad sauntered over.

Michael waved and smacked his hand against his chest. "I-I-I M-M-Michael."

"Pleased to meet you." Chad extended his hand.

Michael responded by touching his fingers to Chad. When the hands fell away, Michael wore the biggest, goofiest expression. His smile pushed into his eyes, nearly closing them in the process.

"Okay, I'm going to help, but if you need anything, you holler." I tousled his hair and placed a kiss on his head.

I probably wasn't the greatest help, as after every couple of swings with the sledgehammer I checked on Michael. He never moved, but his eyes were wide open taking it all in. What did he think about? I imagined the world looked so much different through his view than it did from mine.

"Hey, boss, is it okay if I take a break?"

Chad put down his sledgehammer. Removing his glove and ball cap, he wiped the sweat from his forehead into his hair. "Sure. I could use a break myself."

"Oh yeah?" I dropped my hammer into the tool bucket. "Getting tired of yelling 'Watch where you're swinging'?"

He grinned and grabbed a water bottle from the cooler in the back of his truck. "Something like that." Half the water disappeared as he guzzled it down. "But you did well." A flick from

43

his chin as it pointed to the front of the house. "We separated a few beams."

"And boards."

A sizeable mountain had formed in front of the house composed of rotten beams and splintered floorboards. I no longer had a deck, just pieces of. My house almost fit in with the rest of the neighbourhood.

I dusted off my hands. "Shall we go for a walk, Michael? Get your body moving?"

He grinned and flailed his arms about in excitement. As I approached his chair, he had his arms out, ready for me to pick him up.

"No, you try it." I steadied myself.

Watching him try to stand was soul crushing. He'd pressed his hands into the arms of the chair, which was fairly sturdy, but his arms buckled under the pressure. A small band of sweat appeared on his forehead, growing with each effort. His face contorted into a pained expression with each futile attempt.

After about a dozen attempts, I couldn't watch him suffer further, and to me it looked like suffering, but I needed to wait.

Bearing tightly closed eyes and a downward turn of his lips, Michael mumbled, "H-h-h-helll-p-p-p."

A wave of unsettled bittersweet relief washed over me. He'd get on his feet, and I didn't have to see his pained expression, but no one won in that scenario.

"Okay." I wrapped my arms around his mid-section. "On three. One. Two. Three." I hoisted him onto his feet, and only when he was steady enough to stand on his on, did I let go.

"G-g-good," he said, balancing on his feet with his arms extended out.

"Ready for a walk?"

He took a step forward, moving very slow, even by

Michael's standards. But he never gave up and soon we were walking down the sidewalk, past Chad's truck. We'd take a few steps, and he'd stop and stare at something in the distance. Most of the time, I couldn't even see what he did. It could've been a squirrel but was most likely a bird.

We made it to the end of the block, about five houses away.

Michael became very animated, and I followed his gaze, this time spotting the woodpecker on a tree whose tapping had caught my attention a couple houses back. It started hammering against the bark and with each rest, Michael giggled like a small child, until it started again, and he stopped to listen.

The woodpecker flew away after a few banging attempts, leaving Michael to repeat over on the walk back, "B-b-b-b-bang."

"Yep, that's what the woodpecker does all day. Can you imagine the headache?"

"N-n-no." He reached for my hand, and I was afraid to do more than have him rest it in mine.

The muscles were paper thin, and the bones felt like they'd shift if I squeezed him. He had changed so much over the past few days, slowly withering away. I was glad Monday was his doctor's appointment.

We made it back into the yard, and Chad stopped tossing pieces of board.

"Just wait," he said, running over to the sidewalk leading to the back of the house. A quick survey of the area and a quick sweep, he permitted us to pass. "All clear. Wanted to make sure no small pieces of wood or anything were in your way."

"Thanks."

We hadn't been gone too long, but it appeared that way. Chad had removed the remainder of the beams, adding them to the mountainous pile. I sure hoped I wasn't slowing him down with my help.

"Can I bring you out a drink when I come back out?"

"Sure, that coffee drink was especially nice." He winked, the edges of his eyes crinkling with the smile forming.

"Will do."

"B-b-b-ye, Ch-ch-chad." Michael flailed his arms in a weak wave.

The walk to the back of the house was slow. Poor Michael so worn out, I worried the final fifteen steps would likely take another five minutes. At least. Then there was the issue of the back stairs to conquer.

I sighed.

"W-w-what's wr-wr-wrong?" His chin nearly smacked his chest with the effort to get his words out.

"Nothing, I'm sorry."

"I t-t-take t-t-to l-long?"

"No, it's not that." I held his hand. "I was just thinking about work."

"W-w-w-work? W-w-w-w-why?" Spray flew out of his mouth. He was wearing out faster than I could get him to move. His stutter lengthened, and his lips weren't closing like they should.

Fear spread through me as I worried what would happen if I couldn't get him to move up the stairs. How could I carry him? Yeah, he didn't weigh more than hundred and thirty pounds, but still. I couldn't cradle him, and I certainly couldn't ask him to hop on my back for a piggyback ride, although it would be the easiest way to get him back inside. But he'd have to hop up, which he can't do, or I'd have to bend down, which I can't do - my legs weren't that strong.

Damn, why did I wait so long to get the deck started? I was so foolish.

Michael took another step and nearly fell into me. He was done, and I was screwed.

"Too tired, eh?"

His eyes blinked slowly, and his head bobbed even slower.

"Can I pick you up?"

His face contorted into confusion.

"I'm going to lift you under your knees and under your arms, okay?"

God give me strength to do this. It's fifteen paces and seven stairs plus whatever else to the living room. Please help me.

I braced myself the way I'd watched Melody, although she never picked him up into her arms, she was very balanced at getting him onto his feet. "On three. One. Two. Three."

I lifted under his knees as I tightly wrapped my left arm around his shoulders and hoisted him up. He was a dead weight, and I stumbled backward. And then forward to catch myself. When the balance shifted horribly wrong as I tipped back to correct and overcompensated, I knew we were going down, and instinctually absorbed the worst of it.

My butt was the first to make hard contact with the sidewalk, and my back a microsecond after. It was sheer luck my head didn't crack when it hit, and thankfully Michael landed on top of me.

"Michael," I cried out. "Are you okay?"

My body did what it should have and broke his fall, and pure instinct made me wrap an arm around his head, so it never connected with the concrete slabs.

Please let him be okay. "Michael?"

Michael grunted. "I o-k-k-kay."

I turned my head away from him, knowing as embarrassed as I was, someone else was nearby and could help. I covered Michael's ear and pulled him tighter into my chest.

"Chad!" I screamed out at the top of my lungs.

Heavy feet sounded against the concrete and in a heartbeat

he stood above me, hands undecided about where they needed to go.

"Can you lift him?"

"How? What's the best way?" His voice pitched.

"Under his arm and knees if you can." Suddenly Michael's weight lifted off my body and I scrambled to my feet, my butt stinging as I moved. "Inside."

I beat them to the screen door, opening it wide. "Up the stairs and into the living room."

The door slammed shut behind us, and pushing down the shooting pain, I followed Chad and Michael over to the couch.

I checked his arms for any scrapes and gently but quickly ran my hands down his legs, watching for any signs of aches. Had there been anything, he would've winced. My fingers searched under the mop of hair, feeling for any bumps. All clear. Lady luck had prevented any injuries.

"S-sh-s-sh-sorry," Michael said.

I tenderly wiped my hands over his cheeks. "You have nothing to be sorry for. It's my fault."

I shouldn't have left him outside for so long without moving him around. What I could've done was put him back in the chair for a bit and allowed him to recover. Yeah, that would've been the smartest thing. Instead, I had to be rescued like a friggin' damsel in distress. God dammit anyway.

He closed his eyes, lips mumbling but no sound coming out.

I grabbed a nearby fan and sent a breeze over him. Turning to Chad, I said, "Thank you for carrying him in."

"I'm glad I was here."

I swallowed.

What would've happened if he wasn't? What would I have done then? I shuddered and walked away from the guys, heading into the kitchen. Arms braced against the counter, I tucked my head between them and let the tears fall out. How could I have been so foolish? I was smarter than that.

Dammit.

I should've known better than to have him out for so long, it wore him out. Had the front deck been there it would've been easier. How could I have let it go this long without providing for him? The deck was a necessity to his health, and I'd let him down. Twice in two days. A bigger idiot would be hard to find.

Chad padded his way, his footsteps stopping just behind me. "Are you okay? Did you get hurt?"

"I'm fine." My voice broke though, which betrayed the confidence I wanted to convey. Everything hurt, but mostly my heart. I wiped my eyes against the shoulder of my sleeve.

"You don't sound okay."

How do you tell a stranger how you feel out of your limits, and with each passing day, you worry you're failing your little brother, and the promise to always keep him safe wasn't true? It was too hard to vocalise.

"Hey, you're bleeding. On your arm."

"What?"

I twisted my arm to get a better look. At least that was physical, and eventually a scab would form. I soaked a cloth in cool water and pressed it against my wound for a moment until the sting of it receded.

Coffee drink. Remembering what I had promised, I opened the freezer door and grabbed the tray of frozen coffee cubes. They clinked against the glass, and I added the remainder of the ingredients and pushed blend on the machine. A deafening sound filled the void in the small space. I filled a mug, sealed the top, and twisted around to face him.

Like he'd been stung, he backed up and studied me, searching out my eyes as concern filled his face.

I handed him the mug. "One cold coffee drink." I refused to make eye contact and turned away to clean out the blender.

"Thanks," he said.

When the screen closed again, I let the rest of my angry, shame filled tears fall in the privacy of my home, where no one could see or pity me.

Chapter Six

ichael woke from a light nap in the early part of the afternoon, no worse for the wear, and had an iced tea to drink. I wasn't a fan of the sweetened drinks, but he asked for it, and I wasn't about to deny him. Call it penance I suppose.

The TV played in the background, the ramblings of a daytime talk host prattling on about the merits of composting. Personally, I would've muted it or turned the damn thing off, but Michael was enjoying it, as was Melody - a true blessing in my life. Once I composed myself, I called her up to inform her of the events. I didn't know why it couldn't wait for when she came in for her shift. Maybe I needed confirmation how I wasn't a complete idiot and accidents happened to everyone. Whatever my reasoning was, she said she'd finish her errands and come by a couple of hours early.

I flopped down into the sofa chair nearest Michael, a stab of angriness focused on my butt. Wincing and shifting to get comfortable, I stood.

"You okay?" Melody asked.

"No. It hurts too much to sit."

51

"Since your fall?"

"Yes."

"Your butt smashed into the concrete first, didn't it?"

I nodded and sighed. "Yep."

"Probably bruised your tailbone."

"Awesome." I paced around the room. How long does a tail bone take to heal?

"You should sit on some ice for a bit. It might help." She put the glass of sweetened tea into Michael's hand and held it firmly as he took a drink.

I stopped mid-pace and shook my head. "I don't have time to sit around and wait. I'll just walk it off."

"The ice would—"

I glared. "I don't care about me right now. There are more important things to deal with."

Out the front window, Chad tugged on one of the rotten boards, his foot braced against it as he yanked.

A giggle from Michael shifted my focus back to him.

"I hate to ask..." Melody said, rising to her feet after setting down the empty glass. "But have you considered an assisted living place?"

I spun around and fought to keep my anger in check but failed on letting the vitriol fly. "I pulled him out of an assisted living place. The caregivers were awful."

"They're not all bad."

"Maybe not, but I flat out refuse. I'll never let him into another home so long as I live."

"It wouldn't happen overnight. Trust me. Just getting the process started can take months, and then waiting for a space..."

I grimaced. There was no way he'd be taken from me. Sure, I wasn't the most qualified, but I can hire help. Increase Melody's hours, or maybe hire another Melody. Maybe two. Whatever it takes, but I forbid him going to a home. He's nowhere near that level of care. My twitching arms pulsed with rage, and I curled and uncurled my fingers to disrupt the energy.

"Look..." Her stare fell to my hands. "I can get you the names of other aides, and we can look into finding government subsidies to help out with the finances."

"Do you know how long it took me to find you?"

My eyes fell on Michael. I didn't want to say it, but part of me thought it. *I don't know if we have that much time.*

"You need extra help."

What I needed was the renovations finished. Had it been completed a month ago, today would never have happened.

"Once the deck is done, things will be easier. Much easier." One foot in front of the other, I paced behind the couch. The movement felt good. "In the meantime, can you work extra tomorrow?"

She shook her head. "Not until the evening, but I can still be here at four."

Well, we can have an indoor day, however... My gaze flitted to the window and out beyond. I also wanted the deck built yesterday, so there was that. And it was part of the deal to help out. However, I wasn't feeling sure I should neglect Michael's mental health and allow him to sit in a chair and watch me work, or worse, have Drew Carey babysit. Even though this situation was temporary, I missed our day-to-day activities together. The card games, the little walks, playing CandyLand.

Melody came over to where I stood. "There are emergency services you can use. Respite care."

"Things that all cost money."

Money didn't grow on trees. As it was, Melody's standard pay came from a portion of Michael's government cheques and the rest via a government subsidy, but anything and everything over her regular full-time hours, I paid for out of pocket. I'd managed to keep her additional hours to a minimum this week, thankfully, but respite care sounded pricey.

"I don't know. But you can ask." She retrieved a card from her handbag and slipped it into my hand.

It was like hiring a glorified babysitter because for the most part I'd be here, right? I'd just be outside helping get the deck built so Michael could move in and out a little easier. However, anyone who could help with his immediate needs was going to cost more per hour than I made. The card flipped over in my hands, and my thoughts did the same.

I hadn't really thought through what Chad had suggested in the beginning, had I? Sure, helping him out would reduce my overall cost, but if I had to pay for a respite care worker to keep an eye on Michael since he shouldn't be left alone for long periods of time, was it worth it? Because really, checking on Michael every hour hindered the minimal help I provided.

However, I enjoyed helping with the renos, and it was nice to talk to another adult, even if it was only about the weather or trivial surface topics. It was still adult conversation no revolving around Michael's day-to-day experiences. Was I a bad big sister because for feeling those things?

Sighing, I picked up the phone and spoke to someone from Emergency Services.

# # #

Melody and Michael were having fun as she pulled out the Hop 'n Pop—a poor man's version of Trouble—so I went back to the front yard.

"Hey," I said, approaching Chad, who tossed more deck pieces into the box of his truck, unsure how much more would fit.

There wasn't much left of my front porch and it looked so odd. Like a kid who lost their teeth, and they had a gaping hole in their smile.

"How's he doing?" He thumbed in the direction of the house.

"He's fine. It's all been forgotten in his mind, I'm sure."

"And you?" A rotten deck board pinged off the box. "You're okay?"

"Just a hard hit to my ego." *And my butt.* I pointed to the front of the house. "So, what can I help with? I'll do whatever you need. You can use me for the next ninety minutes until three-thirty, then I need to get ready for work." I rifled through the tool bucket and retrieved a hammer.

He stood in front of me. "How about you pull out those nails? Do you know how to pull out a bent nail?"

Needing to prove I wasn't a wimpy girl, I painfully squatted over a board and braced my foot on. I expertly wielded the hammer and yanked out the bent nail, holding it up like a first-place trophy. "You mean like this?"

A giant smirk spread across Chad's face. "Yeah, I think you've got it."

He started to walk away but stopped and turned. His mouth opened but words failed to come out of it.

"Something on your mind?"

"Nope." He grabbed another stack of boards and tossed them into the box of his truck. "May the odds be ever in your favour."

I pulled out another bent nail and held the hammer in my hands. "You know that phrase?"

"Doesn't everybody?"

My eyes roved over him. Hmm. "Book or movie?"

Maybe he was one of those guys who only watched the

55

movie versions of the book.

"The book. The movies were okay, but the books were way better." A stack of de-nailed boards in his arms, he walked over to the truck.

"I agree." Interesting. The claw of my hammer caught another nail and with a bit of a grunt, I managed to yank it out. "Favourite book of the three?"

He dropped a load into the box of the truck and stopped in front of me. "The first one. I hated the ending of the Mockingjay."

"Why? Oh my god, that was the best part."

"She ends up with Peeta. She should've been with Gale."

I laughed a little too loud. "No way. Peeta is way better for her. He fed her when she was hungry, he's super strong, and he's just a nice guy."

A gloved hand rested on the hip of his blue jeans. "So that's all a girl needs? Someone to take care of her? Maybe for some girls, but not Katniss. Gale taught her how to be independent. He taught her how to hunt and protect herself, and when she was unable, he stepped up to care for her family. Gale was the obvious choice, and it's a little crazy that she didn't pursue what she knew in her heart was the right choice. She settled, and she settled incorrectly."

"Really? Really?" I scrunched up my face and shook my head, and then lined up a couple of boards. I needed to make this nail retrieval system a little easier.

"Totally. A couple like that are destined to be together. Bet you twenty years later, Katniss and Gale find each other, and they're totally head over heels."

"It would never happen. She loved Peeta."

"In her head maybe, but not in her heart."

"Hmmph." I let his theory float in my head.

Debating the merits of Peeta vs Gale certainly made the afternoon fly by, even if the only thing we agreed on was Finnick, and what a good friend he was. To us both, he rocked.

The demolition complete, we finished cleaning the hacked timbers, making sure nothing, not a nail, nor a tiny piece of wood was left behind. Chad was very meticulous in his clean up. He even gave the sidewalks another quick sweep and I wondered if he was going to vacuum the grass just to be sure.

"Well, I think we're done for the day. Clouds are rolling in, anyway."

I looked to the north west, and indeed, the sky was very dark and threatening. The air had been so hot and humid, it didn't surprise me to see a storm brewing. Melody might have her hands full tonight if the storm crackled while I was gone. However, the cool rain it'd bring would be more than welcome.

"What about tomorrow?" I asked, shifting my weight from one foot to the other.

He leaned against the side of his truck, his taunt arms crossed over his chest. "Tomorrow's Sunday."

"That's mighty perceptive of you." He didn't seem as amused as I was with my retort.

"What about tomorrow are you questioning then?"

"Curious what time you're coming over?" I tried to keep my tone light to show him I was joking, but suddenly lost my zest.

"I'm not."

"Oh." I deflated.

The wind totally sucked out of my sails. I had respite care booked so I could work all day with Chad and rest all evening with Michael. Guess I was going to cancel the respite care and hope I didn't get charged for cancelling with less than 24-hours notice.

"On the seventh day, man rested."

"But you've only been here two days, and I'm no religious scholar, but I'm sure it was God who rested." I thought Adam and Eve wrecked the Garden or something. But maybe that was after the seventh day? Ah, who cared. I wasn't into religion.

"I always take Sundays off. Don't you have a day off?"

From work, yes. From responsibilities? Never. "You'll be back Monday then? Around eight-thirty?"

"That was my plan."

"Great," I said, slowly moving toward the front of the house.

The need to get out of there before I did something stupid, or worse, said something stupid, was growing.

"Hey! I enjoyed working with you today."

"That's good." I dusted off beside his truck, making sure it went onto the grass. "See you on Monday, I suppose." A twist of my body, and I headed toward my back door.

"Just a sec." He caught up to me. "I forgot to return your mug, for the iced coffee." So endearing, he stood there, his arm outstretched holding the silver-coloured thermal cup. He pushed it into my hands, and a warm fuzzy sensation travelled up my arm.

I shook it off and took the cup.

"It was delicious. You'll have to share with me your secret."

I laughed. It wasn't a complicated recipe, and probably tasted a little different each time because there was no hard and fast precisely measured ingredients. "It's easy. Frozen coffee cubes, milk, although chocolate milk is better, because then you can eliminate the additional sugar and blend."

"I'll have to remember that." He rocked on his boots. "When you said you have to work, where is that? What do you do?"

"I'm a waitress at this total dive of a place."

He tipped his head forward, the brim of his cap shadowing his eyes further. "That's hard work." A sexy current rivered through his voice.

"Construction is hard work, waitressing isn't so bad," I said sarcastically. I pretty much hated it, and sometimes it was hard to disguise that.

"So, total dive, eh? Well, that would limit it to several places. Centrally located?"

"Hardly." I bridged the distance between us and rested my hand on my hip. "West end."

"Okay. Well… that does narrow it down."

"Good luck."

"What? That's it? What if I wanted to visit you at your place of work?"

"Then I suppose you'll have to do your due diligence." I winked, waved, and walked away.

Chapter Seven

*W*ork, as always, was gratifying. Yes, that was sarcasm. Joy was a delight, singing along to whatever music beat from the overhead speakers. If she wasn't so darn annoying, it may have been cute. Robin, the skinny dude from the weekday club, joined us again, which helped out immensely.

As senior staff, I got the best section, and was kept hopping from one table to the next. Joy got the second best, and Robin got leftovers. He also got tasked with teaching the new hire, Jacob. It was like watching the blind lead the blind. Thankfully, Jacob started at seven-thirty, which I personally found was odd, but it also meant the worst of the rush was over. No more line ups at the door.

I stood beside Niall at the till and watched Robin move to his new table, Jacob hot on his heels. There wasn't much interaction on his part, he simply stood there and nodded at everything Robin did or said.

"Maybe I'm reading too much into this."

Niall was also watching, but his was more of a general surveillance, overseeing the whole of the floor, making sure all was good. "What part?"

"The newb." I tipped my head toward the dining room. "He's been out there for what, ninety minutes, and he hasn't yet taken a table on his own? He should be able to instigate the initial contact and take the orders."

"Maybe Robin prefers to have a shadow?"

"Yeah, well he'd better watch his shadow."

"Still uncomfortable about him?"

I glared at the back of Jacob's head. "I can't put my finger on it. He seems eager to please and yet, he's not showing this go-getter attitude. He can't even make a pot of coffee for crying out loud. It's rubbing me the wrong way."

"Everyone rubs you the wrong way. Don't take it personally." Niall patted my back and headed to his office.

Heels clacking against the tile flooring, I followed him to the office. "Can I leave early tonight?"

"Joy's already leaving at ten," Niall said, rifling through a stack of papers.

"I think the rookie and the day-timer can hold down the fort for a couple of hours. It never gets busy enough to warrant three, and this way, maybe the newb will take a table."

Niall gave me a passing glance. "If it stays this quiet, then ten works. Holler when you're ready to leave, and I'll cash you out."

At least if I was home by ten thirty, I wouldn't have to worry about much overtime for Melody. Since she came at two, it would be only a half hour of OT. Totally doable.

I headed to my section and cleaned a vacated table. A shiny ten-dollar bill sat under a glass. Pocketing it, I grabbed the remaining dishes, which I was proud to say were only a couple mugs of draft and some napkins. It meant I was attentive to my table, removing anything extraneous.

The mugs hit the bus bin and I gave the table a thorough

61

wipe as well as the booth seats. No one likes a sticky or dirty booth to slip into.

I had just dropped the cloth into the sink when a familiar face graced the door.

Apparently, someone *did* do due diligence and found me.

I stepped back before he noticed me. I didn't actually think he'd find me, so I was unprepared. Plus, I was in my uniform; the ugly green, highly unattractive, polo top.

"L6," Joy sang, entering the wait area.

"Can you assign it to Robin? I'm leaving shortly."

"You're off in an hour. You've got time for this." She danced around me and made a fresh pot of coffee, pouring the old sludge down the drain.

I approached the table and held my breath. There he was, all fresh in a navy tee, his sandy-brown hair slicked back. A broad smile filled his face when we connected.

"So, we meet again." His tone layered in good humour.

I broke away from his locked gaze and focused on the other two gents at the table. "I'm Evanora, welcome to Westside, how can I help you tonight?"

"Evanora?" Chad squinted as he stared at my nametag pinned just above my left breast.

"Hey, my eyes are up here," I deadpanned, throwing his comment from our first meet back at him.

"Isn't that the name of the witch from Oz?" his buddy asked. "The bad one?" He wore a baseball cap, but long hairs escaped from the hold and fanned his neck.

"Precisely."

The older-looking dude scowled in humour. "You're named after a witch?"

"Perhaps I am a witch," I said, eyebrow raised as sarcasm laced into my words.

"My girls would be thrilled." He laughed. "You're kind of like Superman. Waitress by night and witch by day."

I stooped lower and slowly whispered, "I may have to cast a spell over you and have you order drinks for everyone in the restaurant." A subtle smirk on my face wiped the one off his. As if I had magical powers. If I did, you can bet I'd find much better uses for it.

"Evanora," Chad said, reading my nametag again, "this is my brother-in-law–"

"Bruce. Bruce Wayne."

Oh great, I nodded my head, a fucking wise guy. "Okay, Mr. Caped Crusader, what can I get for you?"

"A 20 oz draft. Whatever you have on tap. But just one, I'm not sure the few people here are interested."

"No one ever turns down a free beer." I scribbled his order down and made eye contact with the other guy sitting silently beside the wise guy. "And you?"

He didn't look older than twenty, very young, clean shaven. "I'll have the same," he said.

"We ID for anyone under twenty-five, so I'll need to see yours please."

He dug into his wallet and produced his licence, his birth year making him well over the legal age.

My cheeks heated in response. I returned it to him and added a tick beside Batman's order.

"Don't worry, I get that a lot." He shrunk into the corner.

The last name on the ID was different than Chad's but maybe he was Batman's sidekick, Robin. The thought sent a silent giggle through my body, but I kept my lips sealed tight so it wouldn't escape.

"Don't you want my ID?" Bruce Wayne asked, hand ready to fish out his wallet.

"No, I'm pretty confident you're older than twenty-five."

Chad laughed. "Dude, everyone knows you're in your forties."

"Not everyone." Bruce looked up at me. "You didn't know until he said that, right?"

"Give it up," Chad said to his brother-in-law. "She's not biting." He smiled in my direction. "She's a smart girl."

"What would you like to drink?" I asked my contractor.

Chad narrowed his eyes, curiosity dancing in them. "Make it three drafts."

I nodded and walked away, hearing Batman ask Chad how he knew me. My heart pounded loudly in my chest, and I stopped for a quick second. One of the perks of working here was the anonymity. When I walked out those doors, I could be Audrina. But within the four walls, I was Evanora. Although, truthfully, there wasn't much difference personality wise.

I came out of the server station with my tray of beers, and nearly collided with Chad.

"Hey," he said. "I'm just looking for the bathroom."

I tipped my head to the right. "Far corner."

"Thanks." He stopped walking. "About your name?"

"Obviously, it's a nickname. Please don't mention my real name to the others. I like being Evanora here."

"She can't even hold a candle to you."

The tray tilted in my hands from the compliment.

"Your secret is safe with me." The distance between us was too short, and I stepped back for air.

"How'd you find me?"

"I Googled *dive in west end,* and it led me right here."

I rolled my eyes.

"Actually, Batman says they make the best steak bowls in town, and he needed to get away from my sister and the girls."

"How does Tyson fit in, is he a brother or brother-in-law?"

"He's my buddy."

"Oh. Kind of quiet."

"Yes, he is. Do you like the quiet ones?" His eyebrow rose high enough to give his forehead crinkles.

I knew better than to answer.

"I'll give you a tip. He's gay." Winking, he walked away.

Well, it wasn't the quiet, shy dude slinking into the corner of the booth who captured my attention. It was the one sauntering away from me, his cowboy boots clacking on the tiles.

I dropped off their drinks and cleaned another table, pocketing the tip from that one. It was nice having cash as opposed to the credit cards. This way, there was no paper trail at tax time. But I was honest. Inside my nightly envelope are the credit card tip amounts, which I add up every year and submit on my taxes. Most servers didn't and only claimed a small percentage, but I can't afford an audit. Figured if I 'coloured inside the lines', help will be more readily available to Michael when we need it. Maybe. Time will tell.

My second last table left, just before ten. Chad and crew took their time vacating, although we had a good time, the one liners and zingers out in full force. Even Tyson piped up occasionally. It put me into a better mood, but it could've been because I kept catching Chad staring at me. It didn't irritate me the way most guys did it. Rather, it made me feel desired in a soft and subtle way, despite the green of my shirt. Such an awful colour choice. When I dropped off the bill, I bid them goodnight, and keeping things on the down low, I made no mention of seeing Chad on Monday.

However, he did wave as he and his buddies exited.

I sat in the staff booth while Niall cashed me out, carefully watching Jacob. Besides the fact he acted sneaky with his eyes darting everywhere and the lightning-fast pace at which he moved,

I didn't trust him. Standing at the bussing station, he glanced around quickly and dropped something into the pocket of his apron.

I rose from the booth and marched over to where he stood.

He looked me in the eyes, daring me to a stare down.

I complied and shot back the daggers.

"What do you want, witch?"

He could've been referring to my nametag, but not likely. My insides rolled with fury. "What did you shove into your pockets?"

"My hand." He waved its emptiness in my face.

"You're a thief."

"And you have no proof."

It's true I'd have to count all the cutlery and the empty salt and pepper shakers to verify he stole something, but I knew that look. The guilty way the eyes held fear at being caught and they shifted up and away.

"There are cameras everywhere. They'll have the proof I'll need." I walked away, but not before he scanned the ceiling. Busted. I tapped Niall on the shoulder. "Meet me in your office."

"Two minutes." He was bent over the till, the pen in his hand scribbling like mad.

Inside his office, I sat on the desk, tugging down my skirt and pulling my top free of the waistband, letting it billow over me.

Niall stood at the door. "You did well on that last table. They left you a thirty percent tip."

"What?" I looked at a copy of the receipt. It wasn't signed by Chad, and for some reason that made me feel better.

"Good job." Niall sat in his chair and leaned back. "What's on your mind?"

"Jacob stole something. I don't know what exactly, but I watched him." I described what I saw and the resulting conversation.

"I'll keep my eyes on him, but you need to watch your mouth. If he's as shifty as you say, he could slap you with a slander lawsuit."

"Only if it weren't true."

I hopped off the desk and stood at the door, leaning hard against it. When my body realised I was off shift, the weight of the day always pressed on me, and I couldn't wait to collapse on my couch. After I sent Melody home and helped Michael into bed first. There was always something more pressing than my personal needs. Always.

Chapter Eight

J parked my car on the gravel pad behind my house, sleep deprivation and emotional exhaustion hammering against my brain. The morning's appointment had not delivered the good news I hoped for. Almost everything Dr. Grovenor said echoed the articles I'd read on Michael's numerous diseases.

Michael's days were supposedly numbered. There was no exact number mind you, just a gross estimate of a year, two at most. It angered me. And saddened me. I wanted to crumble into a ball and cry for an hour, and yet, didn't want to do it in front of Michael. I don't think he understood what Dr. Grovenor meant.

I smacked my palm against the steering wheel, the pain reverberating up my arm. Inhaling a lungful of air, I opened my door and walked to the passenger side.

Michael had drifted off and I roused him, watching sweet sleepiness crawl across his face. So young and so innocent, it broke my heart over the cards he'd been dealt. Life was never fair.

"Hey," I whispered, crouching down and gently rubbing his knee. "We're home, baby bird."

Jonathan, from Respite Call, pulled in beside us.

My emergency care paid for by hard earned taxpayer

money, thanks to a grant. I didn't question how, but rather, gave my thanks to the citizens of Alberta. A nice bonus was the program paid for the first hundred hours of respite care. Melody deserved some time off, she couldn't always be at my beck and call, even if Michael and I wanted and preferred her.

Needing to test out the Respite Care, I kept my appointment, but limited it to the three-hour minimum. Jonathan was good yesterday, and Michael seemed to tolerate him. Not a complete win, but Jonathan's skills were invaluable. He was strong enough to lift him with ease, and made a killer grilled cheese, according to my brother. But he wasn't funny and didn't enjoy a good game show or even a rousing round of CandyLand. These were important qualities to me and Michael, and Jonathan wouldn't be someone I would've hired full time.

However, I didn't have much say in the matter. The emergency help was provided by a government program, and he had been vetted; complete with a clear Criminal Record check, a Vulnerable Sector, and a Police Information check. In addition to his clearances, I grilled him on his additional certifications. He had his HCP CPR and Standard First Aid Level C with AED, medication administration and his non-violent crisis intervention in addition to his Licenced Practical Nursing diploma. Satisfied with his information, I had stopped the questioning although the side eye he'd given me spoke more to his character than his education.

Still, I didn't trust him as far as I could throw him.

"Can I give you a hand?" Jonathan walked over to where I straightened up, his slight British accent rolling off. He was a tall man with narrow shoulders, and a perfectly manicured beard – he was extremely good looking and reminded me of Riker from Star Trek.

My tailbone was still ridiculously sore from my epic wipeout the other day and unless I was standing or flat on my back, my butt hurt. Much like my ego when I allowed anyone to help me with my brother.

"I've got this, thanks." I brushed him off and turned my attention to Michael.

Dr. Grovenor remained steadfast in his resolve how helping Michael to his feet would not harm him. That satisfied me because watching him was like seeing a turtle on its back struggling to flip over. I hated seeing him suffer.

"On three... One. Two. Three."

Michael was on his feet in no time, and together we toddled over the pebbly driveway and onto the concrete slabs toward the house. Michael walked under his own power, which pleased me.

I braced myself against the railing while I unlocked the door. Holding open the inside door, Michael and Jonathan passed me by, Michael grunting up the stairs as Jonathan assisted him; hands firmly on his tiny waist and lifting him each riser until they reached the top.

Wait a sec? Railing? What the hell?

I stepped back onto the concrete landing and stared at the railing, made from unfinished two by fours. I gave it a hard shake and it barely moved. It was a basic design and yet was more than had ever been there.

A saw roared to life, and a high-pitched buzz filled the air. The responsible party was in my front yard.

I raced back up the stairs and into the living room. Jonathan had settled Michael onto the couch. "Hey, Michael, I'm going to go and help Chad. Are you okay with that?"

A tired nod greeted me. Drowsiness still clouded his features.

"I'll make you a lunch first."

Jonathan tucked another pillow behind Michael's back. "I can make it. Honestly. Go do what you need to do."

My gaze flitted between Chad, who was hunched over a table saw, and Michael, who seemed ready to fall back asleep. "Fine. I'll just be outside. But first, I'll jot down how to make his protein drink."

Jonathan cocked his head ever so to the side. "I know how to make a shake. It's not complicated."

Yeah, but... I sighed and swallowed down my pride. Yes, Michael was my brother, and I knew him better than anyone, however, Jonathan had way more degrees and diplomas than I had. I needed to trust in his shake making abilities.

"Fine. The powder is there." I pointed to his cupboard. The one with all his special needs products, and the list taped on front of it of his medications.

"Go."

I glanced into the living room. Michael was sitting and looking in my direction, having perked up a little. "If you need me, I'm just outside."

The smell of cut wood permeated my senses and took me back to my childhood. Back to when my grandfather worked out in his shop and sawdust blanketed the floor. That scent, always so strong, reminded me of him. I blinked away the memory and waited for Chad to finish running a piece of wood through the table saw.

Gloved hands waved and the neighbourhood fell silent.

"Thanks for the railing at the back door."

"What railing?" He positioned a chunk of wood and kept a hand on the handle of the saw.

I walked closer, my feet leaving footprints in the newly fallen wood dust. "No? Are you telling me some random stranger came to my house after I'd left and built a very sturdy railing?"

"Hmm..." He scratched his head. "I wonder who that could've been?"

I looked around, knowing full well who it was. "Well, I

71

hope whoever it was likes a homemade iced coffee, heavy on the coolness and thick with the sweet."

"If I accepted on this person's behalf, could I have one of those? That sounds delicious." He readjusted the ball cap and removed his safety goggles, revealing a tan line, if you will, of where the sawdust sprayed against his skin.

"Maybe." I leaned closer and brushed a bit off his shoulder.

He stood there, mouth open a fraction of an inch, staring.

For the first time today, I felt a presence I hadn't felt in a while but couldn't quite put my finger on it. It was almost flirtatiousness, but it couldn't be. Could it? The heat rolling off him wrapped around me like the glove on his hands. Day-um. And as much as I wanted to experience more of this, I couldn't. Not now. My focus needed to be elsewhere. To the one person I was responsible for in mind, body, and soul.

I brushed absently at my shorts. "So…" I needed words, something logical. "I'm heading out to pick up a few things for Michael, can I bring you anything?"

"Where are you going?"

"Home care and the pharmacy."

"Oh." He wiped a hand across his brow. "No, I'm good."

He'd hesitated, so I pried. "Is there another place I could stop and pick something up for you?"

"Honestly, I'm good. I brought everything I need."

I looked over at his truck and trailer. It was fully loaded with stacks of timber. "Well, I should be back in an hour, and then I'll come out and give you a hand."

"I'd like that." He tipped the brim of his hat.

"Thanks again for the back railing," I said, wiping my feet through the sawdust. "I truly appreciate it."

"You know," he called out, and I spun around. "That's not up to code.'"

"I don't care. You've given Michael something to hold onto. It makes moving him in and out a little easier."

Chad walked over to me. "No, I mean, how it was before. That wasn't code."

"Good thing I don't have an inspector coming over."

"No but you'll need to when the deck's done. Make sure it's up to code."

I smiled. "Somehow, I suspect you'll already have made sure it will be."

# # #

Seventy-five minutes later, I was back on the gravel pad, a bag full of new prescriptions on the passenger seat, and a wheelchair in the trunk. It had been a long debate with the health care staff, but in the end, we agreed based on Michael's already limited mobility, a wheelchair was the best choice. Not for now, of course, but when he did, I'd be happy it was available, or so she claimed.

She also suggested a chair for the shower so he could sit while bathing, something I hadn't thought of but agreed he needed. Michael had managed so far, but I was right there outside the door, listening for any sounds of distress. As his muscles deteriorated and atrophied, he wouldn't be able to support himself for very long, and a stool was the safest thing.

For a moment, I sat in my car and stared at the back door. Chad worked on the railing, a handful of tools beside his knees as he bent over the top step and attached something underneath the door.

I got out of my car and went to the trunk. The wheelchair was folded but it barely fit into the tiny space. On top of that was the stool which did not fold and part of it went through the spoke in the wheelchair, lodging it in good and tight. I wiggled and yanked but the damn thing didn't budge. I pulled on the chair, thinking if I can just get it out, the stool would be easy to remove. Wrong.

My vehicle rocked, back and forth with the momentum of my twisting, grunting and shaking. How did it manage to get so wedged in? I even braced my foot against the bumper as I pulled, my butt screaming in defiance.

"Fucking let go!" I screamed into the trunk, my frustration peaking.

"What's going on?" Chad said, his voice getting louder.

I hadn't even heard his boots crush the gravel upon approach. "Damn thing's stuck."

He popped his head into the trunk and shook his head. At the passenger door, he opened it, rifling with the seat, and folding it down. "It's caught but I'm going to push down on the front and you pull. Gently."

I tugged a little and the end closest to me rose as the part closest to Chad went down. The wheelchair, with the secondary stool attachment, slid right out.

Damnit, why didn't I think of that?

I carried it over to the grass and set it down, and Chad followed removing the stool from the spoke.

I slammed the lid of the trunk and walked back over to where Chad stood.

He passed me the stool.

"Thanks." I tipped my head to the door. "What were you working on?"

"A brace support. Figured I wanted it sturdier, and a beam securing the two sides should suffice."

Indeed, the wood ran under the lip of the door, attached to the railings on either side.

"You see, I can't attach it to the house, as this type of material…" He ran his hands over the glass in cement look huge in the thirties or forties. "But I made a completely secure structure by running the main beams under the cement stairs between the pilings. However, you may want to back fill in there and compact it down to give more support to the stairs."

I nodded, making a mental note to add that to my ever-growing list of to-dos. "Well thank you for the railings. Please be sure to add that to my total bill." I tried to guess what the cost would be, but I couldn't fathom a number. Damn. Another bill.

"Consider it a gift."

"No, you've already given me a gift with everything you're doing with the front porch." I opened the door. "Please add it to my total."

"Audrina, listen." Chad's thunderous voice caused a quiver in me and I whipped around to face him. "It's not going to cost anything. I'm using leftover pieces from the front. I promise you, there will be no additional charges."

"Thank you, I appreciate that." I stepped inside with the stool in my hands and closed the screen door. "Give me five minutes, and I'll be outside to help."

I put the stool into the shower, grateful it was a free-standing shower and not the kind in a bathtub. At least I wouldn't have to worry about a bathroom renovation yet. But as I looked around the small space, there wasn't a lot of room to navigate in here as it was and that was before the addition of a wheelchair. What would happen when Michael became wheelchair bound, and I needed to get him into the bathroom? If he's immobile, he wouldn't be able to help me help him to the toilet, and I highly doubted I could drag him over, support him, and undress him.

I leaned against the bathroom counter. What was I going to do?

Dr. Grovenor suggested a long-term care facility would be best for all of us as Michael would have round the clock care. The rooms were wheelchair friendly, and the aides were all trained to help with simple tasks like hygiene. Was I going to be the one to wash Michael in the shower? Would Michael be okay with that?

It was one thing to feed him, and clean him, or help him get dressed. It was another thing to assist with the things adults took for granted like hygiene and bathing. What if down the line he needed to wear adult diapers? Was I willing to change them? If not, I needed to look into either having a full-time nurse since it was probably beyond Melody's scope of practice, or seriously needed to entertain the thought of Michael's final days and weeks in a home. The very idea gave me shudders and made my stomach flip. There was no way he would ever go back and be put through the hell like he was forced to endure in his last place.

I stared in the mirror, and in that moment, I hated myself. I was so weak, so out of tune with what he needed. But as his sister, and primary caregiver, shouldn't I be able to handle it?

Well, first things first. He was okay for now. We're talking about things not happening for a good couple of years, no matter what the damned doctor said. He could be wrong about things going south within the year, doctors often were. I had time yet, lots of it. It was the resources to accommodate me hampering any decent plans.

Step one was the deck, then I could move on to the next task. Did Chad do bathroom renovations too?

After a check on Michael and Jonathan, who was encouraging him to drink, I headed outside. "Okay, Captain, put me to work. I have help for Michael, so let's get this done."

"Okay then." He walked to his truck and tossed me a pair of work gloves. They were a little big on my hands, but I'd be protected from splinters. "You up for some heavy lifting? With the braces in place, we're going to lay the boards over the beams."

"Bring it on." I needed to build some arm strength.

Chad caught up and studied me. It was starting to unnerve me just a little how he watched my every movement as if a female was incapable of doing all that a guy could. I'd show him.

"How's your brother doing?"

"He's fine." I placed my hands on my hips and sighed, casting my gaze to the stack of wood. "I'll be honest with you. I appreciate everything you've done for him and us, but I won't talk about my private life." And I wasn't about to apologise for it either. "I don't do small talk."

Well… aside from the minimal conversations we had over the weather, and the latest drama brewing overseas and how he though Gale was better suited for Katniss. Like really? C'mon, anyone who'd read the books, knew Peeta was by far the better catch.

"Don't you ever share tidbits about your life?" He jumped onto the trailer and unfastened the belts holding the boards in place.

I unhooked the tie-down and dropped it onto the ground. "No, actually. I hate sharing my life. It's my burden, and I refuse to put that onto anybody else."

"Why is that? Sometimes it helps to share." He pushed a small bundle of boards, bracing it in his hands. He nodded toward the bottom.

I grabbed my end and walked backwards while Chad pushed it off the trailer. "Not always."

"See, I disagree. When my brother-in-law for instance, the Bruce Wayne you had the pleasure of meeting the other night, has a rough day, he always calls to talk about it. Doesn't mean I'm going to run and fix his problems, it just means he needs an ear to bend."

"Must be nice to have that availability." I rolled my eyes. In my life, it was just me and Michael.

A gentle shrug shifted the weight of the bundle and he stopped in front of the deck.

"We'll lay these over there, starting on the north side."

North side. Smart. Then there was no way to screw up a left and right direction. We dropped the boards, one at a time, across the new deck beams, and Chad moved them into position, butting it up against the house.

"There's always someone around to listen. Whatever burdens you feel you need to carry, you don't have to go it alone."

"Yes, I do."

I tried to share it with my last boyfriend, Marc, but he wanted nothing to do with it. I was stupidly naive enough to think he just wasn't ready to hang out with Michael. What a fool I'd been. All in the name of lust, because it certainly wasn't love.

"You should think about unburdening yourself."

Who did he think he was? I swallowed down my budding anger. It wasn't the time and place, and I didn't need any further delays on this project. If I spouted off and spoke my mind like I really wanted to, nothing prevented him from walking away and leaving me in a lurch. So fine, I let Chad spew his philosophy on what I should do with my life. I didn't need to take it to heart since I had no plans to change it. We were fine. I was fine.

"I'm good."

"You think so now. But you'll just keep putting the metaphorical lid on everything and one day, you'll just explode. And that won't be any good for anyone when it happens." He marched back to the trailer.

I scoffed. "That'll never happen. I have amazing restraint on my emotions." Most days.

"For now."

We grabbed another bundle of lumber.

"But you should spend some time away from Michael. Go for a coffee with a girlfriend or something." The *or something* lingered on his lips.

What girlfriend? My one girlfriend, Katrina, the daughter of my mother's colleague who became my friend, had cut me out of her life. And over what? A guy. How was I supposed to know they were dating? Neither had said anything, keeping it a secret. Until it accidentally came out. After that, it ruined Katrina's relationship with Marc because he had cheated on her. With me. Even though I didn't know he was dating Katrina.

I lost two friends in one shot. A banner start to my year.

"Set them here, and as we screw them into place, we can add more across the beams."

I dropped the heavy bundle of boards on the grass with a thud.

"Tired yet?"

"Nope."

"Good, only eleven more to go."

He was silent on the next few trips, and I wasn't going to say much either. I was seething on the inside but kept it under wraps. It didn't matter if this handyman was beyond handy, he wasn't going to solve all my life problems. Wouldn't even scratch the surface.

"I've seen how handy you are with a hammer, are you as skilled with a drill?"

I rolled my eyes. "Even better."

Extension cords in place, and knee pads secured to my legs totally killing the sexy carpenter look I was aiming for in my shorts, we hunkered down and screwed the boards in place. We got into an easy rhythm of him placing the boards and the spacers while I fastened them in place. Within a couple of hours, I had a deck once again. It was far from pretty as it needed trimming and sanding and a ramp, but it was functional.

I stood and stretched, wincing as pain shot up and down my legs. The bruised tailbone acted like I'd really damaged it. Maybe I should go in and get it checked, but what would they tell me to do? Rest, most likely. And I didn't have the time. There was a deck to finish, a brother to take care of, and a job I needed to work to pay for it all. Rest would come when I was dead.

Dead.

The word hung in my brain like a huge neon light. Death. The end of life. It may not be coming for me anytime soon, but it was driving up and down the main roads waiting to snatch my brother away from me.

I peeked through the front window, checking on my brother and his keeper. Michael was laughing, his head thrown back, his eyes closed. My heart sped, he had the sweetest grin. On the table between them were cards. Were they playing Slap Jacks? It was Michael's favourite. He never moved fast enough to actually slap anything, but he giggled every time I smacked the table.

"No squeaks, see?" Chad paced back and forth, rocking on certain parts. Definitely no noise.

"You've done well."

"As did you. It was a team effort." He pointed to the south end. "Now the hard part begins. Adding the railings, building the ramp, and attaching the stairs."

"Are we building the stairs?" I'd never done that before but was eager to learn.

"No, I have a preform for that. But the ramp I'll have to build."

"Can I help with that?"

"Not right now."

I unhooked the lovely knee pads and walked them over to his truck. "Time for a coffee drink?"

"Music to my ears." His tongue slipped over his lips, wetting them, making them thirsty for touching.

For a moment, I allowed my brain to wonder what that

mouth would feel like on my body, trailing over my neck, down my arms and wrapped around the end of my finger, sucking and pulling… Shaking my head as the embers fired rapidly in me, I walked to the back of the house. Nothing would ever come from this encounter, but I could dream. Another time, another place. Another lifetime.

Chapter Nine

My one full day off rolled around. Wednesdays were the best. It was selfish of me, but those mornings, I ran a little longer and pushed myself a little harder, knowing I could 'slack off' after.

After helping Michael put a clean shirt on after his shower and drying his mop of hair, I whipped up a batch of pancakes, feeling a little giddy at the thought of senseless carbs entering my body bathed in giant puddles of maple syrup. Yum. Michael ate his up, after I cut them into smaller bites and lifted the fork for him. His energy level was low. And it was early in the day for it to be so low.

I carefully doled out his meds and helped him take them.

His big, hazel eyes stared at me the entire time, but he didn't speak.

"What's on your mind?"

A small head shake, and his gaze fell to the fork like his shoulders fell toward the floor.

"It's going to be a great day. The sun's suppose to come out, which means the birds should be out singing too."

A hint of sparkle returned to his somber face.

"Would you like that? You can come outside for a bit and

see the changes on the deck."

He nodded.

"And tonight, how about we go out for ice cream and to the bird sanctuary? It's been a while since we've been there."

"Y-y-y-ah," he said, a bit of drool escaping.

I gave his mouth a quick wipe before I smiled and stood, planting a kiss on his forehead. "Great, it's a date."

Michael was just getting comfy on the couch when a harsh bang sounded on the back door. Heart pounding at the fright, I walked over. It was Jonathan. I glanced to the clock. He was right on time; I'd asked him to come for ten.

"Come in." I gestured.

Jonathan bounded up the stairs. "Hey." The word barely audible. What a jerk. At least he was nicer to Michael. His voice softened to damn near baby talk though. "Would Michael like to go to the mall for a bit?"

Michael looked to me for permission, excitement dancing all over his face. Would two outings in one day be too much for him? I could say no to Jonathan's request, but I didn't want to take away Michael's enthusiasm.

"We'll go for only for an hour or two. It would get him out of this heat and into someplace airconditioned."

The word was said with borderline hostility. Not everyone could afford such luxuries like AC. Fans weren't the coolest, but at least it moved the stifling air around. Besides, it was only ever truly hot for such a short spell. Heat waves here didn't last long.

"You'll use the wheelchair?"

Jonathan nodded.

"And you'll contact me if there's the slightest hint of trouble?"

Michael's smile pushed high enough to nearly close his eyes.

A morsel of fear started building in me. Aside from walks around the neighbourhood, Melody never took Michael out. The thought made her nervous. It was a small strike, one I never held against her. She more than made up for it in other ways. But here was this guy who only after two days wanted to take Michael out. I wrestled with the decision. Yes, he was qualified, but it should be me. And I had plans to take him out tonight. But sweet Michael, he wanted to go.

I swallowed and nodded, forcing myself to smile encouragingly – for Michael. "Okay."

I kissed him on the forehead, and giving a second glance to Jonathan, headed into the kitchen to prepare a drink. A couple minutes later, I wandered into my front yard.

Chad was there, setting up the table saw and everything else he needed.

It sucked he had to pack it every night, but I guaranteed him it wouldn't be there the next morning. Some asshole would walk off with it. How I hated the hoodlums in my area. If it weren't for them, it would be a beautiful place to live, and maybe raise a family.

"Morning," I said, passing him an iced coffee. It had become a pleasant way to start the day.

"How's Michael?" A standard question.

"Off to the mall with Jonathan in a bit." For some reason, the last few days I've felt like I was being watched. I looked to the house half expecting to see my respite care standing at the window. There was no one there, so I returned my attention to Chad. "What are we going to work on today?"

"Lots. I have the railings and the stain for you. I think it would be easier to coat them before they're attached to the deck."

I shrugged, no idea what would be easier. I was the minion, prepared to get the job accomplished as fast as possible. "Sure."

"And if I get the trim and sanding done, I'll have you put

the first coat on the deck floor."

"Aye Aye, Captain," I said, giving him a soldier's salute.

The deck was coming along nicely. Yesterday he added the stairs to the south end of the deck so I could climb up and down, but there were no railings yet, and as such, was still unsafe to be on.

The railings were placed over a couple of work horses, making sure to cover the work area with leftover salvaged plastic. There were 2x2 spindles and 2x4 railings, so many staining them would surely take all day, and maybe tomorrow as well. At least I'd be standing, and my butt wouldn't hurt too much.

Chad sauntered over, the warming scent of his cologne floating in the slight breeze. His ball cap was pulled low, and sunglasses covered his eyes. "I'll set up another station for you."

"Why?"

"Then when you're done staining these, you can move to the next station. By time you finish those, the first set will be dry, and you can flip them over."

"Gotcha."

He busied himself bringing over a bucket of stain and a paintbrush, so I prepared the second set of work horses, replicating what I did with the first set.

My brush stroked up and down the first set of railings, the stain darker than I expected. Chad assured me it would dry lighter as it soaked into the wood. I hoped so.

The saw stopped running, its rhythmic whirring and grinding halting earlier than what he had been pushing through. Familiar voices came from the side of the house and slowly, Michael emerged into view, Jonathan right behind him.

I set my brush on the lid of the can and walked over.

"J-J-Jon t-t-taking m-m-me t-t-t mmmall nnn-owww," he sputtered out, more spit covering me than the stain had.

A rosy glow covered him, the sunlight bringing out the

highlights in his mahogany-coloured hairs.

Jonathan stood close by. "If you can watch him, I'll run get the wheelchair and load it into my car."

Watch him? Really? He's MY brother, and I care for him all the time. Watch him? Sure buddy, no problem, I'll 'watch' him.

His choice of words shouldn't have rubbed me the wrong way, but they did.

"Go," I spit and changing my tune, I stepped closer to Michael. "Want to see what we've been doing?"

"Y-yeah." He wrapped his skinny little arm through mine.

I pointed out the changes, and where the ramp was going to go. All the lines were marked with the angle needed. "It'll be much nicer getting you in to the house. Maybe we can add a porch swing so we can watch the birds. Would you like that?"

"Y-Y-Yeah." His head flopped around, searching the trees.

I walked him over to Jonathan's car, a hot-looking Mustang, perhaps a year or two old. Guess the government cheques paid him handsomely. It was way nicer than mine, but at least I knew mine was paid off.

The saw blade sliced effortlessly through the edges of the deck, causing me to refocus on the man beside the machine. A sawdust cloud all around him, he looked like something out of a dream. So what if it was a weird dream.

Jonathan walked over pushing the wheelchair. When he folded it up to store in his trunk, I stole a peek at the inside. All clean. I wasn't sure what I expected, but this pleased me. Expertly, he lowered Michael into the passenger seat and ensured he was tightly buckled in. Michael's eyes were bright, taking it all in. It made me happy to see him so lit up. I hoped his time at the mall was well spent.

Like some kind of loser, I stood waving at Jonathan and Michael until they turned the corner and were out of sight before I went back to staining the railings, a boring and tedious job if ever there were one. It gave me time to let my mind wander and did it ever.

As much as I spent time taking care to coat the timbers, I couldn't help but admire Chad and his fine form. Everything he did was effortless, or like he was destined to be a carpenter. So much skill and grace, he made it look easy as he smoothed the deck edge, refining the masterpiece of craftsmanship.

# # #

The last of the deck railings, and not of the many more needed for the ramps, was finished with the first coat of stain, I stepped back and wiped the sweat from my brow. Once I got into a rhythm it didn't take long. "Hey, Captain, lunch time?"

He measured out a spot on the ramp and pencil marked. "Sure."

"Great, let's eat in the kitchen. At least we'll be out of the sun." I gave my heated arms a quick rub, they needed a sun break. "I'll meet you inside."

Like a frantic bee, I zipped around the inside of my kitchen tidying up. Apparently putting things away when you're done with them was not listed on Jonathan's job description. I hoped he was less careless with my brother than he was with the carton of milk he'd left out.

A knock sounded on my back door. "Just giving you a heads up."

"Yeah, it's all good." I pulled out ingredients for making sandwiches. "You allergic to anything?"

"Penicillin…" He laughed as he walked up the back stairs. "But I highly doubt you're making lunch with that."

"Yeah, nope."

Moving over to the other counter, he looked at the plethora of pills and pointed. "Unless it's in there."

"Actually, that's one of the drugs he does *not* take."

Amazingly enough. And not recently. There was a bacterial infection in his lungs a couple of months ago, but it passed.

"So many."

"Seventeen different ones." I dropped a loaf of bread, cold cuts, and sandwich toppings onto the table.

Chad leaned against the edge of the counter and crossed his arms over his chest. "He's not okay, is he?"

My vision blurred around the edges, but I blinked it away as I spoke. My Michael was everything. "I keep hoping for a miracle."

"Can I ask what he's got?"

I hesitated and grabbed a couple of plates from the open shelf. "He was born with mild cerebral palsy which affected his speech and thought processes and to a small degree his motor skills, but it wasn't truly diagnosed until he was nearly four. His muscular dystrophy, thanks to an inherited gene from my mother, showed up a few years ago. They're not sure what triggered it, but they blamed the hormonal changes of puberty."

I sighed and faced Chad to gauge his reaction – he was deeply interested and leaned closer to me as I spoke. That had been the most I'd shared with anyone in the longest time, and he acted like he wasn't going to ditch.

"However, he's a trooper."

"Yeah, I can tell. He's always smiling."

"For the most part." *Although I always wonder what he's hiding from the outside world.* "It's not a fancy lunch but dig in." I turned my back to him and rooted through the fridge for a couple cans of pop.

"Holy smokes your back is burnt."

"What?" I nearly hit my head on the freezer as I whipped it out of the fridge.

He rose and stood right behind me, the short distance between us making my tiny kitchen feel even smaller. "Can I touch you?"

I waited and then a sharp sizzle of pain radiated over my shoulder. The sting took my breath away, and I forgot how much I wanted him to touch me because now he needed to back the hell away.

"Wow." His voice pitched in surprise. "That took a long time to go back to red. Do you have any milk?"

"I wouldn't trust it."

"You have a cloth?"

I gave him one from the kitchen sink.

"How about one that hasn't washed dishes?"

"Oh." I retrieved a fresh one from the linen closet.

He ran it under the tap and squeezed it out slightly, unfolded it and draped it over my shoulder. The coolness was heavenly. As he lifted it and blew over my shoulder, the hairs on the back of my neck stood at attention as wave after wave of erotic tension pulsed through my veins.

I needed help. Seriously. So deprived of male attention, a mere breath across my back was enough to send me over the edge. And there was nothing overtly sexual about it.

"Feel better?"

"Oh yeah." The words poured out of me like melted butter.

"Really now?" A tender chuckle rolled out of him.

"I'm a fast healer." I tried to cover up, but I didn't think it worked.

He rinsed the cloth out, re-draped it on my other shoulder and stepped back.

Well, day-um. "Thanks." I readjusted the cloth so it would

stay on while we ate, the dampness of it soaking through the thin straps of my tank top. "Back to our lunch."

His chair scraped on the hardwood, and he took the seat furthest away from me, however he dug in and grabbed four slices of bread, which he opened like a book. He squirted the mustard out in a zig zag pattern across the right sides of his sandwich and spread the mayo on the other half. Multiple cold cuts covered the mustard, and a cheese slice went over the mayo. Before the whole thing closed, he added two slices of pickles.

"What?" he said, looking at me.

I blinked a few times, unaware I'd been staring so hard. "I'm fascinated with oddities. I've never watched someone dress a sandwich like that before."

"It's just how I've always made it. No big deal." He took a man-sized bite.

"You're right, it's not." I rolled a slice of ham around a dill pickle and took a satisfying crunch.

"Oh, you have got to be kidding me."

At hearing the shock in his voice, I searched around for what had triggered the pitch. "About?"

"Do you not eat bread?"

Oh, that.

I shrugged. "Not really, no." Because I had my guilty carbs already in the morning.

"Please don't tell me you've jumped on the no-gluten bandwagon."

I laughed. "Um, no. I'm not a bandwagon jumpee. I just hate the way I feel after I have too many carbs."

He raised an eyebrow. "For real?"

"Honest to God. Sometimes I'll make a PB&J sandwich for Michael, but most of the time he's on a high protein diet, and I find it's easier to eat the same thing and not have to make two separate meals. Mainly I keep bread around for Melody. She loves a peanut butter and banana sandwich."

"That makes some sense." He took another bite, watching me suspiciously.

The need to move away from the stare was high. I lifted the hot cloth off my shoulder and ran it under the tap. With a fresh injection of cool water penetrating it, I placed it onto my other burnt body part.

"Do you ever eat carbs? Like pizza?" He wasn't satisfied with the answer.

"Not so much, no. It's not a diet or anything, it's a lifestyle choice for me. Carbs only make up about twenty percent of my diet." Well, maybe higher if you truly broke it down. It's mainly refined carbs I avoided; breads, pastas and the like.

"Oh." He munched some more. "So, if someone took you out for dinner, what would you eat?"

I rolled another ham and pickle combo, this time with a slice of cheese. "I guess it depends. Where would I be going?"

A crunch filled the space. There was no delicate way to eat it without it being noisy or looking suggestive.

"Say..." He paused as if in deep though and rubbed his chin. "Your restaurant?"

"Well... my restaurant wouldn't be a very exciting place to dine, but if we were there, *hypothetically,* I'd have the steak bowl minus the rice." The pickle squirted in my mouth as I crunched another lady-sized bite. It tasted so good, salty and cheesy. "But really, I can eat anywhere. I'm not that difficult."

"So." His Adam's apple bobbed. "Would you be interested in going for dinner tomorrow night?"

I swallowed, and I knew it was loud because his focus moved to my throat. "I... I can't. I'm sorry, Chad."

"Is it because you're working, or because you have a

91

boyfriend?" He put his sandwich down. "Please say it's not the boyfriend thing."

I laughed. "There's no boyfriend. Trust me. My personal commitments don't allow time for frolicking."

"Frolicking? Really?" He grinned. "I never frolic on the first date."

It was cute, just as he was. "I mean I don't have time. I work a lot to pay for the things to make Michael's life as good as I can. And I feel guilty when I'm away from him. I don't expect you to understand."

I rose from the table and put my plate in the sink. The cloth on my shoulder had warmed so I re-cooled it.

His chair scratched across the floor. "Let me help you." As he took it from my hands, he grazed his fingers over mine longer than was necessary, but the cloth draped over my sun quenched skin quickly dissolved the building discomfort. "I understand that guilt; the guilt of not wanting to do something fun for yourself because you're afraid of missing out."

"How? You have someone you are responsible for?" I searched his finger for a ring, it was bare. Not even a tan line.

"Just my nieces. But my sister's like that. She suffers from FOMO big time. You know, the *fear of missing out*, but it's not a fear of missing what's going on in the world, it's a fear of missing out on what her girls do. She's there for everything from sun up until sun down. It's a rare day if I get to babysit since she mostly drags the girlies along with her. I think her and Batman have gone on six dates in the seven years since they were born."

I'd think it was crazy, but sadly, I related all too well. Since Michael came to live with me in January, dating completely fell off my radar. It wasn't because I didn't want to as I craved the company of another, and I really enjoyed my brain picked by someone other than a medical professional, it just wasn't in the cards. For now.

"All I'm saying is with your helpers, maybe you can take a couple of hours to yourself. Do something for you." He had a twinkle in his eye.

I didn't respond. I couldn't even move. "I take time to myself. Just this morning, I went for a run before you came over."

A curious mixture of shame and anger twirled inside like the start of a raging storm. My fists clenched into tight little balls.

"You think you know how it is, but you really have no idea. You don't know the first thing about my life."

His eyes fell to my hands. "You're right, I don't. I apologise for saying anything." Drawing a breath, he released it as he gathered up the supplies on the table and put them away. "Thank you for lunch."

Jaw clenched, he exited the house, the screen door slamming behind him.

I scrubbed the dishes so hard one plate slipped out of my hands and clanged against the edge of the counter, water spraying everywhere. Drying the floor and grabbing a fresh towel, I leaned against the fridge, banging my head against it.

Michael was important, and I didn't have a fear of missing out. That's not what my fear was. My fear was something terrible happening, and I needed to be there if or when it happened because he was mine to protect. Weird, right? I promised him months ago, when I pulled him from that home, he was safe with me, and we'd live happily forever.

Seemed like I already broke the second promise as forever had been given an expiration date. So much for that promise.

Chapter Ten

*T*he kitchen clean, I headed back outside, two large bottles filled with ice water and a hint of lemon in my hands. I left Chad's on the edge of the stairs and took a swig of mine, dropping it by the work horses. My staining was pretty good. No globs, no trails, no drips. I checked all the pieces twice, readying myself for the second coat.

I'd like to say I read too much into our lunch conversation, but that wasn't the case. I kept looking in Chad's direction, but he never once looked in mine. He had sort of asked me out on a date, hadn't he? I replayed it over and over in my mind. Maybe he was just being nice, and he asked all his customers out, following them to their place of work. Maybe it was part of his brand to flirt with the ones who wrote his cheque. How was I to know?

There was no way I was going to admit he was partly in the right though. Katrina had said the same thing, although not quite so eloquently. They just didn't understand.

The second coat went on much smoother, and I was impressed by how fast I was going through the railings. The stain didn't seem to soak in as much, and as such, the railings were brightening even though Chad had moved the work horses into the shade. I liked the whiter look the railings took on, made them seem cleaner. To me at least. Chad hadn't been so gung-ho about the stain colour, but oh well.

Jonathan's car pulled up in front of the house, the engine revving harshly like he was driving in a hurry.

Panic flooded through me. I flung my brush and ran to the car, opening the passenger door before Jonathan had the car turned off.

I dropped to my knees, repulsion turning my heart black. I hated how my gut reaction was correct. Michael's eyes were red rimmed; he had been crying for some time.

"What's wrong, baby bird?"

"He tripped." Jonathan popped the trunk.

"He tripped?" I glared at Jonathan as he dug out the wheelchair at set it on the sidewalk. "You were supposed to have him in that. How could he have tripped?" My voice pitched, and I fought to control it in front of Michael. I placed my hands on his arms gently, checking out his body for evidence of where he hurt the most. "Where does it hurt?" I didn't know what to touch as I didn't know what body part he'd fallen on.

"M-m-m-m-my armmmm." He wailed.

My focus went over both. "Which one?"

Did he slam his shoulder, did an elbow break his fall? How could he have even fallen? My face heated with surging anger and my body was tense, reading for a fight. I shouldn't have ignored my gut feeling this morning. I really should've paid more attention to it and then this wouldn't have happened.

"H-h-he p-p-p-push m-m-m-me."

NO! My eyes bugged out of my head, and I leaned in closer, whispering, "Michael, look at me."

His hazel greens locked onto mine.

"Who pushed you?"

"J-j-j-j-on." His bony finger pointed to the back of the car.

I stood and yelled for the only other person I knew would hear me. I needed someone to watch Michael while I beat the ever-living shit out the one who hurt him. "Chad!"

Jonathan dashed over to the driver's side of the car.

I had to move quickly. No fucking way was he driving off with Michael still inside. My heart pounded outside my chest.

"Okay, I'm going to get you out. I don't have time for three, I'm just pulling." I wrapped my arms around his waist and weak arms wrapped around my neck.

Chad appeared in a huff. "What's going on?"

It was a quick pull, but I got my brother onto his feet hoping I didn't injure him further. "Hold him please and call the police. This asshole hurt Michael."

Chad slipped his arm under Michael's before he could voice a protest, and I pounded over to Jonathan, my face tight and contorted in anger. My rage channelled into super-human strength and I gave him a violent shove on his shoulder.

"What?" Jonathan said. "He fell."

"Fuck you." I pushed him again. Rage made me freakishly strong, and he tripped over his feet and smashed into the side of his car. "Doesn't feel very nice, does it?" I screamed, getting into his face. The adrenaline spiked, and I felt taller and stronger than ever.

"He stumbled, and I helped him up." Jonathan's eyes did the same thing Jacob from work's did when I busted him. That guilty shift up to the right.

"Great, then you'll have no issues telling the cops that." Chad stood there, phone in his free hand as his other supported Michael. Squaring up his shoulders, he was a good four inches shorter than Jonathan but clearly the more physical build. Jonathan had picked on the wrong person.

My hands curled into tight fists, ready for use. I was smaller than Chad, but when you messed with the momma bird, you were going to hurt. Badly. And I had zero issues with taking the fucker down.

A sob ebbed out of Michael, at once softening the darkness in my heart and ramping up the deep anger. I wanted to make Jonathan pay while at the same time comfort my Michael.

My moment of indecision was apparently all the break Jonathan needed. He gave me a solid push to the ground, and I landed smack on my hip as his tires squealed. I couldn't even throw a solid kick against the body of the car. The bastard drove off.

"You'd better run, you fucking monster," I called jumping onto my feet and yelling as his car peeled around the corner, a car horn blaring as it was cut off.

"Are you okay?" Chad asked from the sidewalk as he held onto my brother.

"D-d-d?" Tears dampened Michael's face, but it had changed a little. It now held a tiny bit of fear in it.

My heart sunk. Michael had never heard me curse or seen me so riled up. Had I scared him? Cautiously, I trekked over, hands extended. "Oh Michael, I'm sorry you had to see that."

He curled into Chad, turning his head away from me, furthering the splinter in my heart. The last thing I wanted was Michael to fear me. I was here to protect him.

Michael cried all the way up the stairs as Chad assisted him into the house.

I managed to get him settled down on the couch but getting answers from him was difficult. With the gentlest of voices, I lowered myself in front of my baby brother, making myself as small as I felt.

"Michael, I'm sorry you saw me get so mad but what Jonathan did was wrong." My anger was disappearing, but tears built in replacement. I blinked a few times to keep them at bay. "The

97

last thing I wanted to do was frighten you, okay?"

He gave a slight nod and stared deeply into my eyes.

"Do you believe me? I love you so much, and I don't want you to ever be afraid of me." I lowered my hand on top of his and allowed my thumb to tenderly stroke the top part of his hand.

"I-I-I-I l-l-l-ove y-y-y."

My heart swelled, further reducing my anger but it did nothing to dampen the oncoming tears. Still, I kept my focus on Michael. If he saw my tears, maybe he would understand how truly sorry I was for frightening him.

"I need to check where he hurt you, okay? I promise to be gentle." I waited for permission, and slowly he gave me another nod.

Lifting the sleeve of his shirt, the distinct outline of a hand wrapped around his upper arm formed and my eyes increased exponentially. I blinked rapidly and twisted to look at Chad, whose facial expression slid right off. I grabbed my phone. Documentation was everything.

Michael pointed to the TV, and grateful for his distraction, I put on the game show network. I continued photographing his back, my stomach washing my heart in nasty bitter bile where a few smaller bruises were forming.

Whatever Michael was enjoying, a sweet laugh escaped him. It kept me focused as I ranted to the Sergeant at the police department.

# # #

An hour later Constables Jones and Fitz had finished taking my statement, and the little info they were able to get out of Michael. The more they asked what happened, the further into himself he crawled, and because I couldn't get much more out of him, they left with what they had. Neither Michael, nor me, had any idea where it happened so they couldn't pull mall security tapes for proof; all we had were Michael's bruises, Chad's statement and mine, and Jonathan's licence plate number.

However, the agency had also been called and Jonathan was reported, with the police promising they'd be in contact soon enough. It was a start, but it was far from enough. As Michael's legal guardian, I could press charges, and planned on it.

Chad sat in the corner of the living room, the cops finished with him. "I should get back to work."

The whole incident took a couple hours out of his day but if he hadn't been here, I don't know what would've happened. I doubt Jonathan would've attacked me, but what if he had? Or worse, what if he had hurt Michael more?

"I'm sorry, but I can't help you further today. I need to stay right here with him."

Michael occupied my every thought and billions of what-ifs played in my mind. There was no place else I needed to be than with him.

"Believe me, I understand." He walked to the front door, and I followed him closely, my focus flitting between the two men.

"I'm so grateful you were there, I can't thank you enough. If anything more had happened–" My vision blurred.

His hand rested on my shoulder, and I winced. Not because I didn't want to be touched, but because the very touch hurt. The callouses on his hand scratched my tender, sunburnt skin.

"I'm glad I was there too. Had I not been holding Michael, Jonathan would be in the hospital."

The tears I'd fought hard to restrain leaked out. I wiped them away, silently willing them to stop. I was making a fool out of myself. Smearing them over my cheeks, I inhaled sharply, hoping for strength.

"It'll be okay."

"No, it won't," I whispered, my heart falling with my words. "Sorry."

I turned from him and stepped over to Michael.

Chad excused himself and headed outside.

The glass of apple juice on the table beside the couch remained untouched. I lifted it to Michael and offered. He shook his head. "You need to drink."

He closed his eyes and his head tipped back. I grabbed the nearest pillow and propped it up under him, making sure the lines in his face softened, then I knew he was comfortable.

"You tired, baby bird?"

It *had* been a draining day, and all I wanted to do was curl up beside him, wrap my arms around him and hold him tightly. But I couldn't. Instead, I massaged his legs in a downward stroke from his knees to the tips of his toes. He'd always found it soothing, especially if he'd been on his feet a lot.

Content he was sound asleep, I needed to share with the one person I did trust to update what happened. Within ten minutes of hanging up, Melody was at my door.

"You didn't need to come," I told her, but the panic on her face suggested otherwise.

"I needed to see for myself that he's okay."

I breathed a sigh of relief and understanding.

Melody was good people. She cared for Michael and not just as a patient but as a friend.

"He's sleeping on the couch."

We walked into the living room, and Melody stood silently over him, taking him all in like I did. I opened my phone and flipped through the images, her gasps hardly stifled.

"I'm so sorry. It was my recommendation."

"You couldn't have known." I patted her arm. "Only

Jonathan knows what went on in his tiny little brain. Who hurts someone like that?

"What a jerk." Sincerity crossed her face. "I really am sorry for having told you to contact him. What can I do to help you?"

I sat down—slowly—on the couch opposite Michael, unable to take my eyes off him. "Nothing. I am going to stick exclusively with you."

"What about the deck?"

I shrugged. "It'll still get built, just without my help."

There wasn't much more I could do. I already needed Melody for my evening shifts, I wasn't going to add to that.

"I can start a little earlier. Instead of four, I can be here by two. We were doubling up when you were needed at work for the double shifts, we can make this work too."

She was right. There were a few weeks when she was pulling double shifts on the weekend to cover me. But with that, I was still coming out ahead after my hourly wage and tips. Her working a couple of additional hours now would need to come out of my savings.

"Thank you for the offer. I appreciate it. I'll figure something out. I always do."

I took in a stuttering breath. The sensations of being completely overwhelmed descended on me; the nausea, the build up of tears, the feeling I had control over nothing. My fingertips tingled and even though I sat on the couch, my heart rate doubled, and my breathing increased. It was akin to a hardcore run and yet, I wasn't moving.

Chad knocked on the screen door. "Is it okay if I use the bathroom?"

My head did a funny sort of nod, it was a back and forth shake which slowly turned into an up and down motion. I probably looked like a bobblehead doll.

"You okay?" he asked as he walked in and stood behind the couch. An intense questioning expression settled on his face.

"I need a minute," I said to no one in particular.

Sprinting into my bedroom, I closed the door and launched myself onto my bed, burying my face into a pile of pillows as deep as I could go. I screamed and screamed.

A hard knock came from the door, and I lifted my head.

"Audrina, it's Chad. Can I come in?"

I shuffled myself into a sitting position. "It's unlocked."

He opened the door, and clicked it close, standing on my side of it. "A little, umm, what's the word?" He rubbed his chin. "Emotionally drained?"

I nodded and rested my chin on my knees.

"I heard you screaming."

The room turned cold as ice and I shivered. "Did Michael wake up?" I'd already scared him once today.

A shake of his head. "No. But come with me, I'll show you a better way." He extended his hand.

"I can't leave."

All I wanted to do was release the pent-up frustration. I didn't need to leave the house for that. I'd just get more pillows.

"Yes, you can." He propped open the door. "Melody, are you okay if I take Audrina for thirty minutes?"

Her muffled voice sailed into the room. "Sure, we're not going anywhere."

"See." His hand waved in front of me. "C'mon. It's thirty minutes, and it'll be good for you. Do you trust me?"

Nodding my head in that weird bobblehead movement again, my feet betrayed me and touched the hardwood floor, curious to know what Chad wanted to show me. My hand slipped into his, scratchier than I expected, but the warmth of it wrapped around my fragile soul.

With a quick check on Michael, who I assumed was having a peaceful nap as he wasn't twitching or moving, I followed Chad through my living room and into the kitchen.

He stopped at the backdoor. "Do you mind driving? I mean I don't mind, but I'd have to unhook my trailer."

"No, that's fine. Where are we going?"

"I'll give you directions on the way."

I was kind of intrigued, and wanted to question him more, but nothing in my gut was setting off alarms.

"Wear those shoes." He nudged at a pair of runners, and we hopped into my car.

We drove for a few short blocks as he called out directions. It didn't feel like we were very far from home.

"Here," he said, pointing to a fenced off area.

"What's this?"

"You'll see."

We walked hand-in-hand up a small embankment and over a hill. There was a crack in the fence, around the empty space resembling a football field, but in the worst condition I'd ever seen. Dead grass and weeds replaced the turf, and the goal posts were a nasty shade of rust. Surrounding the field was once a running track, the lines separating the lanes long since faded away.

I tightened the white kimono-like wrap I'd grabbed to keep my shoulders covered. Even with that, the blistering heat soaked through, but at least it wasn't getting a deeper burn. I already slathered on enough aloe vera.

We hiked down the hill, navigating through mole openings until we made it to the track.

"Now I'm not in the best running shoes, but you are. Run the length of the field, but don't just run, scream as loud as you can, stopping only when you run out of breath."

"You're insane." I loosened the wrap and let it billow.

"Try it. I'll show you." A terrible crackly voice emerged from him as his work boots dragged over the roughed-up track. He screamed and jogged, if you could even call it that, for about fifty metres.

It was the most ridiculous thing I've ever witnessed, and if I wasn't in such a horrible mood, I may have found it funny.

"Your turn."

I stood there with my hands on my hips and shook my head. "No way."

"Think of Jonathan and put all that energy into your scream and RUN!"

Jonathan - Major Asshole – hurt my brother, caused physical bruises to him and emotional bruises to me. I pushed all that hatred and shame down, and letting a scream go, I ran. It wasn't fast, and I wasn't loud. I didn't even get as far as Chad. How pathetic.

Chad closed the distance between us. "Nope. You over thought it. Don't squash those feelings – let them out. Take all your energy and spew it out into the world. Make the goal posts hear your anguish and pain. It's hard to explain but you'll feel the difference."

I narrowed my eyes. This was ludicrous, truly. No amount of sprinting and screaming was going to make me feel any better, however, I did as he asked as I wanted to get back home.

Thoughts lingered on the edges of my brain and my extremities tingled. One foot in front of the other, I pushed off from where I stood, the wrap falling from my hands. My mouth opened, and a high pitch scream escaped as each forceful step propelled me further and further. When I thought all the air was extinguished from my lungs, I came to a stop and turned back to see Chad. He was a good two hundred feet away.

"That's what I'm talking about," he shouted toward me. "Do it again."

And I did.

Many times.

Each time my distance got shorter, but I was starting to feel some sort of emotional control settle in. It was comforting to feel that again. I was surprised at how many feelings I'd held onto.

"Alright, time to get you back. I said thirty minutes." He handed me my white wrap.

A touch sweaty and breathless, I stretched out one leg and then another. "How'd you know about this place?"

He kicked a pebble on the ground, sending it through the goal posts. We *were* only ten feet away though.

"Do you come here?"

His lips remained glued shut.

It was crazy to me, because I didn't really know him, but he never gave off any kind of vibes of having any issues, at least nothing necessitating a full out screaming run. Guess it's true you never knew what battle another person was fighting.

He extended his hand and mine fit into it, and we hiked back up the hill. "This place is abandoned, so no one's around to hear the screams. It's a great place to get out and unwind."

"Yeah, it's kind of crazy how that worked."

"Like a set of pillows but better?" He winked.

I smiled, and for the first time in a while, I was smiling a true grin. "Yeah."

"Some day I'll tell you why I come here, but it will be a longer story than the drive back to your place, and you have someone waiting for you."

Yes, I do. I squeezed his hand. "Thank you for bringing me here. It's just what I needed."

A deep-seated curiosity settled over me. What were the reasons Chad came here? Maybe he was more familiar with my situation than I had given him credit for.

~Chapter Eleven

We arrived back at my house, and I checked on Michael and Melody. Confident all was okay as he was still sleeping, I suggested Melody go home, and hesitantly she left with a promise to arrive a little early the next day.

The whole afternoon had slipped away thanks to Jonathan's indiscretions and in the chaos, I'd left the lid open on the stain and the brush had dried out in the heat of the sun. Could I charge the bastard for lost time and expenses because, one way or another, he was going to pay, and I'd be making an itemised list, starting with everything out front.

"Shall I start on the deck?" I chucked the brush into a garbage bag and set the bad stain—resealed—into the box of the truck.

The sun was on the west side of the house, casting a shadow across the grass. No fear of making my sunburn worse.

"Nah, it's getting late." He glanced at his watch. "It's already after five."

"Can I at least make you supper? I feel after today, it's the least I could do."

"You did make me lunch."

I did?

Holy smokes the day seemed like the equivalent of about four regular days. Sheesh. Not good. Life was spiralling away from me.

"Hey," Chad said, his hand waving in front of my eyes.

"Yeah?"

"You okay?"

"Just thinking. It's been a crazy day."

"Yes, it has."

"So… supper? Yes, or no." I placed my hands on my hips.

The distance between us grew wider. "Would you be deeply offended if I said no?"

"I don't know if I would say deeply…" I aimed for flirty, but I think it came out desperate.

"Can I take a rain check?"

"Time to get home to the wife and kids, eh?" My voice no longer sounded desperate; it was pathetic, and I was ashamed.

A few at a time, he carried the railings over to the deck and laid them out. "I'll be back at eight-thirty tomorrow. Time to stain the deck floor and hopefully attach the railings and finish the ramp."

His reply was terse and moved quickly, storming from one part of the yard to the deck and back again. Suddenly so angry, and he avoided me at all costs. Geezus, and they say women were emotional and flippant. Whatever I said or did to set him off, it wasn't intentional, and I couldn't think of anything in particular so offensive. But there he was stomping around, his face tight with restrained rage.

He left with a "See ya," and drove away while I stood in shock wondering at what the hell just happened.

Screw Chad. My evening was going to be spent better without him. I made a pizza; high carb count be damned. Michael and I ate, and he allowed me to cuddle up next to him, watching

Finding Nemo and Finding Dory until he fell asleep. I needed my life to get back into a normal routine.

# # #

My shoulder's sunburns ached throughout the night, and I tossed and turned. Always one to sleep on my back, the damn things prevented me from doing so, and I woke up in a complete zombie fog. There wasn't enough coffee in the house to keep me awake.

I jogged to the corner store and back, carrying the necessities - coffee and milk. Armed with the supplies, I'd make Chad a couple of iced coffees. Maybe. If he would accept them from me.

The sky was a washed-out shade of grey – perfect to be outside working. Even though the deck had a built-in cover, courtesy of the jut out and overhang, there'd still be some sun filtering in. But only until the sun was high enough, then the whole deck would be shaded.

I couldn't wait to sit on it again in the evening, kicking back and relaxing on my free nights. As a surprise to Michael, I was on the hunt for a cheap deck swing, one fitting the width at the north end, where he could watch the birdies sing. I also needed to get a bird feeder and food. More things to add to my mental list. It was getting longer by the day.

Chad arrived promptly at eight-thirty, and I met him outside.

"Peace offering?" I said.

I handed him a thermal mug of ice-cold coffee drink, although the temperature wasn't so extreme today.

He took the drink and removed the lid, giving it a sniff.

"What? You don't trust me?" I was deeply offended, as if I would poison him. Jonathan on the other hand…

"No, I just love the smell of this. They need to make this in a candle so I can smell it in my apartment all the time. It reminds me of you." He walked to the back of his truck and started unloading the table saw and the other supplies.

"It reminds you of me? Like what? Bitter?"

Scrunched lines appeared across his forehead. "Yeah, because that's what I'm thinking." A foot on the tire, he hauled himself up and reached in the depth of the truck bed, grabbing a black box. "I'm not even going to go there with you."

Oh, well, now it was on, and I thrust out a hip and firmly placed my hand upon it. "Go where?"

He sighed and paused for a breath. "Here." A long stick with a paint roller attached was passed to me, as was a can of stain.

I took it and marched it over to the deck.

"I see your burns look worse."

Somehow, in a weird sort of way, it was comforting to know he was checking me out. Couldn't be that upset. "Yeah, they're quite painful."

"Pop a couple Advil." He carried more supplies over to the deck.

They all seemed to be for me, if I was the only one doing the staining. "I get to paint the deck today, right?"

"You're going to stain it, yes. If you want."

"Then why the roller?"

He sighed and gave me a look as if I were stupid. His tone wasn't much better. "It'll make whoever stains this deck floor easier. And then when it dries, it will be easier to back brush it."

I nodded, unsure if I wanted to help today. If he was going to talk to me like I was a child, I had other more important matters to attend to.

"Did you put sunscreen on?" He was dressed in work jeans, the worn in kind with paint splatters, however, every day he sported a white tee that looked as if he pulled it out fresh from the package each morning. It made his skin so golden and bronzed.

"Did *you*?"

I didn't wear sunscreen. It was dumb, but it clogged my pores and caused breakouts, especially on my face. The face cream I applied had it blended in, but I certainly can't go slathering it on my body.

"I will in a bit." He dug through one of the black bins and retrieved a blue can. "It's a spray, so I don't get greasy hands." He waved it in the air like he was the spokesperson for it. It was cute, and it made a tiny smile dance on my lips. "Here, turn around. I'll do your back."

The cool mist from the spray surprised me but I stopped myself from moving out of the way. Guess I was helping.

"Now you are protected."

"Shall I do you?" I asked. I didn't mean for it to sound how it did, but the reaction I got from Chad was worth it.

"Really now? I thought you didn't frolic? Was that the word you used?" He laughed.

Is it wrong to say I enjoyed the feel of his fingertips on mine as he whipped the can out of my hands? I shook my head and backed away. Clearly, I needed to get out more. It had been too long.

"I'm going to get Michael his breakfast, but I'll be back out soon, and I'll start the painting."

"How's he doing today?" His full attention was on me, concern on his face.

"He's okay, woke up just before you got here."

"I'm glad."

"That he woke up?" I said playfully as I dropped my hands beside my hips. "I get it, and I'm thrilled too, but I don't think he's in a hurry to meet any strangers."

"Too bad." Chad rocked back on his heels. "I mean it's too

bad the jerk ruined that for him. Do you have other care, other than Melody?"

I paused and swallowed. "No."

"No family?"

"No."

There was no need to launch into a discussion about my terrible mother, and the father who left us to pursue a blonde bimbo across the country. Last I heard, he was living the sweet life in Florida, but that was many years ago. He didn't bother coming to mom's funeral in January. Both my parents were only children, and since my father's abandonment, I had no contact with his parents. I don't even remember if he had them. And my mom's mom moved out east, so there goes that *family*.

"Friends?" He was reaching and was perhaps a little disgusted by the lack of people I trusted.

I shook my head again. "To you it may seem like it's a sorry way to live a life, but I'm telling you, we're quite happy."

And I tried my best to voice that happiness, but I don't think I was successful. Maybe because I didn't quite believe it myself.

He narrowed his eyes in my direction and nodded. "Good. I'm happy you're happy." But his tone wasn't filled with warmth, more like sadness. He wrapped a tool belt around his waist, and he walked over to the ramp part and started measuring.

I stood and watched until it felt creepy, so about thirty seconds worth, and I stormed to the back door in a huff.

I'll show you. I am happy. Ridiculously happy.

I helped Michael eat his breakfast and drink a high fat milkshake I would've loved to let slip down my throat. Made with cream and frozen strawberries, and a special weight-gaining powder the pharmacist recommended, it smelled fantastic. With the tip of a spoon, I gave it a taste, and Lordy was it delicious. Some day, maybe.

With the kitchen cleaned, I poured another smoothie in a thermal mug, and hung out by the front door.

Chad sawed and placed a few more boards into their spots, the first part of the ramp coming along. Shouldn't be much longer, a couple more days? Maybe, hopefully into next week. Not because I wanted him to be finished, but because I enjoyed having him around, oddly enough. It gave me something to look at, and truth be told I enjoyed having the company and adult conversation.

"W-w-w-here y-y-you g-g-g?" Michael's eyes locked on me.

"I'm going out to paint the deck." I knew it was stain, but I doubted it made any difference to Michael.

"C-c-c-can I c-c-c-come?"

"Of course. I can get a chair for you to sit in under the tree."

He nodded, and a growing smile emerged. It never failed to warm my heart. "P-p-p-please."

I wiped his chin from the spit and tussled his hair.

"I-I-I l-l-l-ove you."

The words cemented me to the ground and my heart swelled. "I love you too, Michael. Always and forever." I placed a tender kiss on his warm, sweet-smelling forehead.

"H-H-Help?" Slowly, he lifted his arms into the air.

Light as a feather, I pulled him onto his feet, and he shuffled beside me toward the back door. It took us a while, but we made it down the stairs and over to the front yard. He leaned on me most of the way.

He stood for a moment, and I ran to grab his chair, propping it up under the shade of the willow tree. Sitting and smiling, the light breeze ruffled his hair. It was time for a haircut as I brushed the longer strands out of his eyes.

Still as a statue, he searched the trees, and scanned along the fence lines. "B-b-b-irds."

With great effort, he pointed to the neighbour's house where a blue jay sat perched on the ledge of the house.

"I'm sure we'll see more." I hated the lie. The running saw would likely scare off any bird. Double checking on my brother, I sauntered over to the painting supplies and prepped myself for rolling the stain across the first part of the deck floor.

It really transformed the boring wood into a work of beauty. Sure, it was a light stain, and very plain at that, but with a few accessories, like an outdoor rug, the space could be serene and peaceful. Just imagining having a glass of wine after a hard day's work, put a spring into my work, and I rolled the stain on a little faster but not too fast. Chad had instructed me to be diligent and not sloppy.

"Looks good," Chad said but he wasn't looking at the deck.

An embarrassing amount of heat flushed through my cheeks. "You think so?" I leaned against the roller and lost my balance for a heartbeat, stepping into the wet stain. Regaining my balance, I stepped where I hadn't yet stained, and my footprint left a mark. "Damn it."

Chad laughed. "Well, a rug can go right there."

"Shit," I said, and quickly refilled my roller, re-covering the imprint. It mostly worked, but the imprint bleed through. Perhaps when it dried, I'd try again. So much for trying to be sexy.

"Don't," Chad said as I walked over to the stairs. He pointed. Like a rubber stamp, my footprint followed me, growing fainter as I moved to the edge.

"Damnit." I kicked off my tainted shoe, flinging it off the deck and knocking it against the fence.

"Nice kick." Chad retrieved it from the small bush.

"I'll get another pair," I said and returned in a pair of flip flops.

"Seriously, you don't have anything better than that?"

I looked at my naked feet with my unpainted toes. Aside from desperately needing a pedicure, there was nothing wrong with what I wore. Besides, I wasn't about to potentially wreck anything else. I grabbed my one bad shoe and turned it so the bottom faced the sun. "Just until it dries."

He nudged toward Michael. "Are those clothes his good clothes?"

It was a weird question, but I shrugged. "They're not his Sunday best."

Which was really a joke. Aside from mother's funeral, the last time I stepped in a church was eons ago. I just didn't believe there was an Almighty Father who'd let His *children* like Michael suffer with incurable diseases.

"Is it okay if they get a little paint splattered?" He raised his eyebrow, a faint crinkle forming on his forehead beneath the brim of his ball cap.

It took a second, but I saw where he was going with it. Sort of. "Yeah, it's fine."

He walked over to the shaded spot and hunched down in front of my brother. "Would you like to help us?"

Michael's face nearly burst with excitement and his arms flailed out to the sides. Good thing Chad was low enough to avoid being smacked. "Y-Y-Y-yeah."

"Great. I could use a good helper. Your sister keeps stepping on the stain, mucking everything up." He rose and went to prep an area for him.

I hadn't mucked *everything* up, but the statement made Michael laugh and his gaze connected with me.

I shrugged. "What can I say?"

I wasn't sure what he could paint, but I suppose in the grand scheme of things, it didn't matter. Michael was going to help and even if he did nothing more than hold a paintbrush, he'd be thrilled.

And that's all I cared about.

"Okay," Chad said from the northern part of the deck area, where the shade stretched out. He'd set the workhorses at a lower level and had a paintbrush and a small container of paint waiting. He walked over to Michael. "Can I help you up?"

Michael looked to me and up to Chad and back to me.

"It's your call," I said, approaching. If Michael wanted to, I'd support the idea, but he needed to make the decision.

The hesitancy was apparent on his face and he flickered between Chad and me. "Oh-oh-k-k-kay."

I stood right there, just in case, but it wasn't warranted. As if he'd done it a thousand times before, Chad helped Michael onto his feet and led him over to the new area he'd set up. There was nothing for me to do aside from carry his chair over.

Michael sat back, and Chad pulled the work horses closer, explaining what he wanted done. Michael took it all in, and with great pride, held the paintbrush in his left hand as Chad swiped it back and forth across a small plank of wood.

"L-l-l-l-ook," he exclaimed. "I p-p-p-paint."

"You're doing great." I leaned closer to Chad, keeping my voice. "What's he painting?"

"The base to a bird feeder and house. With the small leftover pieces, I'll be able to quickly assemble something wonderful for him."

"Thank you." I couldn't help myself, I gave Chad a quick peck on the cheek - the heat from his whiskery skin singed my lips and I was grateful to the stars for bringing this carpenter into my life.

Chapter Twelve

"Evanora," Joy's singsong voice cut through my daydreams. It had been so sweet watching Chad interact with Michael.

"Yeah?"

"You're in a fog of some kind."

"What? I am not." I gave her a curious look, narrowing my eyes and tipping my head to the side.

"You're smiling, and if I didn't know you better, I'd say you're almost happy."

She wasn't malicious in her tone, and the grin on her face said as much.

"Yeah," Niall said from behind me. "You've been a smiley thing today. It's abnormal." He playfully punched me in the arm. "What's going on? You run a bad driver off the road today?"

"Not at all," I said, scanning the restaurant.

The rush had settled, and my customers were happy, fed and content.

Niall motioned with his chin. "So, what's up?"

"Nothing. Just had a good day with Michael."

A really good day. He painted all the pieces for a bird feeder and didn't even know it. He was just excited to be a part of it.

"We've had so many bad ones, it was a nice change."

"Why? What happened?"

Just remembering a-hole Jonathan sent a surge of anger fueled blood through my veins, and I was insta-mad. My hands clenched into tight little fists, and I ground my teeth together.

"Jesus, what went on?" Niall escorted me to the back office. No one was around, so he kept the door open.

I explained everything that happened, starting with the bad and ending with the good. A shift in my soul with each telling word and by the end, when I mentioned Chad and how he got Michael involved, I was softening up.

"You should've said something before."

"And what would I have said?" I tossed my hand to my hip.

Niall's expression melted into genuine concern. "I don't know, something. You know I could've helped if you needed it. No matter what went down between us, I'm always here for you and Michael. You know he means a lot to me. I'm his big brother for crying out loud."

"Not for the past few years you haven't been."

When Michael was twelve, a gawky twenty-year-old named Niall was matched with him through the Big Brothers and Sisters program and once a week for a couple of hours, they would hang out and do activities. After a while as things got turbulent within my own life, I joined in on their fun. When I graduated high school, I started dating Niall and when Michael turned eighteen, his time with the program ended.

However, Niall still made it a point to see Michael once a month, although over the past year that's dwindled. You'd think with Michael living with me, it would happen more frequently, not the other way around.

He rested his stubby little hands on my shoulder, keeping

the distance manager-to-staff space apart. "What can I do? Do you want me to make some calls?"

I shook my head. I'd done what I needed to and handled it.

"Hey…" He tipped up my chin and looked me in the eyes. "It'll be okay."

"But it's not going to be." I crumbled and waivered a bit but pushed my rising emotional outburst back down where it belonged.

"I think you need some time off."

I shook my head, avoiding his eyes. "I can't afford too, you know that."

"Audrina, your tank is empty." Always metaphorical too, he'd often mentioned keeping your personal tank filled and how the little things can cause it to leak, and when the tank was empty, it was hard to cope. "If you don't fill it up, you won't get very far, and that's not good for anyone. Neither you *nor* Michael." He wrapped his arms around me, his hat switching from a hands-off manager to a compassionate friend. "When was the last time you did something for yourself?"

"I go for a run when I can."

"Pfft. That's not what I'm talking about. When was the last time you did something that wasn't work related or at your house, something truly for you, like a pedicure or a shopping trip or a girl's night?"

Gawd, him and Chad. Were they ganging up on me? I pushed out of his embrace. I knew he meant well, but it wasn't comforting. It never had been. "And what girls am I going to hang out with? Joy? No thanks. Simply too much chipper with that one."

"What about your doctor friend?"

I raised my eyebrow in scepticism, but Niall didn't know the whole story, and I was in no mood to explain it to him. "Anyway…" I shifted my weight between my feet, rocking back and forth. "Right now, I can't. Especially with things being what they are, I can't leave. I don't trust anyone to watch Michael."

"You trust Melody."

"Yeah. And I already max her out, every week."

He swallowed. "What if I watched Michael? I can sit with him or play cards. Like the old days."

As sweet as that was... "I don't know."

His fingers raked through the thinning blond strands on his head. Niall was all of thirty, but thanks to the alopecia, appeared much older. "Want to know what I think you should do?"

I chortled. "No, not really, but I'll bet you're going to tell me anyway."

"Take the weekend off. Melody works the evenings, right?"

Reluctantly, I nodded.

"Great. Now you are going to go do something. Anything. But you need a break from Michael, and you need a rest from here. A couple of weeks ago you were begging for relief, right?"

"But..."

"I'm not asking you to take the time off, I'm telling you." He put his metaphorical foot down with his words.

"The whole weekend?" I mentally added up the lost hours and multiplied it by the tips, going on the low side, and it was a lot. Losing that much income would be hard. "I can't do the weekend. Friday and Saturday nights are huge to me."

So much for the compassionate friend hat, Niall was back in full manager form. He grabbed a pencil with an eraser tip and smudged out my name on Saturday night. "There, problem solved."

"What?" My eyes opened wide. I couldn't believe he just did that. Of all the low down, rotten tricks. "We're short staffed as it is, and I *need* the Saturday night."

"It'll be fine. It's not your place to worry about the staffing situation, it's mine."

"What?" I wanted to laugh out loud, but tiny tremors of rage ran through my veins and helped to keep the laughing away. "Staffing situation? You begged me to help you interview that ass, Jacob."

"Audrina, relax. And for one night, we'll be okay. Plus, it's the labour-day long weekend, and the Saturday nights stink."

"No, please. Don't take me off the schedule." My eyes darted between the pencil and the shift schedule.

Niall sat in the chair and plunked away on the keyboard.

I just glared, a mixture of shock and anger swirling inside of me.

With a couple of quick taps, he erased two hundred dollars of wages and tips I needed desperately. On the screen, a pop up surfaced. "Look," he said, pointing to it. "Staff times for last year."

Only one server stayed past eight, and there had only been three on for the supper.

"The recorded tips."

Another screen popped up beside the first.

It would've been odd for so many to have tipped cash, considering the bills were extremely low. There certainly wasn't much recorded for tips.

"So, with you taking the day off, you're not losing out too much. I'd probably have to send you home early anyway."

"But I…" I scanned the schedule. My name missing from Saturday. My potential earnings erased with the letters.

Niall stood and sat on the edge of the desk, only to straighten himself up properly as his hand reached behind him. The worn-out leather wallet in his hand, he opened it. "About the money thing…" He extracted a few bills and pushed them into my hand. "No strings attached. Consider it a gift."

I hesitated, a lump catching in the back of my throat. It felt like I was going to cry, but I was stronger than that. Swallowing hard, I hoped the feeling disappeared. This wasn't the place or the time.

"I... I... can't." Under control, I said, "I can't accept your money."

"Audrina, listen to me. Either you take the day off and take my money to spend foolishly, or..." A mischievous expression crossed his face. "Or you're fired."

"What?" There's no way he'd actually do that, right? You'd need to have grounds for termination. A surge of panic flew through me. They could probably find reason too.

"I mean it. You are not to step foot in here on Saturday. So help me if you do." He leaned closer. "Don't make me fire my best employee, you hear?"

My heart pounded loudly, afraid it echoed throughout the entire restaurant. I held the cash, a tax-free gift, and felt the weight of it in my hands. What would I do with it? What kind of foolishness would come of it? Could I spend it on something for Michael? Or should I really go get a pedicure or something? The possibility of free money was a crazy thought. Just as was *not* working a Saturday. I couldn't even remember the last time I had that day of the week off.

"We're good?"

Slowly, I nodded and stepped back out of the small space, gratitude swimming in my heart. He'd given me more than just money, he was giving me a gift of time. Something in short supply lately. In a hushed voice and with blurry eyes, I whispered, "Thank you."

He smiled and winked. "Oh, one more thing. Don't go and tell anybody. I'd hate for them to think I had a heart."

"I promise, your secret is safe with me."

"I knew it would be." He waved his hands. "Now go finish your tables so I can cash you out."

# # #

The deck looked so beautiful in the heat of Friday's afternoon with its nicely stained floor, and hardly noticeable footprints, unless you knew exactly where to look. It was all covered by the shade of the house, and the beautiful overhang from which I'd excitedly hung Christmas lights. By the end of Friday's workday, the ramp was complete and ready for a test drive, or at least a walk up and down.

The job was nearly finished, save for the install of the railings and the staining of the ramp. My already limited time with Chad was nearing, and all day long I'd wanted to ask him a question, and all day long, I squashed it because I was afraid.

Michael had haphazardly painted more pieces, but I couldn't figure out how they assembled together. I supposed it didn't matter if Michael was happy. And he truly was. When Melody showed up at three-thirty, he stuttered and spit telling her all about it.

I dawdled, hanging around the front yard when there was no reason; the final bits were in Chad's capable hands. I paced up and down the sidewalk leading from the front to the deck so many times I worried I'd wear down the concrete slabs.

"Are you trying to get in all your steps today?" Chad asked, nailing an edging to the ramp.

I stopped. "No, why?"

"What's with all the back and forth then? You're making me nervous."

"I'm making *you* nervous?"

It was funny, but apparently only to me because he made me nervous. If my heart wasn't a dead giveaway with its relentless pounding, I would've already asked him.

Chad stopped the drill and nodded. "Yeah, you are."

"Just from walking?"

He propped up on one knee. "No, because it's got all the stylings of nervousness. Like you're unhappy with the job, and you're worried about how to tell me."

"How could I be unhappy with this?"

The front porch area had been transformed from a really old house with a just as ancient deck, to something much more modern, and way more appealing. I figured with a few bushes planted strategically in front of the ramp, it would hide most of it nicely. Not that it wasn't esthetically pleasing already. Chad was right, his design was much nicer than the boring old ramp suggestion I had in mind.

"Good, I'm glad you like it."

"I don't like it, I love it. It's truly magnificent."

"Really? It's just a deck." He set the drill down and came to stand beside me. Together we admired the changes.

"This is going to make things much easier for Michael – thank you."

"No, it's I who should be thanking you."

"Well," I started to speak but stopped as I inhaled a charming scent of musk and spice. It was pleasant and relaxing.

Chad opened his mouth, but nothing came out. After a moment of awkward glances, and thrusting his hands into his jeans, he cleared his throat. "I can finish up if I stay late tonight, or I can come back tomorrow."

"Are you asking what I prefer?"

"Yes."

"Well…" My heart hammered in my chest, and I shifted through the possibilities. If he stayed tonight, he'd finish while I was at work. So, if I didn't ask him about tomorrow, I'd lose my chance. If I suggested he come back tomorrow, at least I'd get to see him again and could offer my assistance to help finish up.

Chad laughed and rocked on his feet. "Toughest decision you've made all day?"

I playfully pushed him, the skin beneath his shirt tight. "I was weighing my options."

"Do you do that with everything?"

"Yes," I said, and heat singed my cheeks. "I think it's best if you come back tomorrow to finish up. I can pay you the remainder and make you a final iced coffee."

"Iced coffee? Well that cinches it, then. I'm coming back in the morning." The smile he gave me, the kind that winkles around his eyes and causes a crease to form across his forehead, warmed me through to my core. If I didn't act quickly, I might not get to see it again.

I paced some more.

Chad stopped in front of me. "What's going on?"

"Have you ever wanted to do something, but you were terrified to, just in case it didn't turn out well?" I twisted my hands together and stared at a patch of grass sprinkled with flecks of white paint.

"All the time."

I scanned his face for understanding. "And what did you do about it?"

"I just did it. The perceived is likely worse than the reality."

I swallowed. "I... I..." This was probably why guys did the asking out. Wow, this was tougher than I thought, especially since I'd never done anything like this. I kicked at the patch of grass, keeping my eyes fixed on the greenery, slowly counting the dots of paint. "Are you busy tomorrow night?"

A soft, amused chuckle floated in the air. "Are you asking me out on a date?"

"Yes, but not really."

"I could've sworn I asked you out earlier in the week and

124

you shot me down." He got close and my breath caught in the back of my throat.

"It's just for an evening. Nothing further."

He narrowed his eyes.

An explanation was in order. "My boss gave me the night off. Insisted I take the time off and do something that doesn't include Michael or working."

"And you thought of me?"

My gaze fell to the window. Inside Melody walked beside Michael.

"I don't have any friends to ask. I've managed to fuck up…" I covered my mouth. "Sorry, that slipped. What I meant was I've managed to ruin all my friendships recently. It takes a crisis to make you realise who your friends are."

Because when I pushed them away when Michael needed my attention, they were content to stay away. And aside from Katrina, who comes when Michael needs her, the others have stayed far away.

"What did you have in mind?" He looped a thumb through the tool belt.

"I don't know. My boss gave me some cash to go and spend frivolously."

His eyebrow arched. "Really? That's a pretty decent boss."

"Yeah, he's a good guy. Total pain in my ass at work, but otherwise…" I had to give credit where credit was due. Overall, Niall had a heart of silver, not quite gold, but close.

"So you have no ideas?"

"I have limited ideas. The frivolous cash will only go so far."

He nodded. "Frugal but frivolous. I like it."

"So are you saying you'll agree to go out with me. Just once." I held up my finger for good measure.

"Why just once?"

"Because it's all I can give right now."

"Are you doing this because your boss told you so or because you feel you truly need a night away?"

Answers weighed on me, and I wasn't sure how to answer. "Both?."

"That does make it a challenge."

"How so?"

"Well, if I agree to go, I want it to be fun. I don't want you to go through the motions of having fun. I'd want you to actually enjoy yourself."

"I think I can handle that." I gazed into his eyes. "So… do you want to go?"

He shrugged. "One condition. You plan something, and I'll plan something."

"How's that going to work?"

"You decide what we'll do before supper, and I'll think of something fun after supper."

"And what about the actual supper?" I asked, needing to make sure it was affordable. Dinner options ranged from take out to uber fancy, and I didn't have money for much more than a high-end takeout.

"We'll figure it out."

That didn't help one iota. "Okay," I said, thinking that this may work out well after all. "It's a date."

"Just one little lonely date."

He looked so sad when he said it, but I just couldn't give more. And there was no need to lead him to believe there could be anything beyond. "Just one date." I headed up the stairs on the front porch.

"I'll take what I can get," I heard him say as the screen door closed.

Chapter Thirteen

To celebrate the completion of my long-awaited deck, I jogged up and down the ramp like a child entering a park. Chad joined in and showed me the strength of it by jumping on different sections.

"I built you a sturdy deck."

"Yes, you did."

"Now grab the wheelchair, so you can see its true purpose."

After lunch, Michael asked to lie down, so I'd tucked him for a snooze. "He's still sleeping."

"So, you sit and enjoy the ride."

"I don't know." I couldn't imagine being pushed. It would feel awkward, especially because I could handle walking around.

"Would you prefer to push me?"

I laughed out loud and tapped a finger against my chin. "Maybe."

At least it would give me some practise on manoeuvring it around with some weight in it.

"Go get it." He gestured to the door.

A moment later I returned, easing the wheelchair onto the deck. I propped open the chair and set the brakes.

127

"Whenever you're ready."

He removed the knee pads and dusted himself off. With a solid thump, he relaxed in the chair. "I'm ready."

Unlocking the brakes, I wheeled him down the south side of the deck, and slowly turned around. There wasn't a lot of turning radius, but it was enough for our purposes. I pulled hard to not let the momentum bring him down and a few steps later we were levelling out on to the ground.

"What'd you think?"

"It's very smooth. Nicely done." I patted his shoulders. So tight, so muscular. I let my hand linger a touch longer than was necessary or needed, but it felt nice. When he turned his head to gaze up at me, my hand retracted and held tightly to the steering handles. "Shall we try a return trip up?"

"I would say so. That will be the true test."

I wheeled him around onto the sidewalk and prepared for the push uphill. It went a little smoother than expected, and I was taken aback by the strength I had needed to push a full-grown man up a ramp. However, if I could do it with Chad, Michael, who was a much smaller man, would be even easier.

"Well done," I said as we got back onto a flat and even surface.

"Thank you."

He rose out of the wheelchair so effortlessly; a pang pinched my heart knowing Michael could never do that. He'd always need assistance.

"Now, I know you've said theft is a problem in this neighbourhood, so I installed a bolt here." He pointed to the railing lining the north edge of the deck. There was a metal ring fastened into one of the main railings. "If you pick up a cable lock, you should be able to secure a BBQ or something, without fear of it finding a new home."

"That's awfully nice of you, Chad. Thanks." I hadn't ever thought of cooking outside, especially since I didn't have a BBQ, but it was a nice idea. "I was thinking of getting a carpet to roll out here, and maybe a few planter boxes. Eventually, if I can find one on a wicked sale at the end of season, I'd like to get a swing. Michael would really enjoy that."

"Speaking of Michael, I have homework for you."

"What?"

He trotted down the stairs and over to his truck, returning with a white bird house. It was sizeable and would comfortably fill the wheelchair seat. "You paint on some designs and give it a name. When it's all done, I'll come and put it up under that tree, near the bird feeder."

"Bird feeder?" I searched around until my eyes fell upon it, already hanging in the willow tree.

"Once you start filling it, keep on doing it. The birds will start to rely on you, and you don't want them to go hungry."

"Of course not."

Michael would be thrilled with this, and immediately I wanted to wake him so as to share this wonderful news. However, I let him carry on with his nap.

"Thank you."

"It's my pleasure." He folded the wheelchair after pushing it closer to the door. "Now, I'll invoice you tomorrow for the remainder, and I'd appreciate it if you paid within ten days."

"I can pay you in full now." The money waited in the safe in my bedroom.

He looked at me, curiosity and uncertainty holding the same space. "For real?"

"Yeah, and in cash."

"Okay, great. I'll be right back."

He sauntered off to his truck and came back with a metal

clipboard. He pulled out the quote and the necessary paperwork. Everything was itemised; a running list with purchased items, and another with his clocked hours. He punched a few numbers into his calculator and wrote the total at the bottom, deducting the deposit already paid. For final effect, he circled the total.

"That's a lot lower." My eyes widened.

"Well, you helping out reduced the number of hours I needed to be here. It was win-win for us both."

"Are you sure?"

He ripped off my copy of the bill and passed it to me. "Absolutely."

"Alrighty, I'll be right back." I disappeared into my room after a quick check on the still sleeping Michael. Returning, I passed him an envelope stuffed thick with bills. "My apologies for it being in tens and twenties, but it's all I had. Double check, if you'd like."

"I trust you." He lifted the lid of the metal clipboard and dropped the envelope inside it.

"Do you construct porch swings?"

"Like the free-standing kind? Yeah, of course. They're not complicated at all." He gazed around the deck. "You want it here?" He mapped out an area with his feet.

"I thought maybe here, in a diagonal to the railings." Like an airport worker, I waved my hands in two straight lines, my imaginary lights marking where I wanted it to go.

Chad looked up and searched the ceiling. The rafters were open. "You know, I could make you a hanging one, but it would become part of the house. It would even be a bit cheaper since I wouldn't need as much for supplies."

My heart pitter-pattered faster. With the money saved on the deck, I could afford a hanging swing.

"Could you draw me up a quote? I like the quality of your craftsman ship, and I think I'd like to hire you again." I let the sexiest smile I had in me bubble to the surface.

"I'll draft something and send it to you by Monday morning. Does that work?"

"It sure does."

"I'd do it sooner, but I have a hot date tonight, and I need to clean myself up and make myself presentable."

I winked. "Well, I expect it in my inbox Monday morning."

"You have my word." He tucked the clipboard under his left arm and extended his right hand. "Audrina, it's been a pleasure. Thanks for your business."

He was all serious, and I was a little surprised. Still, I met his hand, and pumped it up and down. "Thanks, Chad."

With a hop in his step, he waltzed to his truck, waved, and drove away.

It was two in the afternoon and Melody would be here soon.

I prepped Michael a high fat, high protein smoothie with extra strawberries, and when I went into his room, he was starting to wake up. "Hey, sleepyhead," I said, tousling his hair. His head felt warm, but nothing alarming. "How you doing?"

"Oh-oh-oh k-k-k-ay." His voice was still sound asleep.

I rubbed his arms in a slow motion. "Shall I help you into the living room?" A lightbulb went off in my head. "Better yet, would you like to see the bird feeder Chad hung for you? I can wheel you over."

It was a slow nod, but it was there.

I ran and grabbed the chair, wheeling it back into his room. Stepping over it, even after moving it as close to the bed as possible, I managed to make it back in front of Michael. A quick grip and he was seated within a couple of seconds. Brakes off, I twisted the chair back out of the room and into the living room. That space was much easier to walk and turn in.

Bumping open the screen door, I pulled him out backwards

and onto the deck. "Ta da." I waved around. "What do you think?"

"N-n-nice." His eyes widened.

"Now check this out. Easier to walk up and easy to wheel up too." I ran down the ramp and back up, throwing my arms out. "See?" Grabbing the handles on the chair and moving very slowly, I wheeled him down the ramp and over to the willow tree. I stood beside the feeder and gave it a little tap.

"B-b-b-b-ird…"

"Yeah, a bird feeder. You helped paint this."

A tired smile split across his face, pushing up his cheeks, but he didn't say anything. He tried to lift his arm but only got as far as pointing his hand, and it curved in the wrong direction.

"We have a bird house that you helped paint too. I'm going to paint little welcome signs on it, and Chad says he'll come back and hang it for us. Isn't that great?"

His eyes remained focused on the new feeder.

He was off in temperament again, but I expected as much. He'd been off since he woke that morning. The two days of fantastic energy had drained him.

"Time to go back in? I have a smoothie ready for you." I was pushing him up the ramp when Melody arrived.

"Oh wow," she said, catching up. "Great job that guy did."

"Sh-sh-sh-sheee h-h-h-h-elp." Michael spit out, irritation high in his voice.

Melody looked at me, her brows furrowed. "I know she did." In my direction, she mouthed, "Is he okay?"

I shrugged. It wasn't uncommon for him to be annoyed at something, but it was weird for him to snap at Melody. I parked the wheelchair inside the house and helped Michael onto the couch.

"Be right back with your smoothie."

Melody followed me into the kitchen. "Are you using that new mix?"

Once out of earshot, she whispered, "What's up with him?"

"He's really off today." I grabbed the smoothie and gave it a quick blend. "He took a nap this afternoon too. Hasn't eaten much, but I can get a smoothie or two in him."

The lid came off the blender, and I inhaled the scent of strawberries.

"I'll give it to him, you go get ready for work."

I hadn't told her I wasn't going in as I felt guilty in using her services for my own pleasure. At least if I were working, it felt justifiable. Besides, this was a one-time deal. Chad and I were going out for one date, and that was it. This way by not telling Melody, there was the expectation to be back home by a certain time but was still allowed the luxury of being around adults that I wasn't serving and taking orders from.

Content that things were good with Melody and Michael, I ran a bath and added my favourite bubble fragrance to it. The water was so silky when I lowered myself into it, I sighed a great relaxing sigh. I drifted away, lost in too many thoughts, but most of them revolved around Chad and a tingling sensation I hadn't felt in a long time focused itself on my core. It didn't take long to work myself up into a frenzy and melt in the tub when the moment exploded.

Chapter Fourteen

*J*ust before five, Chad rolled up in his washed-up navy-blue truck and I walked out front, the two voices inside wishing me fun. Guilt at lying to Melody caught up to me and I caved, admitting it wasn't work I was preparing for but a date. When she inquired with who, Michael's eyes lit up with the mention of Chad's name.

After reassuring her I wouldn't be late, I descended the stairs and met Chad who had hopped out of his truck and made his way up the walk. We both froze when we spied the other.

"You look, wow," Chad began, his eyes roving up and down my body.

Because I had a little time to ready myself, I put some curls into my otherwise flat as a stick hair, and gave it a fluff, amazed at how transformed I appeared. No top knot, shorts and a tank, just a simple hi-low dress in a gorgeous shade of emerald, with a strappy pair of flats. I selected the green hue as it worked well with my skin type, especially the singed skin on my shoulders which I could cover with the wrap I hung over my arm.

Chad himself looked completely different. Gone were the blue jeans replaced with a pale beige set of khakis. His perfectly new-looking white tee poked out from under an unbuttoned navy top. But it was his handsome face drawing the most attention. Without a ball cap covering his head and shading his eyes, I was rendered speechless at the change, especially when he removed the sunglasses. His light brown hair was parted and combed off his head, and his hazel eyes were stunning, taking me all in.

I would've blushed more if that were possible, as it was my cheeks felt like they were on fire.

"You truly look amazing." He stretched out his hand.

I fit mine into his, and clasped my hand shut. "Thanks. You look pretty darn amazing yourself."

"So where are we off to?"

"Well, I've given that a lot of thought."

He laughed as he opened the door. "I'm not surprised."

"And..." I said, pretending to ignore his comment. "Considering I know very little about you–"

"You know a lot about me."

"Professionally, sure, but personally, no."

"Did you find my Facebook page?"

"There wasn't one."

It had been easy to uncover loads out about his business, and I followed all his social media accounts, but anything private was a mystery.

A wry smile crossed his face as he closed my door and climbed in on his side. "It's because you weren't looking in the right places." He

I scrunched my face. "Wrong places?" Tapping my fingers, I listed all the social media platforms I knew. "You, as in you the private person, are not on there."

"You're right, *Chad Lewandowski* doesn't have a private account. But his true persona does." A subtle wink flew in my direction.

"What?" I gasped. The sneaky bugger had a different account. "So what, like Chad the Man? Or something better?"

"No. Like Chad Lawton. Lewandowski is my mom's maiden name, and the name of my uncle, who taught me my carpentry skills." The truck rumbled to life under us. "Where are we off to? What was your well thought out plan?"

I thought he was mocking me, and annoyed, I rested against the door, keeping my distance from him.

He parked at the intersection and waited. "Left or right?"

"Right," I said in a huff.

"Right it is."

He drove for a bit while I continued to call out directions. At one point I asked him if he wanted the name of the place, but he said it was more fun this way.

Finally, we parked outside the little Italian restaurant *Amici Cibo*. Sadly, the owner had died unexpectedly, but his wife ran the place. The food was fantastic and the atmosphere amazing. Every so often, I'd check for hiring's, but they must treat their staff well as they never had job openings.

"We're going to eat first?"

I nodded and hopped out of the truck.

"But I thought we'd event first, then eat and event again." Disappointment echoed in the truck.

"I altered it a little, figuring we'd have more fun with a full belly. After we're done, the place for the event is next door." I pointed down the strip mall.

"I can get behind that."

We walked inside *Amici Cibo* with its Tuscan themed interior, graced with little twinkle lights dancing in the greenery pots spaced throughout the small space. Stone tiles led in various directions along the floor. The main path headed toward the table the hostess led us toward, and another with a gentle turn to the left would lead to the restrooms.

"I'll get your server and be right back," the hostess said, placing menus in front of us.

"This place is quite fancy," Chad said, leaning across the small round table.

"It appears that way, but it's very reasonably priced." I'd been in here a couple of times previously and always impressed.

"Are those pictures of the chain?" Chad pointed to several images of Amici Cibo on the wall.

"Actually, those are pictures of the store fronts in the previous locations around the city until he parked it here permanently," our server said. "Hi, I'm Charlotte, and I'll be serving you this evening." She was a skinny little thing, with bright red curly hair, and a basketball pushing against the fabric of her shirt. "Would you care to start with a glass of wine?"

Chad nodded. "Yes, I'll have the house white."

"Make it two."

"Excellent. Are we celebrating anything tonight?"

I looked at Chad and up to the waitress. "No. It's our first date."

"Well congratulations. We all start there. I'll be right back with your wines."

She disappeared behind an impressive wall of wines.

"This is some place." His gaze jumped from one spot to another, and he twisted in his seat.

"Yeah, it's great." I scanned the menu and settled on an old favourite.

"Do you recommend anything?"

"I like the pasta primavera."

He studied the menu, his fingers tapping against the edge. "Can I be honest?"

"Yes." I swallowed, not sure I wanted to hear the honesty.

He leaned close, his chest pushing into the edge of the table. "I'm really nervous."

"What, really? Why?" I wanted to laugh but decided against it.

"There's just so much expectation and–"

I put my hand up. "Let me stop you right there. There's no expectation for anything."

Chad swallowed and put his menu down. "Yes, there is. This is the only night I have a chance to wine you and dine you, so to speak. If I screw up, there will never be a second date to prove I'm not a muck-up."

"A what?"

"It what my mother always says."

"She calls you that?" And I thought my mother was nasty.

"No, but she does to others."

Our waitress set down our wines, and we gave our orders.

I tasted a sip of the cool, fruity liquid, letting it slip easily down my throat. It was so delicious that if I didn't watch myself, it would disappear quickly.

"Well," I said, putting my glass down. "I don't want you to be nervous, okay?"

He nodded but looked unconvinced.

"No, I mean it. We're going to have a great dinner, and then we're going to go and have a lot of fun. Deal?"

A long blink came my way, and for a moment I worried. About what though, I couldn't put my finger on. Eventually, his expression relaxed, and a smile came back to his face.

I sighed, releasing my own pent-up nervousness. This wasn't a date that would be going places, which Chad understood... now. I wasn't ready for any kind of commitment, and tonight was a one-time thing. I just wish he hadn't put so much pressure on himself. There was really no reason for it.

"All good?" I asked, watching him lean back against the chair, his eyes focused on me.

"You really are direct, aren't you?" His tone laced with a jovial mocking.

"Is there any other way to be? I don't think so." I swallowed a gulp of wine, letting the tingling sensations work their way out to my fingertips.

For some reason, every time I had an ounce of alcohol, I always felt it move out to my extremities. It was the weirdest feeling.

Needing to deflect the piercing stare I was getting, I asked, "What's your family like?"

"Big. Two older sisters, one who's married to Batman and has the twin girls. Then there was me and a set of twins followed a few years after; another brother and sister. Between my siblings, so far, I have five nieces and nephews, and my parents are still together." He took a sip of his wine. "A little different than your family, I assume."

"A little." It was hard imagining everyone in one place. Family gatherings had to be few and far apart. "Do they all live nearby, or scattered all over?"

A gentle chuckle pierced the air. "All within a twenty-minute drive of my parents. Every Sunday we get together at my parent's ranch after church, and the fifteen of us have brunch and chat all afternoon."

"And that's why you don't work on Sundays." It made sense now but seemed kind of abrupt the first time he mentioned it. A little explanation may have been helpful.

"That's why." A smug look crossed his face.

"And you do that every week?"

"Family is important to me. My brothers and sisters are

more than just family, they're my friends, and their spouses too."

It was pretty stinking cool how they all got together like that. It was just Michael and I, and definitely no weekly traditions. Everything went based on how he was doing, and that was a day-by-day thing.

"Has a girlfriend of yours ever graced that family get together?"

The moment the dumb question rolled off my tongue and out of my mouth, I shook my head and covered my mouth. A horrified look crossed his face and caused a flash behind his eyes. Even thought in the next heartbeat it was gone and his composure was back, the damage had been done.

"I'm sorry, you don't have to answer."

"No, it's okay." His chest expanded with the intake of air. "It was bound to come up later anyway if I didn't explain."

I leaned forward, ready to hear whatever it was he was about to spill.

"You know what, never mind." He waved away his thought like it was dust in the air. "Too heavy for a first date."

And *that* conversation was over.

"You go. Tell me about your previous relationships."

I laughed, I didn't mean to, but it fell out of me. "They can hardly be called relationships. My track record isn't great."

"Promising." His smile returned, pushing up the left side of his cheek.

"Yeah, I have a tendency to pick winners." Sarcasm reigned supreme in my tone. "You know, guys who try to demoralise me, or guys who are seeing someone else and they fail to mention it."

"Ouch."

"That last one was my best friend's guy. They were having a secret relationship with each other, but neither said anything to me."

Chad rested his forearms on the table as he inched closer. "And she caught you together?"

"Yeah."

A horrible memory flooded my brain. Not that it was her fault, but she wasn't even supposed to have come home from her parent's house that day. It took me by surprise, Marc too. As did finding out that they were an item.

"It was a great way to lose both a best friend and a potential boyfriend in one fell swoop. One star, don't recommend." I tried to laugh away the dull ache.

"Sounds like everyone had something to lose."

I shrugged.

"Sometimes these things have a way of working themselves out though. Maybe your friend will come back."

"She does, but only for Michael's sake."

"Oh, that was her?"

"That was her." It was sad really, losing a friend over a guy. Very high school drama like, in my opinion. "It didn't matter how much I grovelled, she refused to accept my apologies."

"But you didn't do anything wrong."

"I slept with her boyfriend."

"But you didn't know they were hooking up."

"Still, I didn't do my due diligence." My fingers twitched. "I've made my apologies and I've moved on. Besides my focus shifted drastically when Michael came to live with me."

Chad leaned closer, his eyes moving over my face as I spoke, and his hand gently caressing the top of mine. "It must've been rough."

I stared into the depths of his eyes, daring his past to show itself. For a guy, he was super compassionate and understanding. What had happened in his previous relationships to make him so sweet?

141

Our waitress broke our bond by placing our food in front of us. "If you need anything, please let me know." She waddled away with a smile on her face.

Silently, we dug into our meals, the rich aromas tugging on the pleasure centre of my brain.

"He's lucky to have you."

"Who, Michael?"

"Of course, and he adores you."

Hearing his name, a smile bloomed on my face. He was my favourite person in the whole world. "Well, I adore him. The innocent way he sees everything, how in a rushed moment he'll stop and stare at a bird, watching it as it flies around. I love his outlook on life. Always so happy, well, most of the time." My ray of sunshine, who had a few grey clouds hovering over him lately. "I'm sure all siblings are like that."

He laughed, and a chewed piece of pasta fell out of his mouth. Like coals in a fire, his cheeks turned beet red. "Oh shit." The linen napkin had all the fun wiping the corners of his lips. "Where were we?"

"Sibling love."

"Oh yeah. Not in my house, not to begin with anyway." He made sure to finish chewing before speaking. "My sisters fight like cats and dogs, and growing up so did my brother and I. I can't say I *adore* any of my siblings, but there isn't much I wouldn't do for them. And vice versa."

"That's what I meant." I winked.

"Didn't you and Michael ever fight?"

"No, not really. He was too fragile and it was never a fair fight. I dominated him in just about every way. Kind of took the fun out of it."

"Yeah…" A broad smile crossed his face. "It's fun times getting your siblings into a battle. We still do it."

"For real?"

"Yep. Every week someone tries to goad someone else into an argument or a wrestling match, but it never lasts long."

"Sounds fun." I took a carefully portioned bite and chewed it slowly, savouring the taste of the carbs. The cells in my body rejoiced with each bite, although they'd make me pay for it later.

"It really is. You'll come out one day and see it."

I stopped chewing and stared, his words spoken so casually. I didn't want to remind him how this was just a one-time date thing, but somewhere between the wine and pasta he'd forgotten. It's not that I didn't like Chad. He was funny and easy to talk with, and good looking to boot, but I couldn't share my heart with him, if that's where things went. But they can't. It's not fair to Michael. What if Chad's family was already full, and there wouldn't be room for him? What if his disabilities were too much? Didn't sound like they'd ever dealt with that on a personal level.

Trying to dismiss his comment, I chased my pasta with a hearty swallow of my wine, nearly finishing it in the process.

Our server came back to check on us, a fire-red curl escaping her ponytail. She tucked it behind her ear.

"Can I get a root beer?" I asked her. If I was going to feel bloated and gross, may as well toss a soft drink down the pipe too.

A long, languishing moment passed between us. I spent the time watching our waitress float between tables, a spring in her waddled steps. She reminded me of Joy, eternally happy. As she walked to the back, a handsome guy came out and stood in front of her, rubbing her belly as he leaned in closer. Her eyes closed, and a huge smile covered her face. That couple was deeply in love.

I flipped my focus back to Chad, who had followed my gaze and was also staring at the couple.

"That's nice to see."

"I agree." I pushed my plate away. "They look happy."

"You know, my sister struggles with finding love, but she's quite absorbed in her work so I think that's hindering her."

"What does she do?"

"She's interning in pediatrics."

"Oh wow!"

"She reminds me of you."

"How so? I'm not in med school."

"Working sixty plus hours a week plus all her studying, well, she's let a few things go."

I gave him a sly smile. "Like being in love?"

"Sort of."

"A person doesn't need to be in love to be complete or fulfilled."

He pushed his plate away and dropped his napkin on top. "Do you honestly believe that?"

"I'm not going to deny how it would be nice, but it's not a necessity. Besides, my life already belongs to someone."

"To Michael?"

Tiny morsels of defensiveness built within me. "Yes. He's my passion. No one can love him better than I can."

He nodded and stretched his legs off to the side. "That's probably the greatest truth I've heard from you yet."

"Why do I hear a but coming?"

His back hit the chair, and his mouth opened but nothing came from it.

"No, say it," I said as the rage bubbled. When it came to Michael, I was fiercely protective, and as often as I said I didn't care what people said about him or me or us, I did.

"Forget it. It was just an observation, and I don't know you well enough to—"

"You're right, you don't know me well enough." Anger twisted and flared, and a ribbon of heat flashed across my neck and spread quickly over my face and ears.

The waitress dropped off my root beer and gathered up our plates. "Everything okay?" she asked, her focus on me.

"Just fine."

She stood there longer than needed, but I knew she was assessing the situation. I'd have done it too.

Chad's shoulders were back, and tension corded through his neck as he stared anywhere but at me or our waitress. I was sure a surly expression was written all over my face, but I released my hands allowing them to uncurl from the fist, hoping it would reflect in my eyes.

"Can I bring you a dessert?"

"Just the bill please," Chad said.

Neither of us spoke until she came back with our totals. I presented her with my credit card, and she entered the info into the card reader. "What are your plans for the rest of the evening?"

I was glad customers went up to the till by the door to pay at Westside so I could avoid this incredibly awkward small talk. Still, I fell for it. "We're going to the Scape House down the strip, and then he has something planned for after that."

She ripped the receipt off the top. "I hope it's enjoyable. I've heard great things about Scape."

"Thanks." I shoved the folded paper into my wallet. "Good luck with the baby."

A glow filled her cheeks. "Thanks, only a few weeks left." She gathered the last of the glasses and walked away.

The remaining two ounces of root beer slipped down my throat, cooling my rage with each sip. I stifled a burp and took in a long breath, holding it briefly and releasing it when the tension left my shoulders. Another deep breath, and once again I was in control of my emotions and thoughts. Chad hadn't been rude and didn't deserve my outburst.

I broke the lingering silence between us. "You still want to hang out?"

"Yeah, I do."

"Good." I smiled. "Me too." It was the truth, and there was sincerity in my voice.

He pushed back from his chair and rose. "Then let's play."

Chapter Fifteen

We burst through the main doors of Scape House with sore bellies from laughing so hard and a wee bit of a headache from the panic-inducing fun. Walking away from the party of four we were grouped with, I waved and stood by Chad's truck.

"I'm glad we went," Chad said, a relaxed and joyful look upon his face.

"Me too. It was fun."

For forty-five minutes, I was pre-occupied with solving clues and putting tangram style puzzles together. My thoughts had never waivered, and it truly felt good to engage it in something fun. "You're pretty quick at solving riddles."

He shrugged and pulled open the truck door for me. "Maybe. It bodes well that you enjoy them."

Holding his hand, I climbed in and belted up as the door closed and he got in on his side. I wasn't sure what could top the Scape House, but I was willing to play along. "Now where are we going?"

"Someplace fun." He looked over at my feet. "Are those comfortable shoes?"

"I wouldn't wear them if they weren't." My toes wiggled inside the fabric of my flats. There was a lot of cushioning as I wore the same pair in black for work and my feet never ached after a full shift.

"Great." He put the truck into drive and eased on out of the parking spot.

I took in the surroundings and admitted I was in unfamiliar territory. We got onto a back road leading us away from the city. Giant pine and spruce trees lined the banks of the asphalt, and occasionally, I'd spot a tiny pond through a clearing. Wherever we were going, it was certainly pretty.

He pulled off the road and under a sign reading 'Corn Maze'.

"Have you ever been?"

I shook my head and glanced around. The parking lot was rather deserted with only a few parked cars. A small group of kids yelled and played on a stack of hay bales while others jumped on some sort of huge red balloon tucked into the ground. It was like a trampoline but not quite.

He paid for admission, and we walked over to the entrance to read the instructions. "At each fork there will be a question and the correct answer will take you in the right direction."

"I think we've got this." I smiled, eager to start. Trivia was my strong suit.

After twisting and turning through the paths lined on either side with eight-foot tall corn stalks, we finally arrived at the first marker. I felt like I'd done a complete 360 but had yet to come back to the start.

"First post," I said and grabbed the laminated card inside the mailbox.

If this is your first time through, take the left.

I stared at the card and showed Chad after flipping it over

148

to see where the trivia was

He shrugged. "Maybe it's one of those paths where it doesn't matter what direction you go, they'll both lead to the same spot?"

"Maybe. I wish I'd taken a photo of the design they'd made."

Near the entrance there was an aerial photo of the maze. It would be helpful right about now, if only to verify I was going to end up at the same spot regardless.

"That would be like cheating, wouldn't it?"

"No more that what we did at Scape."

One of our group members had attempted our puzzle before and helped us with a clue we couldn't understand.

"True." He stood at the start of the left path. "Let's go."

We walked further, having to back track a couple of times as we hit a dead end. Had Chad been here before? He was letting me make most of the decisions, but maybe because all of his resulted in returning to a spot we'd been at.

Suddenly, a fork presented itself to us.

"We have to be close, right?" I asked Chad, as if he'd knew.

He nodded and rubbed his chin. "Should be. How 'bout you go that way, and I'll go this way and if you find it, shout it out."

"What if I get lost?"

"You won't. Besides, I'm sure there are guards or something that patrol and help re-direction you." A shy grin crept across his face and spread up into his eyes. "And you can always holler if you need me."

I slowly nodded but willed myself to play along. "Okay."

It didn't take too long before his footsteps faded away. It was borderline eerie how quiet the corn maze became, and a brush of fear propelled me along the winding path.

From out of the silence, and as if he were only ten feet

away, his voice called out. "Found it."

I turned back and retraced the few steps I'd taken and arrived at the fork, taking the other path—Chad's path. I followed it into a circular path and spotted him. Leaning up against post number two looking all smug with pride, he passed me the laminated card.

Go left if you think the sun will set on your right.
Go right if it will set on your left.
Go straight if will set in front of you.

I stretched up on my toes, failing to see over the tops of the stalks. "This should be easy."

The sun was low but hadn't yet set. It was clearly on my left. "So, we go right?"

Chad nodded. "That was my thought."

More twists and turns. Each post we arrived at had a bizarre comment or question, and my pile of useless knowledge was not getting a workout or scoring me any brownie points. Once we took the wrong turn only to end up back at the clue post.

"Guess we should've picked the answer I suggested," but I said it with a laugh.

It had been fun to think we were on the right path only to see we weren't. And Chad, damn him, never appeared unfettered whenever we approached a dead end or a wrong turn. Meanwhile I was batting away at the morsels of insecurity while keeping a smile on the surface. I was having fun but being lost wasn't a thrill for me.

The seventh clue, and the correct answer, led us to a bridge I assumed was near the edge of the field. It wasn't tall but took us above the tops of the corn field; the carved-out maze sprawling around us in all directions. It was a breathtaking viewpoint.

"It's gorgeous," I said, the need to whisper overcoming me.

The sun sat above the horizon, throwing out golden hues into the sky. The fields turned to amber and waved in the breeze.

I tightened my wrap and glanced over to Chad. Hair touched by the rich shades of the setting sun, gave him a natural glow and warmed his skin tone. I was seeing him in a new light, figuratively and literally. He inched his way closer, but not close enough to touch, as if he were keeping the distance out of respect. After all, this was only a first date. And just one date at that.

But I couldn't help myself.

I leaned my head closer to him and closed my eyes, wondering how stupid I'd look if he didn't interpret my signals. It was foolish of me to have worried.

The warmth of his breath greeted me just before his lips brushed across mine, tender and cautious. Pressing back, I kissed him and allowed myself to linger in this intimate presence for several heartbeats. When I pulled back and tossed my focus to the sun as it kissed the edge of the Earth, his arms, strong yet soft, wrapped around me.

We didn't speak, but I linked my fingers through his and held them tight to my side. I may need to work on my one date philosophy, because I wasn't sure how to move on from this. Feet firmly planted on the wooden bridge, I watched the sun sink lower and lower.

"Let's go," Chad whispered into my ear, "before it gets too dark."

"Does it get scary at night?" I stared at the marvelous man before me, seeing him with renewed energy.

"Yeah, but not until Halloween."

"That would be fun."

He raised his eyebrow. "Really, now? A fan of scary things?"

"Totally. Scary movies, horror books. Oh yeah."

"Interesting." Leading me down the stairs and out of the clouds, he never let go of my hand.

151

Bumping our shoulders together as we ambled onwards, we continued on our path, stopping at the ninth post.

If you are having fun, take the right. If not, take the left.

I held the card in my hand, smacking it against the box. "Okay, that's the strangest clue yet."

"Not really. There's a path leading straight to the entrance."

"And where would be the fun in that?"

Not wanting to end our night just yet, I started running down the path on the right, which really wasn't the easiest in flats, but it was still fun to be chased through the stalks by a gorgeous guy.

I rounded the corner and snatched the last card out of the box before Chad did.

Was I on candid camera? A broad grin spread across my face, and I searched the area, as limited as it was, to see if we were being watched. Not seeing anyone, I waved the card under my chin. "You don't need to read this, do you?"

His mega-watt smile could've lit the entire maze. "Nope."

First dates are overrated.

If you agree, go left.

If you disagree, go right.

In two quick steps, he stood before me, charm seeping out of his pores and lighting up his eyes.

"All the clues?" I asked, refreshing my memory about what was on each.

"Maybe."

"Oh, you're smooth." Wondering how, I scanned the area. We'd been the only people in the maze as we hadn't run across anyone else. "Do you know the owners?"

He nodded and gave my hand a squeeze. "It's my parent's place."

My eyes widened and my jaw hit the dirt path. "This is the

ranch you come to every weekend?"

"The one and only, except, we rarely come onto the maze side, except for shutdowns, to make sure no one's roaming after hours. Otherwise, we stay on the private side."

"So how did you…" My heart raced at the thought of being watched and followed.

"My little sister has been a few yards ahead of us this whole time, replacing the cards."

"That's good." I was impressed, but still. "We're not going to… I mean, I'm not expected to…" Meeting his parents was not a great way to end our date.

A look of questioning, and maybe a hint of pleading settled in his eyes. "Only if you want to."

I was damn sure I didn't want to meet his parents. That's a big step. Huge. The other guys I dated, even after a couple months I'd never met their parents. Nope, I couldn't do it. Not today at least. There needs to be mental time to prepare for that, and there's been–

"It's all good. Besides only my little sister knows you're here."

A big gust of air sailed out of me and my hand flew to my chest "That's a relief."

But where she was? My eyes darted between the stalks, looking as far as possible. There wasn't much to see aside from darkness. Had she seen us kissing on the bridge? What had Chad told her about me?

"So, are you going to answer the question?" He nodded to the card I still held in my hand.

"Nope." I cracked a grin. "I'm going to close my eyes, and you're going to spin me around and take me down a path. Only when we've walked away will I open my eyes."

He eyed me and took my hand. "You trust me?"

I took a deep breath. "Implicitly."

# # #

Chad parked his truck in front of my place, and butterflies swirled in my stomach like a tornado, whipping around in a frenzy.

We'd started tonight knowing it was only a one date thing, but everything seemed different now. Previous first dates had ended differently because there was the promise of more. But with Chad? I'd been honest since the start, however, somewhere over the course of the evening, things changed.

Chad had been charming and interesting, and shared about his family but not of his own past relationships. What was the story there? I wanted to find out.

And what of potentially dating? Our schedules didn't mix. He was a day-timer, I was evenings.

I sighed. This was why it wouldn't work. Even if something inside me wanted it to.

"Thanks for the fun evening. It was really everything I hoped it would be, and truly didn't realise I needed so much."

It had been a break from caregiving and a break from work. Plus, I enjoyed hanging out with an amazing guy.

"Feeling a bit better?"

"Yeah. Surprisingly so." My hands twirled together. "Thank you for not having me meet your parents. I need a little more prep time than that."

"You'd be just fine and fit in like family."

I laughed, not believing that. My hand rested on the door.

"I'll walk you up," he said, and hopped out.

More nervous than a kid caught with his hand in the cookie jar, I held his and walked up the front sidewalk and onto the dark deck, having forgot to turn the porch light on before I left.

"You should install a motion sensor for the front. Would make your home a bit more secure. One at the back too."

"That's a good idea." I looked around. Nothing was missing, not that there was much I'd left out.

"Tonight was fun."

I nodded. "Yes, it was." Was he as nervous as I was?

He shifted back and forth on his heels, and had a hard time making eye contact with me.

Or maybe it was me that had a hard time with eye contact. I was so nervous I didn't know what to do besides stare at out feet.

"Thanks for walking me up." A butterfly did a nosedive into the pit of my stomach. Why was this all so awkward?

"Any time." He just stood there as if he was unsure of what to do.

Do I kiss him goodnight? There was no sense in leading the guy on. This was a bad time in my life for relationships of any kind. I suppressed the sigh building in me as much as the desire to kiss him again.

He got a bit closer and as much as I wanted to, I put my hand up to stop him. "I can't." I looked at my feet. "I just can't figure out how to make it work."

"I get it. I do." It was hard to read his face clearly under the shade of the dark. "You've been saying it all night."

"I'm sorry if I led you to believe in more at the corn maze. I was caught up in the moment."

"I'd be okay if you had more moments."

"I wish," I said, my filter busted. "But I can't." I opened the screen door and put my key into the lock. Stopping, I let it dangle and stepped over to Chad. In a low voice, I whispered, "Thank you for tonight. For making me forget my responsibilities."

"Any time."

"Good night," I said and closed the door behind me, my hand lingering on the door as my heart berated my head for being so foolish.

Chapter Sixteen

$\mathcal{M}$elody left with the few details about my non-date date. She handled the lack of info pretty well, shrugging and launching into how their evening was, although – thankfully – not much occurred.

Michael drank a bit and had a nibble of food, but other than that, his caloric intake was very low, which matched his energy level. She was concerned enough to bring it up.

I tidied and slumped down beside him on the couch, covering my feet with the blanket.

"H-h-h- ow w-w-w-wuz," his tongue protruded as he struggled to speak, "y-y-y-y-our d-d-d-day t-t-t." Spit flew in all directions. Words were a definite battle for him tonight. He must really be more worn out than I expected.

"It was great, a lot of fun." I fiddled absently with his hair, wrapping a curl around my finger while I searched out his eyes; they held me with rapt interest, so I carried on. "We went out for supper, and then went to a place where we played games with four other people."

"W-w-w-what g-g-g-gammmes?"

"Had to solve riddles and puzzles. It was interesting.

Afterwards, we drove out to the country and went through a corn maze. I think I could take you there, the paths were hard packed, so it would be easy to push you through in the wheelchair."

He shook his head.

"Not tomorrow, of course, but another day. When you feel up to it." I snuggled a little closer.

Michael surprised me by leaning into my shoulder.

I rubbed and kissed the top of his head.

"Ammm I d-d-d-ying?"

My heart stopped beating, I swear to God it did. I froze and couldn't speak, afraid to breathe for fear it would move me out of the position I was in. The one where I felt I was able to protect him the most, even if Death didn't care. He could snatch Michael when ever he wanted, it didn't matter what I did. Still, I wrapped my arms tighter around my brother and he tucked his head in under my chin.

"Why would you think that?" Although I could list several reasons, I was concerned which one he latched on to.

"M-m-m-el. Sh-sh-she w-w-w-w-as s-s-s-ad."

Lovingly, I stroked his head, once again twirling my finger through his curls. So lucky to have them, whereas I had to spend quite a bit of time to get my hair to do that.

"I'm not sure what Melody's being sad has you thinking…" I didn't dare breathe the word. It was bad enough the energy around us had changed. "We're working on getting you better. You had two amazing days this week, right? You helped us paint." The cheek pressed into me pushed a little harder – he was smiling at that memory. "Chad's going to come back next week and build us a swing for the porch, and finish popping up the bird feeder. Won't that be neat?"

A little head nod into my neck.

"You'll see. It's going to be beautiful, and we'll have so many birds chirping and tweeting."

"G-g-g-good."

A heavy weight pressed upon my heart, and it wasn't the softly breathing being huddled into me. I was scared, and if I was scared, then Michael must be terrified, especially if he was voicing his concern. No one really knew what went on in his mind, and it was hard for him to speak it, so I just imagined what he'd be thinking. I'd always hoped it was simple things--light and fluffy things--definitely not the massive, soul crushing thought that breezed out of him earlier.

A tear leaked out of my eye, rolling down my cheek, and I squeezed him tighter. Death hovered nearby, and for all I knew, he could be pacing outside on the deck, looking in.

But it not tonight.

Or tomorrow.

Or a month from now. Death could fucking wait.

"Would you drink something for me?" I asked, giving him a little nudge.

"T-t-t-tired."

I swiped across my face with my free hand, drying the strip of sorrow smudged on my cheek. "Do you want help to your bed? Or did you want to sleep here?"

"H-here," he said softly, his voice barely above a breath.

I pulled myself out, holding him and laying him down on the pillow I reached for. Flat on his back, his jaw slackened in sleep and opened softly. With the tip of my finger, I closed it, not wanting to give Death an easy entrance into his soul. I draped the blanket over him and positioned the fan so it kept the air around him moving. Maybe it was superstitious or something else, but I saw it as another way of keeping the dastardly dark stench of death away – by movement.

Whatever I could do, I did. I pushed the coffee table to the couch in case he rolled. Double checked the blinds were tightly closed, and the doors were locked and dead bolted. Even the windows. I may have been stifling in the heat trapped house, but there was no way Death was making an entrance tonight. Not on my clock.

Dressed in my pajamas, I pulled a light blanket off my bed and curled into the sofa chair beside him, close enough to hear him breathing and to reach out and hold his hand. "I love you, Baby Bird."

Thankfully when I woke in the morning, all stiff and with the worst crick in my neck, Michael was still breathing. But I knew he would be. Last night had been a test, and we passed. Yay us.

Michael's colour was rosy, the sleep fairy having brushed over him in the night. I inhaled a long full breath and stared at my little brother.

I let my hand fall on his forehead, and surprised at the coolness beneath my fingertips, I tucked the blanket in on his sides. In my whole life, Michael had always slept the same way – straight on his back, face toward the ceiling. He rarely rolled over or moved much for that matter. That was his normal.

My normal was the opposite, thrashing about wildly and sleeping in little bursts. Last night I woke up every twenty minutes, just to check to make sure we had no unexpected visitors. Nights were scary that way; and as I threw open the blinds and allowed the sunlight to flood in and cheer up the space, my fears somehow seemed frivolous.

Wandering into the kitchen, I whipped up a breakfast for one and added more of Michael's high calorie mix to his smoothie. I took a quick lick of my smoothie-dipped finger and scrunched up my face. Blech, it was disgusting, chalky and bland. More strawberries and a squeeze of chocolate syrup went into the blender, turning it a warm pink colour. At least it looked better.

"Good morning," I said to the face staring up at me as I leaned over the couch.

A smell hit me suddenly. A strong, ammonia-tinged smell.

"I-i-i-..." But the remorseful expression said it all. He knew what happened, and there was likely nothing he could do about it.

The coffee table blocked an ability to put his feet on the floor, so really, it was my fault.

"C'mon, let's get you into the shower. Need some help standing?" The smell of urine smacked me repeatedly as I lifted the blanket; he was soaked all over. It had been no trickle by the looks of things.

He nodded, and on a count of three pulled him onto his feet, his pee-soaked clothing touching mine.

"Alright. Let's go." I hadn't released him as I waited for him to feel steady. I was glad I was still holding him as he collapsed back onto the sofa.

Fuck me.

"Too tired to stand?" Yes, please let that be all it was. Too tired.

I rolled the wheelchair into place and transferred him over. It was easier than I expected.

"Drink this, it'll make you strong." I handed him the smoothie, but it slipped from his hands, and I caught it before it splashed all over him. "Can you hold it?"

Painfully, he struggled but managed to clasp it between his wrists, the grip in his hands apparently gone. When he'd taken a half-hearted sip, I set it on the table.

Manoeuvring the chair into the bathroom was no small feat, but we managed.

Thankfully I had the foresight to set the stool into the

shower, and I put Michael—fully dressed—onto it.

Seeing my brother naked was nothing I wanted to see or had prepared for. "Michael, I need to take off your shirt, okay?" I gasped as I pulled the material up and over, exposing bones and tightly stretched skin. To say my heart shattered at the sight would be an understatement.

Standing behind him, I swept my hands over his back while he looked up at me.

God, he was skin and bones.

"You need to drink your shakes, okay?" I used the sweetest voice I could muster, but my gasp had already betrayed me.

He nodded and closed his eyes.

It was a process, however I got him stripped down and into the warm shower, keeping his modesty covered with a small towel. I was soaked more than he, because I was still in my pajamas. Somehow, I got another towel wrapped around him, and used another to dry him before I set him back into the wheelchair. Getting him dressed was a challenge as he was as rigid as a board, but thirty minutes later, he was clean, dry, and smelled much nicer.

Still wet, and leaving little trails of water everywhere I went, I set him up on the sofa chair I'd slept in the night before and encouraged him to drink a little. My hair was plastered against my face, and my clothes stuck to my body, although for once, I wasn't stifling hot. My own thermostat seemed to like this. Ridiculous, given the circumstances.

How did a nurse do this with a patient and not get soaked? I needed to watch a few videos, because attempting this every couple of days was going to be a feat of epic proportions. And that's if I managed to get him to the bathroom on time. Would he need to wear an adult-sized diaper now or was this a one-time mistake? I hoped for a one-time mistake.

The front doorbell rang.

161

Both Michael and I looked at it, foolish as I was thinking it was something nefarious. Wet footsteps following me, I opened the door.

Chad stood there holding a bouquet of flowers. "Oh, I see I've come at a bad time. Sorry."

I glanced at Michael and stepped out on to the porch. "It's been a rough morning."

"You look like you showered in your pajamas."

Yep, they still clung to me, making my breasts bigger and more noticeable than I'd prefer. I pulled the wet fabric from my skin and waved it a bit. A tendril of frizzy, hair fell into my face.

"Everything okay?"

"Nothing I can't handle," I said, shrugging off the question.

"Thought I'd drop this off for you before I headed to church." Chad presented me with the flowers, but he looked beyond me into the living room.

"He's okay, just had an accident I'm working on cleaning up." I inhaled the fresh scent of carnations and lilies, a pleasant change from urine. "What are these for?"

"I'm trying to sweeten you up on the porch swing quote." He chuckled and handed me an envelope.

Bracing the bouquet in one hand, I opened it and read the quote. It was far less than what I expected. "I can't. This is… well, it's too low." I waved the paper back and forth.

"For supplies only. I figure with your help and Michael's, if he wants, it could be an easy project. It's certainly not complicated, and I could use a good painter," he said toward Michael.

"But there's no labour cost."

"Because I'd be working on it one evening this week. What night do you have off?"

I placed my hand across my forehead, the wet hairs sticking

to my hand. Yuck. How absolutely hideous I must appear. "Umm, I think I have Tuesday and Wednesday off, but I'd have to double check."

He smiled. "Do you have tomorrow off? It's holiday Monday."

"No, I work the evening shift."

"Perfect. I have the day free. What about then? Does that work?"

I leaned against the frame of the door, and mentally listed the pros and cons, convinced I was getting better at doing this so quick. There were so many pros; free labour, it getting done sooner rather than later, watching Chad work and move and bend and hammer, having him nearby, nice eye candy, his infectious laugh. And then my mind itemised the cons; leaving Michael unattended if he wasn't up for moving around as I didn't have extra care, and if he did want to come outside, there was still needing to keep an eye on him and attend to his basic needs, my own could easily be forgotten or rearranged, but his were different.

"You know, I don't know." I sighed. "I can't leave Michael alone." And I glanced back to see what he was doing; just resting and watching me.

"You know my sister's a nurse."

"No." My voice hardened.

"You don't even know what I was going to say."

I crossed my arms over my chest and took a step toward the door. "I'm not having a strange person who doesn't know him tell me what I should or should not be doing. We're managing. And I don't need another," I whispered so Michael wouldn't hear, "Jonathan. Thank you very much."

His eyes roved up and down my body and I figured he was giving me a solid assessment. Soaked clothing clinging to my body, a small puddle at my feet, damp and stringy hair. Sure, I was the

163

poster child for having it all put together. Inside I laughed.

"Perhaps, but a second hand is always helpful."

"Not always." I dismissed his comment. Hadn't been so helpful with Jonathan. The ass.

He rested his warm hand on my arm, the dampness drying with an imaginary sizzle. "You don't have to do this alone."

"I'm not." I stared at his face, so honest and sincere. "I have Melody."

"And when you're busy taking care of Michael, who's taking care of you?" The question lingered in the air like static of electricity, ready to zap.

I stomped my foot like a little child. "I don't need anybody to take care of me. I'm doing just fine."

He stepped closer and softened his tone. "And I believe that."

"Then what?"

"I'm just saying."

"Well don't." God damn, I was tired of people thinking I'm incapable. I was a grown ass woman who wouldn't have taken Michael in if I couldn't handle it.

His hand dropped away from my arm, and I instantly missed the connection the moment he let go. All he was doing was being kind and nice, and I was returning the sweetness with a bitter attitude. I was such a bitch.

"I'm sorry, it's just…"

"I know. I get it."

I painted the spot I stood in with my wet foot, making thick circles and rebalanced the bouquet in my arms.

"Better put those in water before they…" He grimaced and stared at his watch. "I need to go." Heavy footsteps sounded on the edge of the deck, and as if hope were a flag, he waved it proudly. "So tomorrow?"

A small smile inched its way to the start of my lips. He was so damn cute, he was impossible to say no to. "Fine, tomorrow."

Twenty-four more hours until I saw his handsome face again. I could make it.

Chapter Seventeen

I debated calling in sick, as I didn't feel like being at work. The only reason I dragged myself into Westside was for the money for a possible trip to Jasper I was going to take with Michael next month. My energy level slacked, and as such I took the slowest section. Of course, all the customers seemed extra whiney and no matter what I did, no one was pleased, but it wasn't in me to plaster on a fake smile and give two shits about these people's lives. As it was, Joy's effervescent-like positivity was too much to handle.

My heart wasn't into being here and leaving Melody alone with Michael, although she could handle anything any incident, I was needed at home.

Apparently, Niall noticed too and dragged me outside to the picnic table for a quick pep talk.

He lit himself a cigarette and took a long, punishing drag. "Tell me about last night."

"What are you, my keeper?" But I laughed.

Of course, there would be strings with his gift, even if it was simply as easy as sharing what I did. Not that it was a big deal, I owed him at least a run down of how I spent his money.

He offered me the cigarette.

"No thanks," I said, shaking my head in disgust.

"Your loss."

"Yes, because on top of everything else I have in my life, adding lung cancer is a big priority." I rolled my eyes and perched myself on the edge of the picnic table, my legs swinging freely under me.

"So… last night."

"I had a good time, thanks. You were right. Is that what you wanted to hear?"

A smug smirk brightened his face. "Why, yes, it is." He jumped up beside me, staying downwind. "But you still seem off."

"One night won't erase my problems and make me forget."

"I never expected that. Not in a million years. I know you better."

"Good."

He took another long breather. "Were you alone, or did you hang out with friends?"

"Gawd, what's with all the questions?" I gave him a playful little nudge in the shoulders.

"All the questions? I think I've asked two."

The parking lot was empty, which I was happy about. If I was going to share, I didn't want extra ears listening in.

"I hung out with somebody."

"A guy?" He dragged out the word.

My feet swung carefree like a child. If only. "Yeah."

"I didn't know you had a boyfriend."

I kicked my legs freely and stretched my arms above my head. "I don't. He's the carpenter who worked on the ramp for Michael."

"I see."

I fiddled with the strings of my apron tied into a neat little bow and stifled a yawn.

"I see you slept well." He raised an eyebrow.

"Hardly. I had an eye on the door."

He straightened up and blew out a puff of smoke. Disgusting. "Trouble in the neighbourhood?"

"No, at least that I can prepare for." I shared with him my woes about Michael.

A sympathetic voice rolled out of him as he leaned against me. "Being the primary caregiver is one of the hardest things I think a person goes through. It's not like taking care of a baby or a toddler where you expect them to gain some independence. It's the reverse, watching them lose their independence, and fighting to keep their dignity. I'm sure doing what you did this morning must've been beyond taxing."

I buried my face in my hands, but I didn't crack. I refused. I just didn't want to see that sympathetic half-smile laced in pity. "It was so hard. I had to see my grown adult brother... naked."

His hand rubbed up and down my back, as he extinguished the cigarette against the table with a sizzle. "I'm sorry you're dealing with this."

I shrugged. Not that I was sorry, because I wasn't. Michael was my responsibility; one I took very seriously. It was just sometimes, things happened and threw me for a loop, but we always managed. Today had been no different, but it drained me in a way I didn't expect.

"Tell me what I can do. What would you like? Anything. You tell me."

"I need a miracle."

"Shit, I'm all tapped out today."

It was such a dumb thing to say, yet, it made me smile.

He pulled me close, his fingers on my elbow as I maintained my stance. "What else?"

"I don't know."

"Well, don't be shy. When you figure it out, you let me know. I'm always around."

I was about to remind him how well that worked out last time, but he covered my lips with his finger.

"I promise you, *this time*, I won't let you down."

I searched his eyes, seeing the truth there.

We had both learned from that mistake the hard way, and it took many months before I could even speak to him without a venom-laced tongue. Talk about a tense working relationship.

"You may disagree with me, but this," we waved a finger between us, "is friendship. And if that's possible, then anything is."

"I wish."

"I know you do." He patted my leg. "And since we're friends, tell me about this carpenter."

"There's not much to tell."

"Of course, there is. Obviously, he's a decent fellow, or you wouldn't give him the time of day. What's his personality like? You hired him, so I know you did some digging."

I gazed away from him and stared at the too-tall grass waving in the breeze. "Yeah, I did some digging. Professionally he's received many accolades. But his personal life is pretty hard to uncover. His business name is a pseudonym."

An easy, gentle chuckle rolled out of him. "I get that."

"Really? It's kind of weird."

"Is it... Evanora?" He gave me a sly look.

I slapped my forehead. "I didn't see it that way."

"You have something in common then."

"He's got a big family, and his parents own the corn maze outside of the city."

"His parents are Lynetta and George Lawton?" His eyes got wide.

"I have no idea what his parent's names are." I narrowed my gaze and tipped my head. "Why? Do you know them?"

"I know of them, if that's them."

I poked him with my forefinger. "And?"

"They're nice people. Huge philanthropists. They own a hotel chain in Western Canada. From what I understand the corn maze is fun for them, and all the profits go to the Children's Hospital or something."

"What? That's it, they're nice people? The way you said their names made it sound like they were mafia or something."

He laughed and lit another cancer stick. "No, definitely not mafia. I'm kinda surprised you didn't already check it out."

The way Niall acted at the mention of the corn maze and immediately knowing the family name raised some red flags. Which was odd because Chad never set off one of them. He was kind and genuine, and always went the extra mile, until his past came up...

I scratched my chin. Yeah, there was a secret hiding there, and I was super curious to find out what it was. But logic took over, how likely would it be I'd find it on the internet, and even if I did, how much would be truth? Even the work reviews I took with a grain of salt, although 99% were great.

"So, did I tell you, we had a manager's meeting today?"

So much for thinking about Chad, and all the internet searching planned for when I got back home.

"Oh yeah, and what did Meghan say?" I braced myself and curled my fingers around the end of the picnic table.

"We went over a couple of things really." He blew a faulty smoke ring into the air. It was ridiculous to see his lips form an O and yet, straight smoke launched out like a rocket. "For starters, she hates being right, and in two weeks, she's switching to nights."

The blood rushed out of my head. "No."

It had been a possibility, especially if he couldn't find extra help. Her taking on the evenings spelled trouble, and I sensed a giant shake up in the weeks ahead.

"And we discussed last night's fiasco."

"What happened?"

"I fired Jacob."

My eyes widened. I knew it. Right from the interview he seemed off. Sure, he looked good on paper, but...

"Why?" My voice pitched in mock surprise.

"Easy there." He stepped back. "You were right, he was stealing. Caught him on camera pocketing Joy's tip money as he helped..." he air quoted the last word, "clean her tables."

"Why the..."

"Before you go flying off the handle, he's already gone. That's why Robin's here. He's switching to evenings permanently."

"When did this happen?"

"Robin agreed to nights after the meeting."

"No, not that, although that's great."

Robin was an okay guy. Hard worker, although the few odd times I've worked with him, his jokes seemed off colour.

"And Jacob?"

"His firing? That was last night." He dusted cigarette ash off his pants when I pointed it out to him. "You should've seen Joy, she was anything but pleased with Jacob."

"I would've liked to. You could probably charge admission since she never gets remotely angry."

"Oh, she was pissed."

I couldn't even imagine what she'd look like angry. Always dancing and singing around the restaurant, it had to have been some sight to see the total one-eighty. "Did she attack him?"

"Not physically, but she followed him outside and cursed him out."

"With real curse words?" No way would she have used

truly shocking words. That was my domain.

He laughed. "It was like something out of Misery. She called Jacob a cockamamie dirty bird." His hands clenched around his mid-section as he hollered in laughter. "As he drove off, she actually gave him the finger."

"She didn't?"

"Come watch the video. It's hilarious."

"I will." Remembering his mention of Meghan and a manager's meeting, I desperately wanted the scoop. "What else happened at the meeting?"

"Well, I managed to buy us some extra time when I told Meghan I fired Jacob. She was going to start right away and turn the transition into a nightmare."

I narrowed my eyes. "What transition? Are you moving to days?"

He was the one comfort, if you could call it that, that made working here tolerable. I didn't want him moving to a time where we'd be like passing ships in the night especially considering we were friends and all.

"Sort of."

"What?" The pitch in my voice was nothing compared to the pitch and roll in my stomach.

"I'm going to train you…"

I held my breath.

"To take over my position, and you will become the daytime manager."

I couldn't breathe.

"It comes with a pay raise which is higher than your tips and wage combined. Plus, it's guaranteed pay. And… you would qualify for benefits; something I think you'll need right away."

"Benefits?" Good thing I was sitting because my legs turned to wet spaghetti. It sounded too good to be true.

"If you want the position, I need to let her know right away." He stood there, expectation on his face.

"And what becomes of you?" I scoured his face, hunting for any kind of tell for a huge impending change.

There was no sadness or anguish, just a twitch on his cheek. What would become of the guy who had been the night manager for years? I think he was born into it, as he'd always been there. Way back when we were a couple, that's how I got the job. I'd often wondered if he thought of Westside as his baby.

"I'm moving on to greener pastures." He walked closer and dismissed my notion of Westside being like family. "I've accepted a position within Lawton Hotels. I'll be their lead restaurant manager when they open up at Halloween."

I swallowed a taste of sadness of him completely leaving and working for Lawton Hotels. *Lawton Hotels...* "Wait a sec..."

"Yep, that's right. That's how I knew. You're not the only one to do some research. I needed to know who'd be writing my cheques."

"So, you're leaving us all behind, are you?" I shook my head, torn between being upset and really happy for him. "Wow, congrats."

He beamed. "Thanks. I'm looking forward to it. A little change of pace from here."

"A little?" Yeah, just a bit.

He would be going from the minor leagues in a one restaurant setup into the major leagues of a huge hotel chain.

"So, you interested in the manager's position?"

"A couple of weeks ago, it would've been a hard no."

Not managing on nights especially, working until one or two am. But daytime? That's a Monday to Friday, nine to five type. A normal forty-hour work week. Which meant... I'd have evenings off, and possibly weekends too. Michael and I could take a trip to the mountains without me having to take a day or two off. And with my evenings free, it opened the door to more moments with Chad. However, it also meant a change with Melody – it would affect her salary as day pay was a slightly lower rate than evenings.

I looked up to the heavens. What was the plan? It was a huge move, yet, it was such a positive one, one I could make work, and more importantly, one that would work for me and Michael.

Maybe there would be more moments of happiness in my life. "Let me sleep on it tonight. I'd like to do some serious research."

"I figured you'd say that."

With a spring in my step and hope in my heart, I walked arm linked in arm with Niall back into the restaurant.

# # #

I entered my house feeling a little lighter, even though my arms were weighted down with manuals. Niall suggested it would be a good idea for me to review the management role and expectations, plus a few packets of the extensive benefits I'd be entitled to; pension top ups, vision coverage, dental, paid vacation days, and that was just the beginning. Having been with Westside for a few years, the benefits would start immediately -- if I accepted. It was so tempting to say yes without hesitation, but a quick review wouldn't hurt.

I dropped the paper paraphernalia onto the table and tiptoed into the very quiet living room. "Where's Michael?"

Melody sat in the chair, channel-surfing like a babysitter. "In bed. He was tired."

I tipped my head back and stole a peek into his room. "When did he go?"

"About an hour ago."

Unusual but understandable, based on how the day started. "How was he overall?"

The TV went black, and she rose out of her chair.

"I need to be honest."

Oh shit. I braced myself against the back of the couch, my heart pounding in fear. My good mood had deflated with her five heavy words.

"You need full-time, twenty-four hour care. He's not well."

I looked back toward Michael's room, not that I expected to be able to see him. "He's just having a rough couple of days."

The remote bounced on the couch after she let it fall from her hand. "He needs more assistance than I can provide."

"You're his aide."

"I'm not saying I'm leaving, au contraire, but Audrina, he soiled himself tonight, and I spent half the night cleaning him up and cleaning up the mess."

"But you're trained to do that." Although we'd never had need for it until tonight.

"Yes, and I did it. But there's nothing here to help with that. There are no *special* undergarments to change him into, there's no soaker pads to absorb the leakage. I'm sorry, it's not in my description to do laundry but I wasn't leaving *that* for you to do later, so I threw out his clothes."

I rubbed my hands over my face and pressed my fingers into my temples where a dull ache announced its presence.

Melody stepped closer and lowered her voice. "I know you want the best for him, but him soiling himself isn't the best. He's losing his abilities."

We still have time. This was a setback.

My voice lowered. "What am I supposed to do, attach a bag to him?"

"That's not what I'm saying."

"What are you saying?" I dug my nails into the back of the couch.

"He's going downhill fast, and you can deny it as much as you want, it's still happening. He's different. He barely talks, it's more of a mumble now. He's not eating. I got him to have maybe three ounces of a Boost, and that's simply not enough to sustain him. It's torture on him, I'm sure, to get his pills in him when he'll hardly drink, right?"

I couldn't disagree and as I recalled the past couple of days, it had taken a fair amount of pleading to get him to swallow them. That was the extent of his hydration too. I sighed and hung my head.

Melody stepped closer and put her hand on my mine. "I'm sorry you need to hear this, but he's going to need a nursing home ASAP."

A bitter taste of bile rose in the back of my throat. There was no way he'd be going to a home. Never. I'd sooner drain my savings and hire a full-time nurse to live with me than have him go to a place where they'd neglect him, or worse.

"Are you going to bathe him?" Her brow arched with her question.

In guff defiance, I placed my hand on my hip and shifted my weight. "I did this morning."

"And?"

It had been weirdness all around, but it got done.

"I'm not saying this to be mean because I adore Michael, you know that, but it's not going well. I left a sheet of resources for you on the fridge. I strongly encourage you to look into and make use of them. For both of your sakes, but especially his. I'd hate to say he's suffering, but I believe he is."

He was having a few bad days, that's all. I straightened myself up and pushed my shoulders back. My voice soured and turned ugly. "Anything else?"

"No."

"Thank you, Melody. You're free to go now."

Like a dog with its tail tucked between its back legs, she left.

I peeked in on Michael and placed a feather-light kiss upon his forehead. Aside from a sweat smell, everything else seemed okay. No urine stench, thank goodness. I double checked all the doors and windows, reviewed the limited notes Melody wrote in our book and stared long and hard at the list of resources she'd left on the fridge. I clenched them in my hand and walked back to my bedroom, peeking in once again on Michael. Secure he was okay—at least as okay as he could be for now—I sat at the entrance to his door and opened my computer on my lap.

Researching anything was like a drug to me, I just couldn't get enough. However, the more I dug into care for Michael, the more my chest hurt and ached as Melody's declaration proved correct. With the proper home care, they could enhance his frailty and intravenously give him his needed drugs, and likely some nourishment, as he likely wasn't getting much.

Between reviewing live-in nurse fees and equipment rentals verses a proper home, which I was still dead set against, my eyes started to burn. I needed to do this fresh and made a mental note to tackle it first thing tomorrow. Start with a phone call to his doctor and then proceed with whatever he recommended from there.

A tear started on the edge of my heart, I was concerned and scared for the future.

I visually searched the living room spanned out at my feet, scanning for the invisible haunt of my nightmares *Death*, but everything seemed still. I wasn't ready to sleep, and yet, I wasn't in the mood for anguishing research. I needed something more lighthearted to keep me going. Typing casually, I let my fingers type Chad Lawton's name into the search bar and hit enter.

Various results popped up tagged to another guy, some actor, but none of them were my Chad. Oh, I laughed, *my Chad.* As if. I kept pushing the guy away. I continued scrolling through the first couple of pages and nothing of interest caught my eye. I added his name plus Edmonton and hit enter.

New results appeared, and I scoured them until I'd read enough.

The lid on my laptop slammed shut. Holy shit.

A lengthy news article about the Lawtons, and the bad luck circulating them. A fire gutted one of their hotels in Vancouver, and a few months later George Lawton had a heart attack, likely from the stress. Then, to top it off, Lynetta and George lost a daughter-in-law in childbirth, and their grandson two days after – Chad Lawton's wife and child.

I couldn't believe what I'd read, although as I dwelled on the information, it made total sense. The screaming runs he made me do, I was sure he did more than his fair share of them as well. How tight lipped he got when I'd asked if he'd brought any girls home. Hell ya, he had, he was married and had a kid. How tragic. No wonder his parents were huge donators to the Hospital for Women and the Stollery Children's Hospital.

I opened the lid again and searched for the dates. How recently had his heart been destroyed?

The one article listed the death of his wife and baby boy over seven years ago, and he was twenty-six at the time – my age now. Fear blew in all around me. Was Betsy Lawton sick a long time? Or was her passing a total shock?

Fingers typed frantically trying to find out anything more. All I got was an obituary for both and a few random write ups in the local paper. It had been news and fizzled away like a leaf in the wind. Although I highly doubt it left Chad as quickly.

A hitch in Michael's breath sent me scurrying into his

178

room. I placed my hand upon his chest and let it rise and fall in a rhythmic motion. Relief blanketed me, and I propped myself up against his bed, resting my head against the foot of his bed.

Content to hear Michael breathing, I allowed my thoughts to wander.

To Chad.

To his wife.

To his baby boy.

He'd been in love once and had the world. When his going got tough, did he hide from the world, or did he ask for help? He was always telling me there was no shame in asking. Had he felt shamed? Ugh, there was so much I wanted to ask, but none of it was my business. If he wanted to share it with me, he would. He almost did once.

Chapter Eighteen

A hard knock rapped from the front door, and I pushed the hair off my face as I clamoured to my feet. Stepping into the living room, I kicked my laptop left on the floor clear across the hardwood where it connected with a crack against the doorframe of my bedroom.

"Shit," I said, but to the door I yelled, "Gimme a sec." I rubbed my eyes to focus and stumbled over, yanking it open.

"Hey," Chad said, looking all fresh and relaxed, his hair slicked back and his sunglasses on. He gave me the once over.

That's two mornings in a row I've greeted the door looking like I either literally rolled out of bed or stepped out of a shower. What must he think?

"What, no flowers this time?" I was joking, of course.

"Actually…" From behind his back, he pulled out a small bouquet.

"I was kidding."

"I'm not. It's to soften you up." He wiggled his eyebrows and made it look as if they were dancing across his forehead.

"Always with the softening up. I'm not that much of a bitch." I rolled my eyes as a smile formed and opened the door.

180

"I've never…"

"I'm kidding." I spied his truck with the trailer parked out in front of my house. "Why are you here again? I feel like I've agreed to something, but I forget."

"The porch swing?"

"Right." I nodded. "Right. Well… you're early."

"It's ten o'clock."

"Ten?" Michael had been in bed for twelve hours. "I'll be right back."

The screen door closed with a bang, and I raced into his room.

Relief settled over me as I spotted him blinking his eyes and focusing on me.

"Hey," I hovered over him, giving him a solid once over. "Time to rise and shine."

Gently, I rolled the covers back and smelled it before I saw it. Not again. However, Melody must've been expecting something because underneath his back side were a couple of folded towels. Once was an oversight, two was a problem, but three? I hung my head. Like it or not, he was losing control of his faculties, and sadly, he needed an adult-sized diaper.

Fuck.

For Michael's sake, I kept my smile firmly plastered on and spoke sweetly and soothingly like I'd seen the caregivers do on the YouTube videos I'd watched into the wee hours. Honestly didn't think I'd need to use their knowledge so soon.

The wheelchair was out in the living room, probably parked there to keep it out of the way. I wheeled it into his room and repeated the bathing procedure I'd done yesterday. It was only a hair easier, but the awkwardness of it has not been erased.

A knock sounded on the screen door. "Hey, Audrina, everything okay?"

"Yes," I called out.

My focus on Michael had been all consuming, I'd completely forgotten anyone was there.

"Can I help?"

Surprised to hear a voice I didn't recognise from inside my own house, I shot up straight, and opened the bathroom door a crack. I peered my damp, frizzled head out, keeping a hand on Michael's shoulders.

"Can I help you?" I said in a snotty tone, glaring at the strange lady standing in my living room.

"I'm sorry, I'm Meredith, Chad's sister."

I narrowed my eyes and glared even harder, trying to connect the invisible dots. "Okay."

"Sorry, I invited her," Chad said, appearing into view. "I told you I had a sister who was a nurse." He pointed to her as if I couldn't figure it out. "And here she is."

Suddenly I felt light-headed and didn't know where to look. He was only being kind, but what the actual fuck? After everything I told him and all the shit with Jonathan, he thought I'd be okay with a perfect stranger? He's off his fucking gourd.

"I'm kind of busy at the moment."

"How can I help?" Her voice was very soft and soothing, and if I wasn't so fucking irritated, I may have responded with a kinder tone.

"I don't have the foggiest idea." I shot a nasty look at Chad and closed the door.

Unsure what awaited me beyond the bathroom, I ran a brush through Michael's hair and replaced the wet towel covering his lap with a dry one and wrapped him in the thickest towel available. I hadn't planned things out very well because his fresh clothes were still in his bedroom.

When I wheeled him into the living room, I didn't search

out who was or wasn't there, my only goal was getting Michael dressed. What would I use as a diaper until I ran out to grab him some? Because I needed to do that, and while I was out, I really should make a few phone calls, the first to his doctor to touch base. Plus, there was Chad and his sister to deal with. My grip tightened on the handles of the wheelchair. Why couldn't there be two of me?

I spoke softly to Michael and mentioned step by step what I was doing. It felt so weird, but the video assured me it would let the patient know so they wouldn't get frightened. And I didn't want that from him.

A few minutes later, I wheeled him into the living room, grabbing a few towels from the closet cabinet on my way.

The sister was in my kitchen bustling around, alone or not I wasn't sure. Once I got Michael settled, I was going to escort her out and have some very strong words with Chad.

I placed two fresh towels over the sofa chair seat and moved Michael into it. Surely it was more comfortable than the wheelchair. "Would you like the tv on?"

His eyes connected with mine. Whatever was happening to his body, there was nothing wrong with his eyesight. It pained me how he was losing motor function and yet he was still there in his mind, as much maybe as he'd ever been.

I flicked on the tv, finding the game show network. My lips found his forehead, and I planted a tender kiss on them. "I'm going to get your pills and breakfast."

His arms flailed, smacking against mine. I grabbed his hand, and he squeezed me. It was similar to a grasp, but I understood the gesture; he was trying to hold my arm. Gently, I uncoiled his hand and placed a kiss into his palm and rolled it up.

"Be right back." I needed to get nosy Nellie out of my house but froze when I passed the entrance.

The sister had breakfast on a plate in her hand. "For you."

The plate had an omelette and a piece of toast.

I was touched. No one had made me breakfast since, oh I don't know, grade school? I stared unbelieving at the plate.

"Eat while it's hot." She pulled out a chair and set my plate on the table with a fork. No older than mid-thirties, she had the warmth of a grandmother, and spoke just as softly.

I blinked many times.

She walked closer and patted my shoulder. "I'll keep on eye on Michael while you get your nourishment." She pulled out a chair and positioned it. "If you sit here, you'll also be able to keep an eye on him."

"I… umm…" I fell into the chair harder than I should've. The sudden jolt rocked my tailbone, and I winced in pain. Leaning to the left, I crossed my damp legs. I still hadn't had a chance to change. "Thanks."

The eggs smelled wonderful, and I placed a morsel into my mouth. It tasted good too. As if I hadn't eaten in a week, I scarfed it down and dropped my plate in the sink all the while the sister talked to my brother, telling him she was a nurse.

Finished, I spied her sitting beside Michael, laughing at the game show. I walked over to her completely dumbfounded. "Ah, excuse me."

"Yes?" She rose.

"What are you doing here, I mean like overall? Why did you come today?" I asked as nicely as I could considering this stranger just made me a nice, hot breakfast.

"Chad suggested you could use a nurse, and today's my day off."

"I don't need a nurse." But I wasn't making eye contact with her, instead I was searching the front yard looking for Chad.

"I specialise in elder care, and I work for Assisted Life."

I was familiar with the name; it had been one I'd surfed for info through last night. My hands fell to Michael's shoulders, and I lovingly stroked my hands from his neck out over his shoulders. "He's hardly a senior."

"No, he isn't. You're about twenty-three?" She spoke to Michael.

Lucky guess. "Twenty-two," I answered for him.

"And in his state, with limited mobility, I can assist you. With whatever you need. I can keep my eye out for him while you change."

The bottoms of my jammies were still damp and clung to my leg, and it'd be so nice to slip into dry clothes. And maybe also run a brush through my hair. "Five minutes, that's all I'll need." A peck to Michael's cheek and I was off.

Three quick head peeks out of my room to check on him and four minutes later, I emerged in shorts and a tee, with my hair piled on my head in a top knot. "Thank you."

I gave Michael a once over. He was okay, and as far as I could tell, she hadn't laid a hand on him. Understandably, I was super nervous about anyone touching him.

"Now, what can I do? Chad said he was working on a porch swing with you, for Michael, and we weren't leaving until it was done." A sweet chuckle similar to Chad's rolled out of her. "So, make use of me. I can run errands, I can cook, I can clean. If you don't tell me what you need done, I'll just start figuring it out and go from there."

"I... ah," I started babbling and stopped myself. Taking a deep breath, I focused on Michael. His needs were important. My hand smacked against my forehead. Geezus. In the rush I'd totally forget his meds. "Pills. He needs his pills and a smoothie."

"Allow me, please."

She followed me into the kitchen where I stopped at the counter and pulled out his morning dose.

Since she was a nurse, maybe she knew. "Are you able to get him to take these? I haven't had any luck."

The small dipping-sized container in my hand held nine different pills.

"Of course. Do you have a straw?"

"No. Maybe?" I rifled through the junk drawer. Chopsticks, yes, and a lighter too, which was weird as I never smoked, but no straws. I shook my head. "Nope, but I'll pick some up. Does that make it easier for him?"

"It can."

I retrieved a cold can of Boost from the door of the fridge.

"Warm would be better," she said, sweetness lacing her words.

I dug a warm one from the pantry and shook the hell out of it. These things were gross on a good day and drinking them cold only made it tolerable. Having to drink a warm one would be like torture to me.

"Please." She took it from my hands.

She poured it into a wide mouthed glass and walked over to Michael, the container of pills in her other hand. Expertly, and one at a time, she managed to get all his meds into him. Blown away wouldn't even begin to describe my feelings. There may have been a tinge of jealousy too because I'd never had much success with it.

"How're you doing?" I asked my brother.

He blinked a few times but didn't try talking. His lips didn't even attempt a mutter.

Torn, I needed to go grab some personal effects, but I didn't want to use the sister as a brother-sitter either. My hand rubbed the back of my neck. "I'm sorry, in the craziness I've completely forgotten your name."

"That's fine. It's Meredith."

"Meredith, right." I sat on the edge of the armrest and tried

186

to collect my thoughts. But they were as scattered as fall leaves on a windy day. "I need to get a few things for him. I hate to ask..."

"Make me a list, and I'll zip out and pick it up."

"I couldn't ask that of you. I was going to run out." Maybe. Or find an online delivery service because I didn't really want to leave him alone with her, especially if I wasn't within view. Did Shoppers deliver?

"Nonsense." She walked over to me, placed her hand on my shoulder, and gave it a soft run. "I think you'd be more comfortable here."

That was truth, and I nodded in approval. "Let me give you some cash." There was still a small stack in the wall safe.

"Catch me when I get back. Now what would you like?"

It was all too good to be true, and when things like that happened, I froze, waiting for the other shoe to fall I suppose. Sliding off the armrest, I sat on the couch, flipping my gaze between her and Michael. Until Chad knocked on the door.

"How's everything going?"

Meredith turned to her brother. "Things are going well."

Unable to speak, I stared slack jawed.

"Are you okay?" Chad asked, walking closer. "You're very pale."

"I'm just..." I didn't know what I was. Surprised? Definitely. Overwhelmed? Completely. Scared? Totally. Tears started to blur my vision.

Meredith hunched down in front of me. "It's okay, honey." Her voice, like warm melted butter, leaked into my crusty exterior.

I buried my face in my hands and fought to control my emotions as they bubbled to the surface like a fast boil.

"Chad, why don't you show her what your plans for the porch swing are?" She gave my knee a rub and rose.

"Yeah, sure," he replied, curiosity in his voice, until it was replaced by genuine whispered concern. "C'mon, Audrina. Give me your final approval on the plans." His arm wrapped firmly around my shoulders.

"Michael," Meredith said, "do you like The Price is Right?"

Chad led me out to his truck and opened the door. "Climb in."

"I don't want to leave."

"We're not, just climb in." He held the door for me. "I'm going to close the door and you let out any screams or yells you want."

"What?" I said, wiping away the tears.

"Just let loose here where Michael can't see you nor hear you fall apart." With a quick nod, he closed the door.

In shock I stared at him through the glass as he walked away. I was going to let it out, he wasn't going to be a witness. He placed a chunk of wood under the saw and fired it up, the ear-splitting sound covering any possible screams.

But I couldn't. I wanted to. Each time the blade came down I tried again. But nothing came out. Defeated, my feet touched the concrete and inched their way over to Chad. "Thanks."

"Do you feel better?"

"No. Nothing happened."

"Nothing?" A surprise inflection ribboned in his voice.

I shrugged. "Guess giving myself permission to lose it backfired."

"Well, it worked in a way. Michael didn't see it."

"Would it be a bad thing if he did?"

Of course, it probably would. He'd want to know why I was crying, and you didn't need a Ph.D. in Rocket Science to figure it out. Yeah, it was a good thing I got out of there.

"You know, and this sounds awful, but whatever happens to Michael, you'll still be alive, and you need to make sure you take

188

care of yourself or you'll never get over it."

That was awful, and even if it was the truth, it still stung. How could I ever get over it? A vision of Mother flashed in my head. Okay, fine. That one didn't take long. I was more upset about being an orphan than I was at losing her. Guess it made me a total bitch, but whatever. Losing my brother though? That was a horse of a different colour.

I looked at Chad's weathered expression, the deep personal pain in his eyes. "How long did it take for you?"

His hands fell to the sides of his jeans. "You searched."

Busted. "Yeah, but there wasn't much information." I bridged the distance between us, inhaling a whiff of aftershave or cologne, never quite knowing what the difference was.

A measuring tape came out and he placed it on a piece of wood, pulling it along and marking whatever length he needed with a pencil.

"Years."

My hand fell upon his shoulder, all tense with grief and pain, if I hadn't already witnessed it settle into his expression. "I'm sorry for what happened."

For a brief moment, he glanced at me, his bottom lip quivering for a fraction of a second, but he reeled it back in. That type of restraint was tough, and I knew from first-hand experience.

"Want to talk about it?"

"Want to talk about Michael?"

Breaking eye contact, I glanced to the house. "No."

"Did she make you breakfast?"

A smile inched onto my lips. "Yeah."

"Eggs and toast?"

I nodded and faced him.

The pencil made scratching sounds on the wood. "She did that for mc too."

"I told you though, I don't need help."

"Would you believe me if I said I had purely selfish needs in having her come with me?" His hip rested against the saw table and his arms crossed over his chest.

"I might or I might not."

He laughed. "I enjoyed building this deck with you. I'd love your help with the porch swing too."

"And you figured by bringing your nurse sister here I'd come out here and help you?" I raised my eyebrow. "Instead of being in there where I could help Michael." A rush of anger fuelled my words as my arms crossed in front of my chest and I tucked my fists into my armpits. "And you think that after what happened with Jonathan, I'd welcome a stranger's help?"

"You see, if Michael comes out, my sister can keep on eye on him while getting some much-needed sun. She's kind of a ghost. They can sit over there." He pointed to the filtered shade under the tree. "And Meredith can talk his ear off. She likes birds too and can name most of the regional species."

There weren't any birds nearby, but I sort of saw his plan. "So, her being here is beneficial to her as well."

"With her here," the distance between us closed, leaving only a few inches of heat, "it benefits everyone. It's win-win overall, and how do you say no to that?"

Fresh minty breath tickled my nose.

"How do I say no to that?" I gazed into his eyes, admiring the flecks of amber and brown nestled around the hazel halos. So mesmerising.

Rough, callused hands graced the edges of my arms, electricity ramping up the speed of my pounding heart. My breath caught in my throat and my eyes fluttered to a close as he drew near.

"Audrina," a strong voice from up above interrupted the soft brushing of his lips against mine. "Do you have any undergarments for him?"

For him?

For Michael, right. Shame replaced the heat between Chad and me. My main focus needed to be on my brother, not on kissing the carpenter. I stepped back, filing Chad's desire-filled face into the far regions of my brain.

"Just a sec," I said to whoever wanted it to be intended for them, bounding up the stairs and into my house. "They're on my shopping list." I whispered to Meredith. "His aide used folded up towels."

"Okay, well, how about I run out and grab those things. I know what to get."

I supposed she did. After digging out some cash from my safe, I gave it to her, along with a note of the few things I remembered off the top of my head. Really, when those thoughts hit, I should've written them down immediately.

"If it goes over, I'll pay you when you get back."

She looked admonished.

"Please," I said with a plead.

Tucking it into her purse, she said, "I won't be long." A few moments later, the screen door closed, and I heard her yell, "Be back in a bit, Chadwick."

Chadwick? That's different.

After first sneakily watching out the window and doing some admiring, I sauntered back over to Michael. I ran my fingers through his hair, and it must've felt nice as Michael's face softened and a warm glow filled his cheeks. Tenderly, I continued the motion while listening to an over-crazed contestant scream and yell over the car she just won. Some people had all the luck.

My hands ran over his neck and out over his bony shoulders, the muscles as thin as a sheet of paper. Such a contrast to Chad's.

"Does that feel nice?" I asked Michael.

In response to his nod, I gently placed his arm across my lap and rubbed toward his heart, having read somewhere how it was a positive feeling on the body to send the stroke toward the heart. At first, I thought it was bullshit, but the more I did it, the more Michael relaxed; his face loosened and the strain around his eyes disappeared.

Was he in pain? Could he feel his muscles disintegrating? Were the bones rubbing against each other? He'd changed so much in a week, and really, so much in just a few days it was mind boggling.

I stroked his other spindly arm and sang a little song I suddenly remembered from our childhood. I imagined our mother sang it, but I couldn't picture her doing it, but someone had to have. A sitter perhaps? It didn't matter though. The words from *All God's Critters* rolled out of me as if I'd sung them daily. They came out off tune and likely out of sync, but somehow it was calming.

Michael closed his eyes, and I alternated rubbing his arms, paying attention to making sure each got an equal amount of love while I continued singing.

A knock sounded on the door. "I'm back." Her voice like a whisper.

"Sorry, I didn't hear you."

"That's a beautiful song."

Embarrassment filled me fast as I wasn't a great singer and really, it was meant only for Michael.

Meredith came into the house and set a few bags on the couch. "He looks very happy."

Michael's face had taken on a youthful, childlike look, serene and peaceful. He blinked at me, and I saw the love in his eyes.

I smiled the most genuine, love-filled smile I had. It wasn't hard. Michael was my everything.

"Should we?" Meredith held up a package of adult undergarments.

Bam, one flick of the packaging, and I slammed back into reality. "Let's go."

Chapter Nineteen

*I*n the span of a few days, my brother had gone from partially self-sufficient to a complete and utter dependant. Would I be enough for him, or would it be in his best interests to hire another full-time nurse? Could I even afford something like that? Would I have to let Melody go because her skills were not high enough to help him with his barely functioning motor skills?

Discouraged, and not wanting to dwell on it for the moment, I threw myself into the porch swing construction with Chad – the perfect distraction I needed. Although it was only temporary because every fifteen minutes or so, I was checking on Michael and Meredith.

"Ever sliced a length of board in a table saw?" he asked, the long board balanced on his hand.

"Of course, but I suppose you'd want to show me anyway?" I winked and walked closer. Years ago, I had taken shop class, but only because home economics wasn't as interesting.

"Not at all." He lined up the wood and kicked the saw on. Sawdust flew all around, creating a tan coloured cloud. It came out the other end and he showed it off.

"Anyone can do that," I said in jest.

194

"Great, try this one." The toe of his boot nudged a piece on the ground.

I turned around and slowly bent over, picking it up and wiggling my tush as I rolled up. As I stood, I burst out laughing. "I can't do it."

"Do what?" He wiped the sweat from his brow with the back of his hand.

"Try and act all sexy like they show on tv. I just can't. I have more self-respect than that."

"Aww, that's too bad. I rather enjoyed the show." He kept his distance though. "Take that board and cut it to forty-eight inch lengths."

I grabbed the tape measure from the top of the carry case and measured out the length. Like I'd watched him do, for good form, I checked the length twice, my marks lining up perfectly. Donning the work gloves, I held the board and fired up the saw, vibrating as the blade cut effortlessly through.

"Ta da."

He took the board and inspected it. "Nicely done."

"Thanks. It's not the first one I've ever cut."

"You'll put me out of a job."

I pouted. "I hope not."

My gloved hand covered his, and his gaze dropped to it. Neither of us pulled our hand away, and I didn't know about him, but I wasn't in much of a hurry to do so either.

Meredith popped her head out the door. "It's getting close to lunch time. Shall I make you both some nourishment?"

I laughed inside my head as I wasn't sure how much *nourishment* she'd find in my house. "I don't have much for groceries."

"I'll manage."

"Can you give us a good hour until it's ready?" Chad yelled

to the front door. "I'd like all the staining done so it can dry while we eat."

"Sure thing."

He placed boards across the work horses, and I mirrored his actions on the second set of workhorses. Another set of work benches popped up, and I added pieces across them.

"Same as with the railings. Two light coats are better than one thick one."

"Got it." I grabbed a brush and began.

It was easy to get distracted watching him work. And bend over. And slap stain across the wood. The board was having all the fun as he stroked up and down. The more I watched him, the hotter my cheeks flamed.

"Are you finished? The table's set," Meredith called out.

"Excellent, I'm starving." He walked to the trailer and pulled out a mid-sized cooler.

My heart stopped beating for a second; had I really been so into admiring Chad and painting rails that an hour had passed without my noticing it? How selfish was I as I hadn't once thought about Michael, or gone to check on him? Had I missed anything?

A blue cooler swung through the air as he walked back to me. "What? You didn't think I'd expect you to feed us, did you?"

Well… the thought had crossed my mind.

"I brought lunch for us all." He carried it past the front porch and walked along the sidewalk to the backyard.

I followed. "The table's inside."

Surprise was not the right word for what I stumbled upon as I entered the backyard.

Under the shade of the huge willow sat a makeshift table, with two folding chairs set around it, and an old stool. The table looked like a door set up on two work horses. I lifted the edge of the tablecloth, wondering where *that* had come from, and spied the worn door. It had been an old one from the basement, taken it off months ago and set it by the fence in the back yard. Someone had fashioned it into a table.

My mouth turned to cotton, and coherent words failed to form. All I managed was, "When?"

"Before we started, when you were inside with Michael. Meredith helped me." Chad balanced the cooler on the stool and set out picnic food—finger sandwiches, cans of pop, personal sized bags of chips and a container of fruit. "Got to have the healthy part, the nurse inside would insist upon it." He winked.

"I'm speechless."

In amazement he set up three places, each in front of the chairs and stool.

"We're coming," Meredith's voice rang out behind me, and I spun around as she wheeled Michael into the backyard.

He was as lit up as a Christmas tree, arms flailing about.

"He's already fed."

"What did you feed him?"

She smiled. "I got another Boost into him, along with his lunch pills."

My mouth dropped in exasperation. "How'd you know which ones?"

"There's a long list hanging above them, all colour coded with times beside. You're very efficient."

Sheesh, maybe I should consider hiring *her*. That's probably more food in him than I've managed lately, and his meds too. If I wasn't so happy Michael was getting some nutrition, I'd probably be a teensy bit more jealous of her ability to take care of him.

"Looks good, Chad." Meredith pushed Michael to one side of the table and sat close to him after snagging a couple quarters of sandwich. "Are you going to sit and eat, honey?" she asked me.

"I... ah, yeah." I took the vacant spot with the best vantage point – Michael was in the center of my radar.

It was like the sunshine filtered in through the branches of hanging leaves and focused all its light on him. It cast a golden glow around him and warmed the pale skin on his cheeks.

"Help yourself." Chad pushed a clear container of sandwiches toward me. "Nothing much. Just ham and cheese. I'm sorry, I don't have any pickles here."

"No, this is all perfect, thank you," I said, my voice threatening to crack.

Swallowing down the emotions bubbling to the surface, I took it all in. The strangers dining with me who were no longer strangers as somehow they had taken me in, walls and all. Chad was better with Michael in the ten days he'd knew him than all my previous boyfriends combined; Niall aside. And Meredith? In a mere few hours, she had brought life back into my brother, at least given him some much-needed nutrition and medications. Maybe after a couple days, he'd bounce back, and things would improve.

"Are you going to eat?" Meredith asked, nudging a plate into my elbow. "You've just been sitting there staring into space."

"Yeah, thanks." I grabbed the container and took a sandwich quarter. With a smile, I sunk my teeth into the meaty taste.

Meredith lifted a drink to Michael's mouth, and as his lips sealed around the end of the straw, the dark liquid moved up higher until it disappeared into his mouth.

I just stared. It was great. A small victory all because my brother was drinking. "I don't suppose I could hire you for the week?"

"Who me?" Chad said, bearing a giant smile.

"I'd like that, truly, but I meant your sister."

"Damn." He snapped his fingers. "I picked the wrong career."

"Not at all." A shy grin formed but I twisted my head to speak to Meredith. "Do you have any availability for the next few days? You've done so much for him already."

"Aw, any of us nurses would. It's the job. We take care of our patients."

"And he's not even your patient." I let my gaze travel back to Michael.

"I can give you the number for the company I work for, and you can take it from there."

I suspected she had a long list of patients vying to be with her. Her demeanour was so calm and caring, and it reflected in Michael. It still caught me happily off guard to see him with a touch of colour in his cheeks. Perhaps she'd be able to make some recommendations on nurses at her work, and I'd get someone awesome, not like Jonathan.

"It's ready," Chad said, as he hoisted the last chain onto the hook he'd screwed into the overhead beam. "Want to have a seat?"

It looked so comfy, and to think, I helped build it. And there it hung in sweet perfection.

"I want to, but I don't."

He cocked a brow. "Because you'd planned on only using it as a decoration?"

"No, because I think I should wait until Michael wakes up from his nap, and he can join me."

After lunch, he'd nodded off, so Meredith moved him into his bed for a more restful nap and every time I peeked in on Michael, she was keeping busy. I had a feeling my living room was dust free.

"How about I test it out with you?" His hands were tucked into his pockets and his eyes were lit up.

"Hmm…" I looked at the hooks in the ceiling and at him.

"Trust me, it'll hold. And if it doesn't, you can blast my poor skills all over social media."

"Tempting." I wiggled my brows. "Let's."

Slowly, I lowered myself into the seat, Chad sat beside me, keeping a respectable distance. My feet just barely touched the floor, but it was all I needed to gently push the swing back and forth. Instantly the motion relaxed me.

"So?"

"Five stars. It's perfect." I patted his thigh.

He placed his hand on mine and linked his fingers through. "This has been a lot of fun. I've never enjoyed going to work as much as I have over the last few days."

The compliment warmed my cheeks and flooded my core. "I'm so pleased."

"Look, I know you said this wasn't a good time, but I'm willing to wait. It's been so long since I've…" His thumb rubbed the top of my hand. "It's been a while since I've been excited to hang out with a female."

"You have your sisters and sister-in-law." I joked, but the weight of his words pressed down on me, and I desperately needed the lightness to come back in.

"Yeah, not quite the same." He twisted in his seat but never took his hand off mine. "What I'm trying to say is… Is I like you." His Adam's Apple bobbed in his throat, and he pulled his teeth over his bottom lip while casting his gaze overhead. "I know you need space and time, and you feel like you can handle everything on your own, and I'm not discounting that because I've been there, but I want you to know I understand what you are going through."

The pulsing in my veins threatened to drown out his words, and I took a deep breath in hopes of controlling it. It didn't work.

"But you don't have to go it alone, I'm here for you however you'll take me. I just enjoy your company, and it's such a nice change from family and buddies."

I stared into those precious eyes filled with sincerity and honesty. "Well, if we're being truthful, I like your company too."

"Why do I feel as though there is a but coming?"

The eye contact ended when my gaze fell to our hands. "Because as much as I want to devote myself to you, I just can't. My personal needs are secondary right now to what Michael needs from me. He needs me to be focused and make sure he's well taken care of. He's my responsibility."

"And it's an admiral one, believe me, but you can still take care of your own needs *and* Michael. I promise I won't let you fail on that."

"But I don't know how to juggle both. Maybe in a few weeks when I start working days, and our schedules sync up. Maybe then."

He sighed, and sadly, I understood all the pain in that sound. It killed a part of me to have to wait for the future, but Michael came first. He needed to. I rested my head on the back part of the swing.

"Being a grown-up sucks."

The twinkle in his eye returned if only for a moment. "Only sometimes. A lot of the times, it's actually pretty good."

I gave his leg a solid pat and pushed myself out of the swing. "Let me get you your cash." Before he could stop me, and tell me all the words I wanted to hear but knew I'd discourage, I dashed into my room, away from the heart-breaking, sweet intoxication of his warmth.

Chapter Twenty

*T*uesday, I woke up to a text message from Chad.

Left something on the porch. Make sure you bring it in.

Curious, I went out and searched around. On the porch swing was a white box with a blue string around it. Once inside, I opened it, spying four cupcakes I couldn't wait to sink my teeth into. And after getting Michael up, clean and fed, I did taste one.

Heaven tasted as sweet and sinful as it looked – the light pink strawberry frosting a perfect compliment to the dark chocolate cake, with a ribbon of fudge in the middle. I put two into the freezer, and kept one in the fridge for later, and after a long day of putting out fires at home and work, it was the perfect treat for a midnight snack.

Wednesday, I got a mid-morning text.

Popped your receipt into the mailbox.

I fumbled through the stack of mail piled in neglect, tossing the flyers and junk mail. A lone blue envelope, thick as a card, bore my name. I tore it open. Indeed, there was a card in there, with the words *Thinking of You*. The receipt for the porch swing was taped to the left-hand side. A handwritten note was crawled across the bottom.

Hope your day blossoms into something beautiful.
Enjoy the sun.
–C

Later that day, I got a surprise flower delivery from Beautiful Blossoms. Unfortunately, the guy tried delivering it in the middle of Michael having a full-blown crying jag where nothing I did settled him down. The driver left the flowers on the front porch and scurried away as fast as I'd ever seen someone leave.

It was a moot point, as try as I may, I couldn't comfort Michael. He wasn't hot, and he wasn't cold. He didn't want to be touched until I gave him some space and then I couldn't leave. I encouraged him to eat but he pushed away any food I brought to his lips. Words failed him, and I couldn't decipher his grunts. It was an uber frustrating day. The only thing that settled him, was practically carrying him to the swing and rocking with him secure in my arms where he whimpered until he fell asleep.

After a sleepless Wednesday night, another text from Chad came in.

Craving steak bowls big time. The guys and I are coming in. Just couldn't wait any longer to see you.

My heart nearly burst reading his words, and I fanned myself with the phone. It was still many hours until I headed into Westside, but I couldn't wait to see him either.

I pulled out my sexiest pair of underwear and matching bra. Even if he couldn't see it, it would raise my confidence, and everyone says confidence was sexy. I just wished I felt as sexy as I tried to pull off. Maybe I had to ditch the dirty and damp shorts and tee I wore, as I still hadn't found an easier way to clean Michael without also getting wet.

Michael sat on the sofa, and I curled up on the sofa chair beside him, flipping through my phone and checking out social media. Michael started murmuring, which was odd because he hadn't said more than five words since Monday. His mouth was slack, and a low groan rolled out.

"Hey," I said, jostling him just a little.

His arm was hot. Real hot. Not a natural hot either.

"Hey," I said, panic rising in my voice. "Michael!"

I stood over him and touched his face. It nearly burned my hands. Lifting his shirt, the heat rolled off him and water would've sizzled had I had any to drip on him.

I rubbed his face, encouraging him to look at me, but his head rolled back, and his eyes with it. "Michael! Michael!"

There was no response. His pulse was hard to find, but it was still there.

"Holy shit you're hot."

He made me hot just touching him. He hadn't felt warm at all, at least not more than normal an hour or two ago. How the hell does one heat up so fast?

"Michael?" I grabbed my phone and dialled 911, throwing the phone on speaker.

"911, what's your emergency?"

My voice shot into the stratosphere. "Please send an ambulance. My brother has a sky-high fever."

"Ma'am, what's his fever at?"

"I don't know, but his skin is so hot. He has cerebral palsy and is in the final stages of muscular dystrophy. Please," I pleaded, the crack forming in my tone, "send an ambulance. NOW!"

I spit out my address.

"We have one dispatched, please stay on the line until it arrives."

"Come on, Michael, please respond." I grabbed a wet cloth from the bathroom and ran it over his face, sure I heard the drops sizzling. "Come on."

As I ran it over his chest, the heat changed the temperature of the cloth in my hands.

The dispatcher's voice crackled through the speaker. "Ma'am, the ambulance is less than a minute away."

"Have them park out front, there's a ramp they can use. Please hurry."

I rewet the cloth hoping the cooler water would rouse him and he'd blink open his eyes and everything would be okay.

"Michael, please."

I held the cloth over his heart, the rapid pounding pulsing up into my palm.

The wails of the sirens approached, and I opened the front door, racing back to cool down my brother. He felt hotter than he did just a couple of minutes ago.

"In here," I yelled to the voices pounding up the walk.

The first one through, an older man, walked directly to Michael, pulling out a funky white device and scanning it over Michael's forehead. It beeped. "Forty point five," he said calmly to the other attendant as he crossed the threshold. "Has he had this long?" he asked me.

"No. He was fine at breakfast. Maybe he had a slight fever when he had his shower afterwards as he was shivering a bit in there, but I turned up the heat." I slapped my hand across my forehead with a resounding smack. "Oh my god, did I cause this?"

"No." He checked Michael's blood pressure and pulse, both way beyond what was normal for him.

Panic built in me impressively fast.

"What meds is he on?"

I sprinted into the kitchen and wiped all his meds into the makeshift pouch I created with the bottom of my shirt, carrying them over to the paramedic. With a crash, I dumped them all onto the couch beside Michael, and rapidly unloaded all about his diseases, and everything the doctor said at his last appointment.

The medic flipped through the pills, tossing each after reading them. "Nothing out of line. Did he take anything? Did you go anywhere?"

"No, he hasn't left the property in at least a week."

An elastic was wound around Michael's upper arm, and the medic unwrapped a needle. "Going to start a line and give him some saline."

I closed my eyes, the tears falling over Michael. "I'm so sorry."

I couldn't bare to watch the guy poke my brother in an attempt to find a vein.

"Got it," he said and the elastic unsnapped.

Still no response from Michael.

"C'mon, baby bird," I cried over him, a sick feeling building in my stomach. "C'mon." I held his head in my hands and ran my thumbs over his brows.

"We're transporting," he said to the other medic, who disappeared from the doorway.

I kept up with kisses on his forehead, each one wracked with guilt over the mysterious reasons for the rapid rise in temperature. "I'm here and I'm not going anywhere."

The other paramedic opened the door. "Transport here." He wheeled the bed into my living room, filling the space almost instantly with the length.

They moved the coffee table out of the way and angled the couch to slide the gurney closer.

"On three. One. Two. Three."

Feather-light Michael was lifted, and the saline solution bag was held by the lead guy.

"You can come with us," the medic who worked on Michael said.

I grabbed all of Michael's meds, my purse with his health info tucked somewhere inside, and my phone, following the guys outside and into the waiting ambulance.

"In front," the one guy said, and I climbed into the passenger seat while the two of them spoke in a language I didn't understand and fussed over my unresponsive brother.

The younger guy hopped into the driver's seat and put the truck into gear, flashing red and white lights reflecting off the parked cars alongside the road.

I closed my eyes and sunk into the seat. What would cause his fever to spike so high and so quickly? What infection suddenly raged a war within him? How fast would the right antibiotics bring it down?

"Hey," the driver asked me, startling me out of my head after he radioed the hospital with all his medical jargon, leaving me completely in the dark. "Is there anyone you wanted to call? To have them meet you there?"

Who would I call? We had no family. I shook my head in response to his question. Oh shit, work. Probably best to text Niall directly. My thumbs moved quickly, and I sent a short and unpleasant text to my boss. I wasn't coming in today, nor tomorrow, and we'd see about the rest of the weekend.

Niall called me back almost as soon as I hit send. "What's going on?"

"Michael's very sick and we're enroute to the hospital."

"Which one?"

"I don't know."

"Ask."

My hands trembled as I twisted the mouthpiece away. "Excuse me, what hospital are we going to?"

"The Alex, it's closer."

I repeated it verbatim to Niall.

"I'll meet you there."

"I don't know where we'll be. Give us a bit, and I'll text you to let you know."

"Promise?"

"Promise. We're friends now, right?" I ended the conversation and with shaky hands, tucked my phone away.

We pulled into the ambulance bay at the hospital, and a team of blue scrub-wearing people waited for us. It was like a scene out of a movie—the kind I hated watching for this very reason. It scared me, as it was all out of my control, and made me feel weak and freaked out about everything.

They wheeled my brother through the ER where a blast of hospital smell – that nasty ammonia type clean—hung in the air. It stabbed me in the nose and I gasped for breath. Past the waiting room they walked, and into a small curtained area, sealing me off from my baby brother.

The tears fell fast and free, and I stood there listening to doctors talk about my brother as if he was just a body and not a living, breathing human. Medication names floated around, and someone listed his diseases and low oxygen and high pulse and a bunch of other things I didn't understand.

A nurse walked by and stopped in front of me. "I'm sorry, you can't be here." Her voice was warm, with an east-Indian accent, making her sound like Russell Peter's little sister.

"That's my brother." I touched the curtains separating me from my brother, in case she wasn't sure who I was referring to.

"Come," she said, and put her arm around me. The heat

from her was nice as I didn't even notice I was cold.

"I'm staying right here."

"They need you out of the way. We're just going to go over there." She pointed to a couple of chairs against the wall. "Okay?"

I nodded as she retraced her tiny steps back to where my brother was.

She poked her head behind the curtain. "The sister's with me." And she returned to me. "What's your name?"

"Audrina."

"And your brother's name?"

"Michael."

"Good strong name." She pointed to the chair, and as I fell into it, terrified I wouldn't be able to stand much longer, the air whooshed out of the cushion. "How old is he?"

"Twenty-two. His birthday is October sixth."

My body went numb. He wouldn't make twenty-three, of that I was suddenly sure. Even the doctor had said when *it* would happen, it would be quick. Things had certainly moved quick over the past couple of weeks.

The curtain opened enough for me to see a couple of blue scrubs.

"Please, I don't want him to be alone. Can't I stay there?"

"Let me check." She marched over to the group of blue scrubs and her lips moved but I couldn't figure out what she was saying. Occasionally, someone would look in my direction. Walking back to me, she stopped. "Soon, they tell me."

I watched and waited, and in trying to calm myself, I counted to thirty. Repeatedly. So many times, I lost count. My nails were chewed right to the quick, and I managed to pick a raised bump on my arm until it bled and pressed a tissue from the box hanging on the wall onto it.

Eventually, the curtain pulled back fully.

The nurse led me over.

Two blue scrubs with long white jackets stood on either side of my brother who was blanketed in a blue plastic tarp-like thing with a rainbow of cords running beside his head, up to a machine to his right.

"What's going on?" I whispered.

The doctor came close and turned me away from seeing my brother.

I fought to turn back and stared at the body covered in the blue plastic, it was impossible to see his twisted limbs. Even the frailness of his bone-thin arms were hidden. His face was relaxed, and his eyes were closed. To an outsider, he probably looked like he was sleeping. But I knew better.

"What's this?" I fingered the blue 'blanket', the coolness chilling me further.

"We're trying to lower his body temp."

I nodded and rubbed his toes which protruded from under the blue. He still felt hot, even across the tips of his feet. But warm was good. He was still alive and for that, I breathed a sigh of relief.

"There's minimal brain activity however, and we suspect it's from the rapid rise of heat."

I turned my focus to the doctor, trying to understand what he was saying.

"He's not responding to treatment."

I blinked back a rush of tears and swallowed the ache in my throat.

"What... does that mean?" I asked slowly and quietly, holding my brother's foot, the only thing I could touch from this point.

His hand patted my shoulder. "I'm sorry."

"You're sorry?" A strong voice bellowed out of me as I pushed him out of the way and went to the head of the bed. "You're sorry? You're the doctor. Make him better. I want a second opinion."

"Is there anyone we can call for you?"

"Yeah, another doctor," I said tersely and bent over Michael. My lips graced his forehead, tears dropping onto his face. "Oh, my baby bird." I cradled his face between my hands. "I love you so much."

The monitor beside him blinked, the green light peaking with each heartbeat. They were rapid, numbering in the low hundreds.

"Stay," I whispered, the most selfish word I've ever breathed out.

It wouldn't be the best thing for him, especially if there was no brain activity, but I couldn't bear to have him taken away from me. He was the one constant.

I saw him every day of my life, how would I be able to face a future without him? I was there when mother brought him home. I was there, proclaiming to anyone who would listen that he was *my* baby. I fed him and played with him, and when I came home from school, he was the first person I talked to about my day. When mother put him into the home, I walked over daily for a visit. He was my baby bird, and I wasn't yet ready to let him fly.

My back pocket buzzed and after ignoring the first few, I finally checked. A text from Niall and Chad.

Remembering I promised him an update, I texted Niall.

In the ER. Not going home. Not good.

I stared at the text from Chad. *Can't wait until supper. What about lunch?*

The thought of food sitting like a lead weight in my stomach made it flip and sour further. Yeah, not going to eat.

I texted back. *Not a good day. We're at the hospital. I'll talk to you later.*

I flipped my phone to silent, not wanting to get into any more discussion about it.

A nurse popped her head into the room. "Can I get you anything?"

"Yeah, that second opinion. I'm still waiting," I said without blinking an eye.

Her round little head disappeared and the patter of her feet down the hall grew silent.

I was starting to believe we were at the back of the ER or something, in the land where patients were forgotten. There was no activity in this area, no voices, no beeps from other machines. Every time I checked to see if a doctor was coming, the hallway was vacant. Eerily vacant. I shuddered.

I lifted the blue plastic bubble wrap off Michael's hand and held on to him, the heat from it not as intense as it had been. My hand softly pulled down the length of his hand from the palm to his fingertips. Side by side our hands were identical, the same shape, our fingers the same length. Even our thumbs bent out the same way. Retrieving the phone from my back pocket, I snapped a picture of my hand holding his, and deleted all the notifications of incoming text messages.

I went up to his head, and finger brushed his curls. His forehead was cooler; it didn't burn my fingers like it had before. I glanced to the machine recording his pulse and it was slowing down.

Ninety-five.

Eighty-eight.

Eighty-two.

His pulse was returning to normal but the more sensible part of me knew the harsh, oncoming truth.

Oh god, no!

I kissed his forehead, my tears trailing into his eyebrows.

212

Wiping them away, I checked the monitor once again.

Seventy-one.

Sixty-two.

I squeezed his hand – his cool, limp hand – and a painful ache rose in my chest. Gasping for air, I tried to push the intensifying pain deep. "I love you," I whispered.

Forty-three.

Twenty-nine.

My lips graced his cheek, and a sobering thought rolled out. "It's time to fly, baby bird. Spread your wings and go." Sobbing into his chest, I placed my ear against it, feeling the weak beat of his heart.

The monitor's flashes of peaks and valleys became a straight line.

No more beats beneath my cheek. No noises. No hollow sounds.

Death had silently arrived and carried my brother away.

Wrapped in a hug, I held my brother tight, crying over him. A hollowness replaced my heart, my own beating with less strength.

A nurse remained, not speaking, not moving, and suddenly I hated her. I hated her for not doing something. Anything. I hated the blank expression upon her face, as if she were devoid of feeling, like a robot. Probably part of the training, and I hated that too. The longer she stood there, the harder I hugged my brother.

"Miss," she said, her hand on my shoulder. "We need to–"

"Shut up." I winced as the words rolled out of my mouth. "Please, just stop."

"Where is she?" a voice said, curtains rolling back with a snap. "Audrina," he said breathlessly. Chad's hand fell between my shoulder blades.

I buried my nose into Michael and tried to inhale his sweet smell, but it was long gone replaced with a deep medical stench. In shock, I pulled back and stood up.

The nurse opened her mouth. "We need to–"

"Give her a moment." His rough hands smoothed my shoulders as he rubbed them. "Audrina?"

Heaving from breathlessness, I straightened up, the ache in my chest radiating out to my extremities. It hurt to breathe. It hurt to blink. It hurt to cry. I turned into Chad, his arms wrapping tightly around me, holding me up from collapsing on the floor.

"I've got you," he whispered into my ear, and tugged me out of the space and into the vacant hallway.

"Michael," I cried, my heart splintering into two.

He squeezed tighter, his cheek against mine.

A low click came from behind me, and I opened my eyes to see robo-nurse unhooking the machines, the wires still draped over his shoulders.

"Let's move over here," Chad whispered, his grip warm and comforting.

Another click echoed, and the distinct sound of rubber wheels moving over flooring filled the air. The bed creaked and groaned as another nurse pushed it out into the hallway, away from us. From me.

I fought to break free from Chad's grip around my waist, screaming and yelling while pushing against his firm chest. "That's my family."

But he never let go.

Chapter Twenty-One

The corridor was endlessly grey and silent, aside from my feet dragging along the floor and the clomping sounds from Chad's work boots. Staying silent, he held me close, and I was grateful for sharing space without having to share thoughts and words.

I'd followed Michael as far as I could, until we reached the double doors restricting us access. No, I wasn't medical personnel, I was his sister, and I knew what he needed.

"He needs a clean shirt. The one with the blue jay on it. And don't comb his hair, he liked it messy like that."

Chad squeezed me harder, but I wasn't going to fall apart. Not here and I wiped away my fallen tears.

Slowly, mumbles and voices became clearer as we stumbled along stopping at a desk. Nurses and doctors milled around.

I was somehow back at admitting, and I tapped the counter. "Do I just leave?"

"Just wait." Robo-nurse walked behind the desk and chatted with someone in a white coat.

A deep bubbling pain started in my chest and expanded

215

outward. It suffocated me, and I gasped. Feeling the softness of Chad's shirt against my cheek soothed me a little, but I had to remind myself to breathe.

Chad's firm hands rubbed up and down my back, and I counted each one, zoning out deeper with each downward stroke.

I rocked back and forth, clutching his cotton shirt in my fists, and closing my eyes.

"Audrina?" His voice came from a million miles away. "The liaison worker needs us to follow her."

"What?" I lifted my fifty-pound head and blinked the admitting area back into focus.

"This way." My hand firmly gripped in his, he led the way.

One foot in front of the other, the hardness of each step rippled up my body. I followed the person in a nice pant suit I could only assume was the liaison worker.

"Audrina," a voice from my past called out behind me.

Turning my head to match the face with the voice, I spied him walking in through the emergency doors and up to the triage desk. I pushed out of Chad's embrace.

"Niall." I ran into his arms and buried my face into the crook of his neck. "Oh my god, Niall." Giant sobs flowed out of me, and my body shook against his.

He rubbed my hair. "Oh, Audrina, I'm so so sorry." Arms I'd once fought against now held me together.

"My baby bird," I cried out, my sobs growing in strength, "has flown away."

I stayed there, letting the world fade away, my heart breaking as Niall's chest rattled under me. I wasn't sure if it was his tears or my own that puddled on my cheek.

A brisk tap on my shoulder, and I looked over to the source. Robo-nurse.

"We need you to move this to the room down the hall."

Right, heaven forbid anyone in the waiting room see a public display of heartbreak. I wiped my eyes and separated myself from Niall, gasping for breath again.

Chad's strong hand rested on my lower back. "Breathe."

I hated that I needed a reminder, but I listened to his voice as he counted it out for me.

"This way," the nurse said.

Behind my head, two male voices spoke. "I'm Chad Lawton."

"Niall Underwood." Another hand landed gently between my shoulder blades. "I'm Audrina's boss."

"It's nice of you to come here and support her. She'll need all she can get in the next little while."

I drowned out the rest of the mumbles and wobbled my way down the hall, stopping at the entrance to a room. Bathed in neutral beiges and creams like it had been hosed down in top-of-the-line hotel décor, it should've been comforting. To me, it was a clinical space filled with brochures and handouts and tissues. Where many family members had likely been given the worst news of their lives. A room where I was about to hear all the things I didn't want to know.

# # #

After meeting with the hospital liaison worker, and vaguely listening to what would happen next, Chad escorted me back to his truck with my hands full of papers and bullshit. To the hospital, Michael was simply a body to deal with and ship off to the funeral home, and as soon as I knew which one I preferred, to let them know. Because this was the most important things to deal with at the moment. Not how I was going to move on. Not how to figure out how to breathe and move. No, the funeral home was most important.

The ride back home was a muted quiet, as if I were under water. Voices were muffled, and I couldn't even guess if it was Chad, the radio or something else since I really didn't care. My hand constricted every so often, a warmth touching against it. The scenery out the pickup window became a blur of greens and the skies held a hazy shade of grey and mourning, like the clouds were ready to cry but desperately hung on for the right moment. Sort of how I felt.

Hanging on.

Barely breathing.

Heart still beating, but to a lonely, pitiful rhythm.

My baby bird was gone.

The gentle lull rocking me stopped, and I blinked and swallowed to clear the fog. I exited Chad's truck, putting one foot on the ground at a time. And froze.

My beautiful house stared down on me, the windows in a slow, sad blink with the blinds half drawn. The new deck face smiled pathetically like a grimace.

Chad's arm wrapped around my shoulders, his lips sealed.

Without warning, I couldn't move. Forgot how. In the span of a few hours my home, my sanctuary, had morphed into something sad and unwelcoming. The desire to rush up the steps and greet the beautiful face inside was gone in a heartbeat.

A vehicle pulled up behind Chad's truck, and Niall sauntered over to where I stood. "Are you going in?"

I shook my head and backtracked a couple of steps.

"Do you want to stay at my house?" Niall asked, stepping in front of me and blocking my view with his round, balding head.

Again, my head moved from side to side.

"What is it you want?"

A hard lump formed in my throat. "I want him home." Chad's grip tightened around me, but I held myself up. As much as

I wanted to break down and well, break, I wasn't going to.

Not here. Not now. Not this way.

Niall moved back and forth until I focused on him. "You know that can't happen."

I closed my eyes. "Shut up," I said softly. I wasn't looking for a fight, I just needed him to stop talking.

"Audrina." His voice warm and oddly soothing. He wasn't mad.

"Just please, shut up. You asked what I wanted." I stepped back again until my legs hit the running boards of Chad's truck.

"Take all the time you need. The first time's the hardest," Chad said.

I turned my head and opened my eyes. He stood there looking as lost as I felt. His eyes were sad, and the sparkle wiped clean. The bright smile he usually sported was flipped upside down and his shoulders rolled inward. I wanted to cheer him up and make him feel better, but I didn't know how.

My gaze travelled back toward the house as a sigh erupted deep in my chest and blew out of me with great effort. The depth of sadness deflated me further as realisation that the newly constructed deck wouldn't be used anymore, at least not by Michael—its intended recipient. He hadn't even had a chance to truly enjoy any of it because I had delayed too long in getting it done.

God damn it!

A phone rang, its tone muted as it was in someone's pocket. It would stop, only to start up again.

"Is someone going to answer that?" I growled.

Chad angled his body away from mine. "Sorry."

"Forget it." I shirked out of his grasp and headed up the walkway, pausing as a flock of small birds flew away from the feeder. My legs gave out, and I crumpled onto the sidewalk.

Niall rushed to my side and knelt beside me, Chad right

behind him. "Audrina?"

A sob tore out of me.

It was *his* bird feeder. He'd been the one to paint the boards and he'd been so happy to have been a part of it. His smiles were infectious. I'll never forget how wonderful that day was, that wonderful memory making day. And that's all I had left now – just the memories.

Giant, painful aches settled into my soul, stomped on my heart, and squished my lungs. I wrapped my hands around my chest, trying to desperately hold myself together.

"No!" I said, my tone blunt and surprisingly strong. "No!" I pushed away Niall's hands and slapped a hand against the cracked sidewalk.

A small pebble had buried itself in my palm and scratched its way across my face as I attempted to piece myself back together. I was stronger than this. I could make it into my house and tough it out. I didn't need anyone to hold me up or carry me or lift me. One foot in front of the other, I climbed the stairs and unlocked my front door.

"There you are," Melody's voice called out when I stepped inside. Her joyful expression hit the floor the instant she laid eyes on me. "Where's Michael?"

My vision blurred again, and an arm reached around me as the feeling left my body.

"Noooo," Melody cried out. Tears instantly streamed down her face and she wrapped me in a hug.

"I'm so sorry," I whispered. I wished I'd called her while I was at the hospital, and at least given her a little lead time. She was expecting an evening with him, and now…

My stomach gave a little roll, followed by a bigger flip. I covered my mouth and pushed myself to the bathroom and heaved into the toilet, just in time.

220

Feeling as physically drained as I was emotionally and mentally, I curled myself onto the cool bathroom floor and pulled a towel over myself. My eyes fluttered shut as visions of Michael flickered in my head like an old-time movie. The past twenty-two years. The special bond we shared, his smile, the curly mop of hair, the way he said he loved me that final time.

Chapter Twenty-Two

J marched into the server station, wrapping my apron around my waist, and giving it a solid yank.

"What are you doing here?" Niall strutted over to me, and firmly reached for my hand.

Narrowed eyes met his gaze. "I'm working. I'm scheduled to start at four."

"You know we've covered your shifts."

I heard him, but I wasn't looking at him. Instead, I started making a fresh pot of coffee. Who had let the coffee get so low?

He tugged on my hand, a gentle yet persuasive pull. "Come with me."

"I'm busy. I'm making coffee. I can do this." With a shake, I yanked my hand out of his and tore open a packet of coffee. The smell used to be wonderful, now it turned my stomach. Mind you, everything turned it lately. "Stop staring at me, Joy," I barked out.

Since I'd walked into the station, she hadn't removed her happy little eyes from me, and it was pissing me off.

"Now." Niall's voice echoed in the small space.

I threw the package into the garbage and stormed ahead of him, grunting with each step.

He closed the door to the tiny office. "You shouldn't be here."

Lifting myself onto the edge of the desk, my eyes darted around the space, landing on the restaurant surveillance monitors.

"You should be at home."

The room darkened as I closed my eyes. "I've been home all day long, Niall. For the past four days I've been home. I've been planning a funeral for the twelve people I think would show up. I've been going through his things and packing up his clothes. But I can't do it anymore. I needed to escape."

Opening my eyes, he stood in front of me, hardly a breath of space between us. A weird instinct, like the desire to be comforted without judgement, pushed my forehead against his chest, the soft fabric covering the slight cushion of thick skin.

"Please. I need the distraction."

His hands found the knot at the base of my neck and he gave it a rub. "Chad was coming by this evening to help you out, remember?"

As if I didn't know. "I'd texted him before I left to tell him I was working."

Bless him, he'd been great popping by each evening to check on me.

"Did you eat today?"

"No." My stomach hadn't kept much down since Thursday. I tried a smoothie, but it brought back too many memories. It soured in the pit of my stomach and burned on its exit.

"I'm not letting you go onto the floor in a weakened condition."

I lifted my head to glare with the little bit of energy I had left. "I can handle it, and I've *been* handling it."

"Eat something, even if it's just a little, and I'll let you work through the dinner rush."

"Is that an ultimatum?" My eyes narrowed into thin little slits.

"You tell me." He raised his brow.

I hopped off the desk. Going home wasn't an option, not right now.

"Place your order with Trigger, and I'll bring it out to you."

"Fine."

Despite eating a quarter of a Coririki Steak Bowl, I barely made it through the supper rush. Exhaustion overwhelmed me. A couple sat in my section, and I leaned my hand on the back of the booth they sat in, my other hand over my heart.

"Miss, are you okay?" the lady asked.

I closed my eyes quickly and took a breath. "I'm going…" My hip rested against the edge of the table. "I'll have someone else take care of you." The air around me was suddenly chilly as I stumbled to the back and paused at the entrance to the kitchen. "Niall?"

He popped his head out of the office and raced over. "Jesus, you're pale."

I gripped his arm. A voice I didn't control fell out of me. "I want to go home now."

"You can't drive like this. Just rest a minute."

As I was ushered into his chair, Joy called back for Niall.

"I'll be right back," he said, kissing the top of my head.

I rested my heavy head against the back of the chair, zoning out to the sounds emanating from the nearby kitchen.

"She's right here." Niall's voice brought me back into the present, and I opened my eyes to Chad hunched in front of me.

"What are you doing here?" To say I was surprised to see him was an understatement.

224

"I was supposed to help you tonight."

My weighted hand waved through the air. "I'm fine, really." But I shivered, even as Chad shrugged out of his jacket and wrapped the weight of it around me.

Niall whispered, "That's why she's sitting back here. Because she's fine." He smirked and walked away.

I glared at the back of his head. Jerk.

A sad expression cut across Chad's features. "First day back's a bitch." He extended his hand. "C'mon, I'll take you home."

A sigh larger than me, escaped in a strong puff, and I found myself nodding at him. On wobbly legs, I managed to right myself and hold his hand. His warm, strong hand.

He walked beside me and opened the door to the truck, waiting until I was belted before he closed the door. A moment later, he was in the driver's seat.

"You know," he said as he started the engine, "my first day back was the worst. I was working with this company during the boom times, and we were so busy. I'd already taken a couple weeks off and felt I owed it to the boss to came back."

I turned my head to stare out the window as he spoke.

"That day, stupid me, I thought I could handle a full shift. And to them I did. I was a machine all day, and popped up a full floor, fueled by determination and pig-headedness. But that night, I couldn't move. Couldn't think. Couldn't do anything really. I ended up taking another few days off, but then I eased myself back into it. The human body is a remarkable thing. It truly tells you when you've done too much." He was quiet for a few heartbeats. "If you listen to it."

I twisted to face him, a spark of rage flickering. "The human body is not remarkable. It's so fucking fragile, and it withers and breaks. It creates fevers out of nothing and cooks your insides. It attacks you and makes life very difficult."

225

"That's the anger talking."

"That's the disease working. If the human body was so amazing, we'd surely be able to fight and resist the very things trying to break us down."

"It's okay to be angry."

"And I'm okay being angry." In fact, the flicker had ignited into a full out fire. "The doctors failed to do their jobs. They did not keep my brother alive, instead, they let him go. They didn't even try." My voice weakened.

Chad reached over and squeezed my hand. "I know."

There was something powerful about those two words. He wasn't discounting my opinion, like Melody had. Over and over, she kept reassuring me the doctors did all they could. It didn't make me feel better because I'd asked for a second opinion, and no one came. They'd abandoned my request. Assholes, all of them.

Chad shook out of my hand and quickly changed the station.

"No, go back."

I knew that song. It was an old one. A *really* old one. About how the singer was saying the burdens weren't bad because it was his brother. The lyrics played and wove a thread of hurt through my heart. The words were so powerful.

"The load doesn't weigh me down at all. He ain't heavy, he's my brother."

It had been truth. Whatever burdens society thought Michael had, they were mine to shoulder as family should. His problems didn't weigh him down, and I was more than happy to take them on for him.

Tears welled as an achiness spread. Had I given him the best life I could? Was there anything I would've done different? Was he as happy as he could've been? Had he hurt on his final hours?

226

How I hoped not. He'd suffered enough, and I hoped his last day was a pain-free one.

I blinked and wiped away my sorrow. I wasn't the only one in the truck who hurt or had hurt. "Can I ask, about your wife?"

A small smile thinned his lips. "What do you want to know?"

I shrugged. "Anything you want to share."

There was so much I was curious about, but I didn't want to push it. Trudging up memories wasn't always a pleasant experience.

He parked his truck in front of my home and killed the engine. "Let's go inside and I'll tell you anything you want to know."

We walked into the house, passed a couple garbage bags full of clothes, and a pile of items I needed to return like the wheelchair and the stool for the shower.

"You were busy today."

"Not really."

"What are you going to do with all those bags?"

"They're all his old clothes. I kept a couple of his favourites, but I really don't need the rest. Donate them, I guess? I don't know really. However, I'll need to return the rentals."

"Let me take care of the donations. I know a place that can put them to good use." He focussed on the bags.

"That would be great, thanks."

He popped open the door and dropped the two bags onto the deck. "I'll take them home with me later."

I rummaged through the fridge not finding anything of interest. "Do you want something to drink?"

He stopped at the wall dividing the living room from the kitchen and leaned against it "I'm good, thanks."

A lightbulb went off. "Ah-hah." I stretched and reached for

the bottle of vodka stored at the top of the cupboard, wiggling it back and forth once it was in my hand. "No?"

"No. I'm driving."

"Suit yourself." I set a glass on the counter and filled to the halfway mark. Without a second thought or hesitation, I guzzled most of the clear liquid down my throat.

"Easy there," Chad said, removing the drink from my hand.

"I needed that."

"Alcohol won't solve your problems, and it won't help you with your grief."

"But it'll numb the pain." And it needed it to work fast. Hurt and aches built impressively fast over the past couple of days.

Such sincerity formed on his face. With a tender thumb, he stroked my cheek. "There's nothing wrong with allowing yourself to feel the pain."

I broke free of his gaze and his hold and headed into the living room. I stopped behind the couch where I stared into Michael's empty room. As much as I had packed up his clothes, I'd left his bed untouched and unmade, leaving it the way it was.

A hitch formed in my breath and a dull ache blanketed my heart. "Oh, my baby bird," I whispered and covered my chest with my arms.

Chad moved behind me, and without a word, rubbed my shoulders and neck. Each stroke magically untied the knots and soothed the rough edges.

I rolled my head forward. "That feels nice."

"Yeah, not much beats a massage."

My eyes softly shut, and I leaned into each rub and caress. The alcohol I'd downed drifted through my system. On a good day, I was a cheap drunk, and it took so little with my low tolerance to make me feel it. On a bad day, and an empty stomach, it took no time at all. Between the pressure of the massage and the four ounces of alcohol, I was starting to feel pretty damn good.

I moaned.

Chad worked a knot at the base of my neck and a flush of heat rolled through me as it loosened.

I braced myself against the doorframe to allow maximum pressure. "Oh, sweet hell, that feels amazing."

"I'm glad you're enjoying."

I turned around and pushed him over to the couch, straddling my knees on either side of his hips.

He stared at me with a hunger in his eyes.

Without hesitation, I caved to my emotions and pressed my lips to his, the roughness not something I expected. My arms wrapped around his head and through his hair while I inched my body close to him, enough to nearly fuse our bodies together. The intensity in my kisses roused something in him, strong enough to feel between my legs.

"Oh, Chad," I whispered into his ear and flicked his hot lobe before gently nibbling on it.

Two strong hands gripped my shoulders and pushed me back.

I righted myself and stared down at him. "What the hell?"

"I think we should wait."

My eyes once burning with lust and desire, narrowed at him. "You wanted me to have more moments. Here you go."

"And that's fine, but not like this."

"Not like what?"

"You're slightly intoxicated."

"So what?" Until a moment ago, I was feeling lighter than air; something I hadn't felt in a very long time.

"Not like this." He shook his head.

"Not like what? Not like me?" I pushed myself off and dropped onto the other couch, a sofa chair. I pointed to the front door. "Get out."

He didn't get up and head to the door like I asked, instead he moved closer, lowering himself to his knees. "Audrina, I want you. I want to explore what's blossoming between us, but not tainted. Not while you're under the influence."

"I said get out." I lowered my head into my hands, covering my face.

Raging hurt coursed through my veins, along with tendrils of pain. Ears wide open, I listened as he stood and padded his way to the door. A creak as it opened and then silence after the inside door was pulled closed.

Knowing he was gone, I sobbed openly, curling myself into the couch and covering up.

Chapter Twenty-Three

Niall sat in the chair beside me and gave my thigh a friendly pat. "How are you holding up?"

All I could do these days was shrug. I just bid adieu to a red-eyed Melody and her girlfriend as they walked outside with Chad. With knowing so little people, I had a small service in my home, rather than a totally impersonal one in a funeral chapel.

From the viewpoint in my oversized chair, I scanned the living room, stopping for a moment on the 8 x 10 of Michael, hanging on the wall between the bathroom and his bedroom. He had such a euphoric look on his face. I took it not long after he moved in, while he was watching his favourite show. I figured it was only fitting to see that smiling face, with his unruly mop of chestnut-coloured hair and his dark eyes glistening with happiness, from anywhere in the living room since he'd spent a lot of time there. That's how I wanted to remember him, and how I wanted everyone else to as well.

I peered past the lingering guests into his room. Michael's urn—hand painted with birds—sat at the head of his bed, on the bookshelf under the window. I could just make out the sky-blue colour background on it from my seat.

Niall gave my knee a rub. "You should eat." He held a plate of cheeses and fresh fruit.

Always with the eating. "I'm not hungry." My voice was barely above a whisper.

"I know you're not, but still. A little food in your system…"

"I've no desire to eat."

I glanced out the window, watching as the rain poured down. At least the clouds could release their tears. Despite an overwhelming bloated feeling of needing to release mine, they refused to fall. Instead, a blanket of numbness settled over me. Which I didn't mind – it allowed me to sit in the corner and let the world mumble by.

Normally I'd play hostess, but not today. Food and drinks were set out in the kitchen, along with a book of condolences the funeral home gave out. Guests were free to come and go as they pleased, there was no hard feelings either way. Niall had taken over as the host and had said a few choked backed words on my behalf.

Feeling as uncomfortable as I was, given the circumstances, I hardly moved out of my chair. Smiles were impossible, and even a frown seemed like an extraordinary task.

Robin sat beside me. "I'm really sorry for your loss."

They all said it, or some variation of. I knew they meant well, however, at the end of the day, they'd be going home to their happy homes, and I'd still be here in my Michael-less house.

"Thanks," I mumbled, unable to make eye contact.

A little blue bird had captured my attention as it sat on the fence, twisting its head and staring into the house.

"If you need anything…"

"I'll let you know."

The bird hopped along the edge, almost as if it were locking eyes with me.

Robin's hand gave my shoulder a squeeze and he left,

whispering incoherently to another lady. Could've been a girlfriend or a sister for all I recognised.

Joy and her main squeeze said goodbyes after a long, uncomfortable hug. That was the only time I ever saw sadness on her face, and I felt bad for her. Some of the kitchen staff had come by as well, giving the friendly condolences and heartfelt handshakes or hugs. Meghan had even sent her condolences via Joy while she covered for Niall. But the little bird stayed for a while, hopping back and forth. Eventually, the slamming of the screen door must've scared it, and it fluttered away.

"Everyone's gone?" I looked right through Niall.

"Chad's just walking his sister out, but he'll be back."

"Okay." I rose and headed into the kitchen. "Clean up time."

As I stood against the counters, there was nothing to clean up. My kitchen was tidier than it was before the service started. The tray of sandwiches were wrapped. The fruit and veggies platters with dip were long gone. Even the trash can under the sink was empty, a fresh bag in its place.

Ready to coat my dry and scratchy throat, I grabbed a red, plastic cup and opened the freezer to grab an ice cube. I paused and stared. It was full of food containers. Curious, I grabbed one, and read the label. *Lasagna. Reheat 3 minutes.* Another read *chicken with rice.* There had to be two dozen containers stacked inside.

I closed the door and looked over at Niall.

"There's some in the fridge too." He opened it and pointed them out.

My voice cracked. "What? When? Who?"

He closed the door. "Everyone. Chad suggested they bring a meal already proportioned and pop it into the freezer. Said something about it being handy for the first few weeks when the interest to cook is gone."

How sweet. It'll be nice to have something easy to eat whenever the desire to eat kicks back in.

"He's a good guy, Audrina. Better than I ever was."

"It was a different time. I no longer hold anything against you." I reached out for a hug, which he reciprocated, and I melted into it. "I'm sorry. For being so angry about it all the time, and not forgiving you." A hard lump formed in my throat and it hurt to swallow. "It ended up hurting Michael more than anything else." I pushed my eyes into his shoulder to push the tears back in – now wasn't the time to let them fall.

He rubbed my back. "You know that's not true. We had lots of good memories together. Recent ones too."

I nodded. Niall had been instrumental in helping me when my mother died, and I gained guardianship of Michael. However, even before she passed, he'd been the one who planted the seed about Michael moving in with me – a decision I never regretted.

He pushed out of the hug and pointed to the table. "There's a pile of cards for you to read through later."

"From who?"

They were all addressed to me as I sorted through them. Envelopes of every colour. I seriously didn't know that many people, and judging from the stack of cards, it was more than who attended today.

A small smile tugged at the corners of his face. "Believe or not, there are a lot of people who care about you."

That was a surprise. I never gave anyone the chance.

"Korey and Shayne send their condolences as well."

"Who?"

"Jasper and Jade."

Oh right, them. Forgot their real names since I really only knew them via their work nicknames, and it wasn't like we hung out or anything. But Jasper was a good friend of Niall's.

A new ache formed in my heart as I stared at the pile of cards and thought about the meals stacked and stored in my fridge. Michael's collection of friends were a loyal count of two; Melody and Niall. The people who showed up today, or sent in their support, hadn't done it for Michael, they'd done it *for me*. To support me. And that was the biggest surprise of all. The ache deepened with that reflection.

"Let's go sit on the porch and grab some fresh air. It'll do you a world of good." He led me into the living room and pulled the blanket off the back of the couch, wrapping it around my shoulders. With a gentle push, he sent me toward the door.

The screen closed with a bang, and I curled up in the swing, pulling the blanket around my naked feet. Niall sat and gently swayed the swing. The cool air breathed across my cheeks as the rain pattered and bounced off the edges of the deck. The deck built for Michael. Who only used it in passing. A deep breath shuttered out of me.

From the corner of my eye, Chad walked the sidewalk and to the edge of the stairs. He climbed them, and removed his dripping cowboy hat, setting it on one of the folding chairs.

"Sorry I was gone so long."

"It's okay. I figured you'd left," I said, my voice raw and scratchy.

He moved slowly, as if he were afraid of what I'd say or do. "I wasn't going to leave without making sure you were as okay as you could be."

Niall stood and walked a few paces away. "I'll let you two be. If you need anything, Audrina, please don't hesitate. Otherwise, I'll be in touch tomorrow."

"Thank you. For everything."

"Of course."

I waved as Niall descended the stairs and disappeared

around the side of the house. My focus returned to Chad. "I'm...
I'm doing okay."

There wasn't anything I could do to bring Michael back, I
lived in the real world enough to know that. At least today I did.

"May I?" He pointed toward the vacant space on the swing.

The contact between us since I'd kicked him out had been
minimal, reduced to a few texts at best and the air felt charged with
awkwardness and a smidge of tension. "Of course."

Chad sat beside me, his arm resting on the back of the
swing, the other on his lap. It clenched and released as if he was
fighting his own nerves.

It was up to me to break the tension; after all I'd been the
one to put the wedge between us. "Niall showed me the fridge and
freezer. I can't thank you enough for that."

His gaze fell to the floor. "It's the least I could do."

"No, the least you could do would be nothing at all." I
offered a hint of a smile. "I'm sorry. For the other night. And for
today. I'm really out–"

"Shh." His finger fell across my lips. "You don't need to
explain it to me."

"Been there, done that, eh?" I tucked my arms under the
blanket as I was getting rather chilled.

A pained grimace showed on the left side of his face.
"Yeah."

"Want to talk about it?" I for one wasn't in the mood to talk,
but I wasn't in the mood to be alone either. Figured, if he talked,
he'd stay longer.

"What do you want to hear?"

I shrugged but wasn't sure if he could see it. "Whatever you
want to share. I'm sure you had pleasant memories. It wasn't all
bad."

His grimace shifted into a true smile, although his eyes held a tinge of pain. "No, it wasn't all bad. Just the opposite. Betsy was my high school sweetheart, and we did everything together. Did you know she was an engineer?"

I shook my head.

"Of course not." Chad ran his fingers through his hair. "We had the most amazing destination wedding in Mexico. Ten fabulous days in the heat in the dead of winter. We'd talked about kids, but we wanted to wait a few years. However, He had other plans for us." He looked toward the heavens. "She created this neat way of telling me. Ever so nonchalantly as she was making supper she said, '*So Julia and Corbin are expecting in November. On the twenty-second. It's three days after us.*' And it took me a minute to hear what she said."

"Wow, that's pretty sneaky. Corbin is Batman, right?"

He nodded. "She had a relatively easy pregnancy compared to Julia, since Julia was carrying twins. However, one night Betsy started complaining about a brutal headache and an upset tummy. I thought it was the flu, but I took her into the ER anyway." He paused. "At the Alex."

The hospital Michael never came out of.

"A few tests later, and she was in the OR delivering our son." His head hung low as he breathed heavily. "She didn't survive the surgery. She never met her beautiful boy."

That did it. Fresh tears fell as an ache in my heart for him spread. How awful. I reached out my hand to him. "Oh, Chad."

He squeezed me back, linking his fingers through mine. "Tristan was born sixteen weeks early and had a huge road ahead of him, but sadly, God called him home to be with his mother just forty-three hours later."

I was beyond crushed. There had been no warning, no goodbyes. I'd been living the past few days in deep grief, but at least I got to say goodbye. I'd held Michael while Death stole him from under me, but Chad never got that chance. In the blink of an eye, his whole world was snatched away.

"I'm so sorry." I lifted my blanket and snuggled over to him, draping us both in the warmth of our sorrows. Leaning my head against his chest, I sighed; a soul crushing, painful sound. Chad did the same.

"How long has it been?"

"It was seven years on July 30th."

My cheek nestled against his shirt, and I placed my hand over his beating heart. "How long..." I couldn't ask.

"For what?"

"Until you felt whole again?" There I asked. Grief affected everyone differently, but I wanted a general idea. There was no manual for what I was going through; for what he went through.

"Years." The words were laced in the saddest sound.

"Years?"

"Probably not the answer you were hoping for, but yeah."

The swing swayed back and forth. It was a nice motion and soothing too. Michael loved it, and it had been the only thing to calm him his last night on Earth. Remembering that frustrating day and how nothing else had worked burned at me. I had tried to be patient and to work the problem, but I got nowhere. Had he been suffering all along and I'd ignored it? Had I taken him in to the hospital, would he still be here?

"Oh god," I said, as the possibility of being the reason for Michael's demise settled over.

"What's wrong?"

"It's all my fault." I tossed off the blanket and scrambled out of the swing. "Michael's death. I could've prevented it."

Chad walked toward me, tipping my chin and staring into my eyes. "That's not true."

"It is. The night before, he'd been whimpering and hurting.

I couldn't go away and yet I couldn't be near. He was either too cold or too hot. He wanted to eat until I gave him food. He was all over the map. If I'd taken him in..." My legs gave out, and I crumpled onto the floor of the deck. "He'd still be here."

I pounded my fist against the wood, hitting it harder and harder each time until I finally gave out and my hand brusied.

The deck certainly wasn't going break; Chad had constructed a solid piece of work.

"I was supposed to take care of him, and that night, I failed."

Chapter Twenty-Four

Chad

*G*rief is the weirdest emotion. When my Baba died, we'd all been expecting it, but it still hurt when the Good Lord called her home. But Betsy's loss... and Tristan's too, there was no warning and the grief was like a double-edged sword. I had to maintain composure around my family and friends, as it's the male way. I wasn't allowed to openly cry and grieve, and I didn't—except when I was alone.

But seeing Audrina curled up on the floor, banging her fists, well, I understood that kinda pain. In its purest form.

I hunched down on my heels, keeping a safe distance from the flying fists. She needed to let it out, but she didn't need to be alone. Finally, the hammering stopped, and she curled into herself.

"Audrina, it's okay."

Her great big sobs rendered her speech incomprehensible, but hearing that kind of soul-gutting pain, triggered a lot of flashbacks to a darker time in my life.

"Come on."

I scooped her up and she wrapped her delicate arms around my neck. She'd probably prefer to walk herself in, but I doubted she had the strength. I opened the door, and with the toe of my boot, held it open while I squeezed the two of us into her living room.

I set her down on the couch and kicked off my boots. Her house was no barn, and I wasn't going to take the chances of scuffing up her hardwood. Brushing the hair off her reddened face, I stroked her cheeks. Finding the right words to say was awful.

So many had been said to me at Betsy and Tristan's funeral, and in the days, weeks and months following. They all meant well, but they were all the same.

Call me if you need anything.

We're here for you.

We're sorry.

She's in a better place.

Her job on Earth was done.

At least she's not suffering.

God will take good care of both of them.

Yeah? And what about me? I'd been preparing to take care of them. I had done all the weird midnight cravings, and I never once complained about it. I enjoyed taking care of her every whim and desire; she was growing our baby after all. We'd painted the nursery, and I built the cradle for our room. Just that day, I had finished sanding it.

But no one reaches out in grief and asks for anything, at least I didn't. I wanted the two things I'd never have again.

Just like Audrina.

"It's not your fault." No matter what she thought, she did not cause Michael's death.

I took in the crumpled form before me. God, she was beautiful, even with the blank expression robbing her emotions. What I wouldn't give to see that smile of hers cross her face.

It'll take time. Lots of it.

And I can wait.

It took years to get over Betsy and Tristan's loss, and even longer to figure out when I was ready for the feminine touch and warmth. And not the well-intended contact from friends and family, but the kind that grows within your heart; that's what I wanted. And I was sure I'd found it in Audrina.

God, she was so unexpectedly different than Betsy. Audrina was a take charge kind of person; a leader not a follower. Tenacious to the core, she often pushed aside her own needs to care for others, her brother at the very top of that list. I adored everything about her.

"What do you need?" I asked gently.

Her eyes were closed, but she didn't seem to be sleeping.

"I don't know." She moved beside me and sighed.

I rubbed her arm. "You just let me know. Whatever you need, whenever you need it." I had no issues being her errand boy or her chef or house cleaner.

"Thanks." She turned her head away and looked to the outside. "If you don't mind, I think I just want to be alone for a while."

"Want me to grab supper? Give you some peace and quiet?"

She shook her head. "Not tonight. I need to be alone. Completely alone. Every night this week, you've been here, or Melody, or Niall, and as lovely as that is, I need to be here by myself. I did it before he moved in, I can do it again."

"You're sure?"

I didn't agree leaving her alone was the best thing, but I needed to trust in her. After all, she knew herself better than I did. However, I could text her later. Just because she didn't want me here in the physical sense didn't mean I couldn't check in with her.

"Absolutely." She said it with such conviction there was no way to doubt it.

"Okay then." I rose and slipped my boots back on.

She followed me to the door and held the inside door open. "Thank you. For respecting my wish."

"I'll talk to you later?"

She shrugged. "Maybe."

I cocked my head to the side. "Maybe?"

Her chin tucked into her chest and her hair fell across her shoulders. "I can't do this right now. I can't start a relationship when my heart is in a million pieces. I don't have the strength to be something I'm not. Please don't make me."

"Audrina," I said, trying hard to keep the desperation out of my voice. "I'm not expecting anything more from you than who you are."

"That's the thing, I don't know who I am any more. I used to be a daughter. I used to be a sister, and now I'm none of those things."

My finger found the sweet spot under her chin, and I tipped up her head to search her eyes. The irises had a greenish hue to them, and the white of her eyes had pinked up. "You are all of those things. That's never changed."

"But it has." A hitch caught her voice. "I'm sorry. I can't do this." She put her hand on my chest and stretched out her arm with a push.

"It's the grief talking. I know, I've been there."

"Please, don't try to change my mind. I need my space." Her head shook from side to side. It was tiny, but it was there. "I'm sorry, but you have to go."

"Audrina." I stepped out onto the front porch and watched as the door closed, cutting me off from the one I was ready to give my heart to.

# # #

"You finished it?" I stood beside the box Mom had set across the bench at the family table.

"Just last night. Have a peek." She skittered around the kitchen, no doubt putting out a variety of snack food.

Julia and Corbin were on their way over with the girlies.

The box was heavy in my hands as I transferred it to the floor and lifted the lid. Securing the fabric in my hands, I hauled out the homemade quilt and spread it across the bench seat to get a better look at it.

"Oh, mom, it's lovely."

"It wasn't that hard."

"What's that?" Julia's peppy voice echoed in the large space. She walked over and immediately ran her hands down the length.

"A quilt made from Michael's t-shirts."

I had attempted to stitch two shirts together, but I didn't make the straightest lines. Some of the pieces had wiggly lines between, but Mom said it gave it personality. Well, there was a ton of personality after I finished putting five of the shirts together. You'd think by then I'd have figured it out, well, you'd be wrong. This was no fence building, or deck project. The detailing on this needed to be more perfect. Thankfully, Mom swooped in to save the day.

Julia stepped back and checked out the blanket as a whole. "Did you do this?"

"Most of it."

Sewing had been so far out of my comfort zone, but I couldn't let all those clothes go to waste. That night, the night she was getting rid of the bags of clothing, I took them home first and kept all the t-shirts before donating the rest to our church youth group. A couple shirts I remembered him wearing, and the one with the paint stains was in the first row. I hoped it brought back happy memories.

Julia nodded. "It's nice but huge."

"Yeah, I got a little carried away."

There were so many, it was hard to narrow it down. I selected fifteen of Michael's shirts and cutting out the squares from the front and the back—it made a nice checkerboard type pattern.

"Either that or you were expecting it to cover the two of you." She wiggled her eyebrows and gave me a friendly punch to the shoulder. Sibling or not, she was still a girl and she knew I've never smack her back.

"I've seen her–" And I stopped myself before I said something more that would ensure a good deal of ribbing. "She has a queen-sized bed. I wanted it to fit." I wanted her to feel Michael giving her a hug and reminding her she's never alone.

"Oh, it'll fit." She turned her back and headed over to Mom. "I'm going to go run through the maze. Can you keep an eye on the girlies?" Her finger pointed out to the backyard.

They were happily bouncing on the trampoline.

"Corbin's just tinkering with something on the car."

"Yeah, go ahead." Mom walked over and held up one end of the huge quilt. "You did a great job, Chadwick. I'm sure she'll love it."

I gave it another once over. "I hope so."

"Have you heard from her?"

"Not really."

Mom grabbed the other end and together we folded it up and set it back into the box. "Not at all?"

"She's replied to a few of my texts, but that's about it."

"She needs a bit of time still."

"It's been two weeks, Mom." I pushed the box off to the side and sulked down onto the bench.

A tsking came with her words. "Need I remind you, it was months before you came out of your shell." She sat across from me.

"That's different."

245

"Not really. From what you told us, and what Meredith said, she was quite devoted to her brother, and truly, her whole world revolved around him and his needs. I say her taking a couple of weeks to return is hardly unexpected. She's had him in her life for what was it, twenty-two years? That doesn't fade within a couple of weeks. Her hollowness will last a long time."

She was right, and I knew it.

"Did you respond to requests from anyone to go out after Betsy and Tristan?"

I hung my head. "You know I didn't."

"Exactly. I'm sure she appreciates your check-ins, even if she doesn't have the heart to do much about them."

"Oh, he's checking in all right." Corbin's voice carried across the kitchen.

I shook my head and narrowed my eyes. He'd better keep his mouth closed.

"He's sent her flowers a couple of times, and he's checked on her at work. And had us check on her too."

Mom glared in my direction and shook a finger. "Chadwick."

"I just needed confirmation she was functioning, that's all." I could've killed Corbin. That was supposed to be private.

Laughing, he sat beside me. "It's innocent. Mostly. We've never sat in her section though. Either she didn't know we're there, or she ignored him." He smacked me across the shoulders. "Ain't that right?"

"I'm hoping she just didn't know we were there." Otherwise, it's devastating to think she'd be ignoring us. "But she acts so robotic. And her friend, Niall, he won't tell me much."

"You've asked?" Corbin gave me a questioning look.

"Just once. He knows who I am though, so it's not like I'm some crazy stalker."

All he'd share was how she came to work as scheduled, did her job, and went home. Niall had lunch with her a few times, but she didn't speak much. I worried for her.

"Dude, you need to let up. If she wanted you as more than a texting buddy, she would've said something by now."

"Not necessarily." My mother's voice had all the warmth of a homemade apple pie, but I wasn't biting.

"Anyway, I'm not anxious to discuss the lack of reciprocation with you both. If you'll excuse me." I grabbed the box as I had plans to deliver the package soon. I just didn't know when, or how.

Chapter Twenty-Five

The air was getting colder, and our brief autumn had come to pass. That's how it was here – the season was over in less than three weeks. It didn't matter if the Autumn Equinox was two days away and we were technically still in summer. Being this far north, it was over. And the way the breeze blew with a little more zest to it, I shuddered to think how bad the upcoming winter was going to be.

With the heaviest blanket I could find, I made my way out to the porch swing. It had become my most favourite place to relax. There, I listened to the birds, and sometimes if I was really paying attention, the little bird from the day of the funeral, which I discovered was a Red-breasted Nuthatch, always came by. I'd done my research and learned most will fly south for the winter unless they had a steady supply of nuts and seeds and a shelter to call home. So, I made good on keeping the bird feeder full.

Seeing the bird reminded me of Michael, and I nicknamed him my little Michael-bird. It was crazy, and probably something I should discuss with my mental health expert but still. It kept coming around, and usually hopped along the deck rail. It never seemed frightened of me.

Chad parked his truck out front. After weeks of texting back and forth, I agreed it was time for him to pop by for a visit. Despite needing the distance, which he respected, I'd really grown to miss him.

"Hey," I said, tucking my socked feet under the blanket.

"Hey." He ambled over and motioned to sit beside me, moving a pillow out of the way.

Over the past few weeks, the swing had become my sanctuary, and by the addition of big fluffy pillows, it allowed me to sway and stay curled until it was time for bed.

"Thanks for having me over."

"It's all good."

"How's work going?" He tipped his hat back.

It was dark on the porch, and hard to see directly into his eyes.

Candles or a string of lights to brighten the space would be ideal and I made a mental note to add it to my list of things to do. Oh, where were we? Work. Right.

"It's easier than I expected moving into the management role. I'm not on the floor as often." I shifted a little and the swing moved. "I'm sure one time I saw you and Batman there, but I got busy behind the scenes and when I came out, you were gone."

"I hope you didn't think I was stalking you."

"Never crossed my mind, in fact, it was nice to see a familiar face."

The air was getting colder by the moment. We both sat there, neither of us speaking. No sounds. Just the creaking of the cold chains suspending the swing rubbing each other the wrong way.

I picked at the fray around the edges of the blanket. It used to be so easy to hang out with him. Now it felt forced and awkward, and I wasn't sure what to say or do. Most definitely I didn't want to talk about work or how I was coping. I'd talked enough with the shrink Niall had suggested. She suggested to start by having friends over and trying to pick up where I thought my life had stalled. But where do you start when you're empty and alone? I shivered.

"Are you getting cold?"

"I'm always cold lately."

"You should head inside where it's warmer."

"Nah, I like it out here. This is a beautiful deck and a wonderful swing. It gives me a great view of the bird house and bird feeder." Something akin to a smile worked its way across my face, it wasn't as large but was bigger than nothing. However, it was dark now, the sun having set before Chad's arrival, and I doubted he saw it.

"That being the case, I have something for you. Can I give it to you?"

"Sure." It was a rare day indeed when I got a present, and the thought of it warmed me up a bit.

Chad moved across the deck and down the stairs at a good clip and walked over to the back of his truck. He opened the end gate and pulled out a big box. It looked too big to fit under the box cover. With the great big package in his hands, he came back onto the deck, stooping down to set the box on the floor.

"Can I turn on a light?"

"Sure."

It wasn't the nicest of porch lights, but it faintly did its job.

"Go ahead open it."

"Okay."

I tore the bow off the top and pulled up on the edges of the lid while peering in.

What the...? Michael's t-shirt, the one he wore when he painted the bird feeder, stared up at me.

"How?" I reached in and pulled out the rest, standing when

I couldn't hold it all up. It had a serious weight to it, and I couldn't get it all out of the box. Each square was one of Michael's shirts. "Oh… wow! I thought you donated these."

He tipped his head. "Most of them, yes. But I kept some, especially the ones I remember him wearing, and turned them into a quilt. A big quilt."

"It's … wow. I don't know what to say."

I ran my hand over them, flashes of buying them sparking in my head. He didn't have many shirts when he moved in, so we went shopping at Wally World. He wasn't interested in the regular shirts, he preferred the graphic print ones, even if he didn't know what Zelda was, or who was Captain America, those were the ones he wanted. And now they were here beneath my palm.

"Thank you." Tears built up fast. "It's lovely."

Chad held the blanket, and I grabbed at the bottom to see which other shirts he'd picked out of the bag. A whiff of cologne that could only belong to Chad tickled my nose, and as I ran my hand over the bottom, I inhaled deeply. Lingering within the layers was a hint of Michael.

I blinked away the blurriness and swallowed down the lump in my throat. There was a music shirt, and the shirt I'd picked up for him when we took a drive to Jasper a couple years back. It was a pun with a deer saying he'd fight with his 'bear hands'. He was opposing a bear who said, 'oh deer'. It had made me giggle, and Michael said he wanted it. It still had the same effect on me.

"I don't know what to say. Thank you." I sat down and pulled it over my lap. The weight of it was comforting, and I tucked it all around me.

Chad slid into the vacancy beside me and rocked the swing with a gentle push off from his feet. It had been a long time since I'd felt a flicker of happiness. He placed his arm around the back of the swing, almost like an invitation to snuggle in closer.

I shook my head and stayed in my spot. "I can't. Sorry." My hands ran over the shirts. "This isn't a gift ..." The words didn't want to come out, so I forced them. "With strings?"

"Oh, heavens no."

Relief blanketed me faster than ever.

"This I made for you because I like you. A lot. And I wanted you to have something to always remember Michael by."

I went to open my mouth but stopped.

"Yes, I know you have these other things..." He waved about, pointing to the frayed blanket hanging on the back of the swing. "But one more never hurt."

No, it didn't. This one would be with me always. It was easy to move, unlike the swing which was part of the house, and the feeder and bird house which also belonged.

"Thank you. I really love it, Chad."

He shifted in his seat and clasped his hands on his lap. "I'm trying to give you the space I think you need and yet, at the same time, trying to make sure you're not going through this alone. But I'm lost somewhere in the middle."

I dropped my gaze to the blanket and ran my fingers over a couple of flecks of paint.

"But I don't know what you want, so it makes it tricky to move forward."

"I know what I want, but I don't know how to make it work. The capacity to be more than what I am right now is overwhelming. I can't be a girlfriend when I haven't figured out who I am." Life had handed me lemons and I still hadn't figured out how to make lemonade.

His lip curled down in a sad smile. "I get that, but here's the thing, time doesn't wait for anyone. It does what it wants, when it wants." A quick shift and the swing moved with a bit more force. "I certainly didn't want Betsy to die, and I never dreamed I'd lose a child. Our pregnancy was a surprise since we were going to wait another couple of years before starting a family. We weren't financially ready yet. But fate intervened, and I've never regretted that."

An achiness for his hurt cozied up beside my own. "What are you saying?"

"It's simple. Sometimes, waiting for the perfect moment for all the stars to align, or the signs to line up, or whatever it is you are waiting for, never happens, and by time you figure that out, it's too late – the moment had passed by and you're never able to reclaim it." His long legs kicked at the rug near the door. "I was most certainly not ready for a baby, and even though it's what did Betsy in, I'm no longer gutted by the whole thing. Because for those 43 hours, I was a dad. And those were the most amazing moments in my life."

A lump formed in the back of my throat, and I forced it down. "So, you're saying if I don't act now and be with you, that it might never happen?" I wasn't a fan of ultimatums and being told what I should and shouldn't do.

"I don't know." He shrugged. "I enjoy being with you, I've never hidden that. You're so different than Betsy, I find it intriguing. And as much as I love all these unexpected moments with you, I can't wait forever for you to decide you're interested in finding more moments with me."

"Are you telling me I have a deadline?" I narrowed my eyes.

"No, but sometimes it's worth it to go with your gut." He raised an eyebrow. "I've loved every moment with you, the good and the sad. You need to trust in your heart, Audrina. It'll never lead you astray."

"I no longer have a heart, I left it behind at the hospital," I said as sadness broke through my voice. "I have nothing else to give you or anyone else who happens to walk into my life, and I won't apologise for that. But if you are going to rush me into something I'm not ready for, then things will *never* work out between us."

Hurt and disappointment lingered on his face long enough to announce clearly how I'd said too much. He rose, his heavy footsteps scratching over the surface of the deck as he grabbed his cowboy hat and placed it on his head. "You have plenty to live for and you are not as alone as you think. And I'm not trying to pressure you into anything. I'm trying to be the safety net I think you need."

"I don't need anyone or anything."

"That's a sorry way to live. A very sad existence indeed because everyone needs someone." With a tip of his hat, he retreated and made his way over to his truck.

I grabbed the blanket and stormed indoors, plunging the porch into darkness as I locked the door and flicked off the lights.

Damn it, who did he think he was? He thought after working with me for a few weeks that he knew me? He's wrong. Dead wrong. I had no one.

No father.

No best friend nor boyfriend.

No mother.

And now, no brother.

Maybe to him it *was* a sad existence, but it was my life.

My heart, although broken and hollow, still beat, and I placed my hand over my chest to prove it. Beneath my fingers, it plucked along, one pump at a time. But it was no where near capable of loving another. That much I knew. Too many scars lined it, reminding me of the hurt and pain.

Chad. He tried and maybe down the road... It ached to think of the sadness dripping from him as he walked off my porch, but it was better this way. By his own admission, he'd taken a long time to heal, and I didn't need him to come down to my level when he'd worked so hard to overcome his own void.

Maybe that's all I needed—time and more of it. Wasn't that the expression? Time healed all wounds.

Well, maybe not all. There was still one wound time hadn't fixed.

After a quick search, I found my phone laying across my bed, and I sat beside it. The phone flipped over repeatedly as my mind made sense of what my plan was, trying to figure out if in the grand scheme of things, it was worth it. Had there been enough time?

It didn't take long for the pros to win out, and my fingers to dial the number.

Chapter Twenty-Six

J'd never felt more nervous in my life. I sat in the tiny café in a worn-out wing back chair, a jazzy number playing on the overhead speakers. A rich aroma of coffee and steamed sweetened drinks permeated my senses, making me wish I'd ordered a macchiato as opposed to the peppermint tea I held between my hands. My stomach was in knots, and I figured this was the best way to soothe it. I was about to ask for forgiveness about an affair I didn't even know I'd been a part of. However, it was time to step up and be the bigger person.

Chad's thoughts still echoed in my head; how not needing anyone was a sorry way to live. It had been a week, and I couldn't get the words to vacate my brain. I didn't want a sad existence, I wanted everything I'd put on hold. A career. A boyfriend, and I hoped after the coffee meeting, maybe I'd have my best friend back, at least in a form that was more friendly and less hostile.

The bells on the door rang and a tall, slender blonde entered the establishment and locked eyes with me. "Let me grab a drink."

Katrina walked past me to the counter. If things hadn't changed, she still enjoyed a grande iced cinnamon dolce latte, but I wasn't about to make assumptions.

A minute later, she shrugged out of her coat and hung it on the nearby coat rack, water droplets creating a small puddle. The rain hadn't let up for a few days, and I felt as though I were drowning. I missed the sunshine.

She leaned back into her red chair and crossed her legs. "What's up?"

"Thank you for coming." I ran my thumb around the rim of the cup, letting the heat warm up my nearly frozen hands. Cold feet syndrome didn't just affect feet. My gaze moved from the brown liquid up to her green eyes where a lot of anger sat, along with curiosity. I inhaled sharply. "Ever since Michael's passing, I've been re-evaluating my life, and trying to fix the wrongs."

"Before you begin…" She inched herself closer, a hint of cinnamon on her breath from her latte. "I'm so sorry about Michael. I needed to tell you that in person. It just didn't seem sincere over the phone, besides you didn't really seem to be listening anyway."

I remembered her calling before the service, but if she said more than four words, I forgot the rest. "Thanks." A burgeoning ball of sadness lodged itself in my throat.

"I would've come to the funeral, but I was stuck in a conference in Vancouver I couldn't get away from."

I shook my head. "It's all good. Nothing you could've done anyway."

As it was, the day of his service was a grey, misty blur. All I remembered was the little blue bird who perched on my window ledge.

"You weren't responsible, you know."

My vision focused on her razor sharp.

"I read the hospital records."

"You got them?"

Crying to Niall one night over how Michael's death was because of my failure to properly care for him, he suggested I contact the hospital to get his records. Since I was the legal guardian, it was fairly easy. All I had to do was pay a small admin fee and have the records sent to a doctor. Katrina's name was the first doctor I thought of. A blossom of hope welled up inside me with her comment.

"There was absolutely nothing you could've done. His diseases had progressed rapidly at the end, and it was a combination of them ending his life."

Tears prinkled, and I gripped the mug of tea a little tighter. "Thank you."

"The doctors did what they could do, but there wasn't anything they could do either."

"So my second opinion…"

"Wouldn't have changed a thing." Katrina reached for my hand and gave it a squeeze. "And probably would've taken away those last few minutes you did get with him. The nurses report said you practically crawled into bed with him."

I tried. The suffocating feeling tightened in my throat. "Did he suffer?"

"Not in the hospital, no. His final hours were peaceful."

Although it should've made me feel better, it didn't. Just because he wasn't suffering at the hospital didn't mean he wasn't in pain at our house. The dull ache started spreading the length of my body again.

"Audrina, you did the best you could. He loved and worshipped you. I'm positive, you just being there with him these final months were the best of his life."

I looked into her eyes and gave her a weak nod.

"And I'd never lie about that." One thing I admired about Katrina, even if it sometimes came as a blow was her honesty.

"Thank you. I appreciate you saying that. Michael was the world to me."

"I know." She leaned back in her chair. "How have you been coping since?"

"Are you asking me as a professional?" Because I'd had enough of answering that.

"No." A smile firmly plastered onto her face, pushing the apples of her cheeks up nice and high. "As a concerned..." she breathed out, "friend." She reached for her drink and took a long sip.

I wanted to press her for more information on what changed since she hadn't acted like a friend over the past nine months, and then I spotted the reason on her finger. A stunning solitaire. "You're engaged?" Of course, love would soften her.

"Yeah. Just last week."

"To Marc?" I shook my head a little hoping it wasn't him; how they hadn't made up and took their relationship further.

The secret guy I'd been seeing. The one who begged me to keep our fling secretive. Apparently, Marc had done the same with Katrina as I later found out. It was her discovery of us together that ended our friendship. She refused to understand she was just as guilty since she'd been his secret mistress as well.

"Oh, god no. You think I'd give that rat-bastard anymore of my time? After you whimpered off, I told him where to go and how to get there." She laughed and tipped her head back in her easy going way. She wasn't holding on to the tension about the situation like I was.

"If that's what you did, why did you blow me off? I tried repeatedly to get in touch with you and explain things."

She sighed, a great big heavy sigh and rolled the bottom of her latte around in little circles. "Truthfully?"

"It's what you're good at."

"I was so embarrassed." Her chin tucked into her chest, and her gaze fell away.

I too, had been greatly embarrassed, but I kept my lips shut. For far too long I'd been hoping to hear her side of the story, and honestly, it made me feel better she'd at least held some shame over her part in the friendship dissolving.

She tipped her head and looked at the ceiling. "I mean, can you imagine? I was the valedictorian in high school, the one who completed high school a year early, I was at the top of my class in med school, and had several prestigious schools seek me out, so I'm smart."

Internally I rolled my eyes. Prestigious? Really? I wasn't sure the U of A ranked in the top ten best schools ever, but I let it go. I was finally getting somewhere with her explanation.

Katrina carried on. "If I'm so smart, how did I get roped into a secret relationship for so long? How did I not see what was going on? I was stupid."

"Hey," I said offended. "I didn't see it either. His story was believable. His schedule conflicted with mine aside from that one night a week. Besides, he always texted me during the day from work. It had felt real."

It really had. We had plans to go public in the new year.

She snorted. "Yeah. It was work all right. Keeping us all thinking we were his one and only. Jackass had a girl for each night of the week."

When Marc confessed, I learned I was the Wicked Wednesday girl, and Katrina had been the Friday Night Fling.

I pushed back a little in my chair and wavered on what I to say next. There was nothing to stop me from speaking my mind since that had been the reason to contact her in the first place. Only now, the tables were flipped. I wasn't going to apologise.

"So, your embarrassment, that's what kept us apart?"

She gave me a slow, sad nod.

"I was in the same boat as you. I'd been roped in, I fell for him hook, line and sinker as well. We could've put each other back together instead of tearing each other apart."

Her gaze drifted away from our cosy spot in the coffee shop. "I know, and I'm sorry."

All these months it was simply embarrassment holding her from reaching out? Not anything less trivial? Not that she'd gone back to him and was now engaged. Or discovered she was pregnant, or something along those lines. It had been her wounded pride? I hadn't done anything wrong, and yet, before her admission, I'd been willing to accept the blame for our friendship deteriorating.

"You're sorry? That's big."

"What? Where do you get off?" She contorted her face into a confused state.

I shot myself forward in my chair, pushing the table between us toward her. "I'll tell you where I get off. At the next station, lady." Months of tamping down my emotions over the way Katrina had ended things between us without an explanation fired up to the surface. "Did you know I'd been worried these past few months thinking I had done or said something to put a wedge between us, only to find out it was you and your stupid pride? I felt horrible over what happened. Horrible. I worried about you and tried to find out how you were doing, and how you were getting over him. But you didn't care that I too had been wronged with Marc's indiscretions. Your biggest worry was how someone as smart as you claim to be made a stupid mistake. Well, I'm here to tell you your biggest mistake wasn't with Marc, it was with me. I was your friend, your best friend, and I tried hard after his big reveal to keep us together. But you, Katrina, you pushed us apart. I needed my best friend after that whole fiasco, and I really needed a friend's support after Michael." I reigned in the crack in my voice and snatched my tea off the table. "We're done. Since Michael has died, I have no need for your professional duties in my life and you

261

clearly don't value our friendship. Goodbye."

I squeezed the cup in my palm and deposited it into the waste can by the door. I had asked for a get together in hopes of reconnecting with my former best friend, but I'd been wrong. She wasn't my best friend. When the Marc thing blew up, only one friend stood by my side. Niall. And when Michael passed, two were there in heart and soul – Niall and Chad. Only thing was, I was no longer interested romantically in Niall, but along the way, he'd become my best friend.

The one I was really into, I'd pushed away like Katrina had pushed me away. Damn foolish pride.

Well, no more. Pride can kiss my ass. I knew what I wanted, I just needed to find the appropriate way to make it right with him.

Chapter Twenty-Seven

J wanted Chad. And I could make it work. It was important. He wasn't someone to slot into my life, he was the reason for the smile on my face as I recalled the sweet gestures and the way he let me be without me being alone. He had so much more going for him than Marc ever did.

But it was more than that. More than just schedules. Chad had seen me for who I was, a messed-up person who valued responsibility over enjoyment. Okay, valued was the wrong word, but it was close. He never walked away when I was drenched from having showered Michael and was frazzled over some problem. In fact, he went out of his way to work within the inch of space I allowed him into. And how does one apologise for keeping him at arm's length, and attempt to make it up?

I knew who I was. And it didn't come with a title like a daughter, or best friend or girlfriend. I was a person who wasn't afraid to stand on her own, who stood up for what I believed in, and who more than anything, wanted to be with Chad.

He'd been the one to gave me the push I needed, and it made me want him even more.

But how to tell him? Sure, I could just walk up to him and

say *hey, let's give this a go. I understand what you were trying to do,* but I didn't think it would go over well. Whatever I needed to do, it needed to be big, not just for him, but for me too. The problem was—what? What could I do to announce I was ready to make a leap of faith with him?

I could show up at his work. Nah, that was stupid.

I could send him a text and tell him how much I needed a screaming run. And as much as I did, I was pretty sure he wouldn't respond.

It needed to be something bigger. Something romantic and unexpected. However, I'd need to enlist in help for that as I'd never be able to pull it off. *Help.* The word hung in the air like a neon sign. What had Chad been saying all along? How there was nothing wrong in asking for help. And I was terrible at that. So that's what I needed to do.

But first, I needed a plan.

On the kitchen table sat a notepad. I wrote the word *moments* on the top piece of paper, since that was the word Chad said I should have more of. I liked it. It looked pretty in cursive. My pen made a few circles around it while ideas swirled inside my head. And each thought connected nicely to the thought preceding it. Yes… it could work. It could work very well.

# # #

A week later, in the early afternoon, I tried to hide my minor nervousness as I sat in Lynetta Lawton's kitchen. The sunlight brightened the space filled with a giant blue/grey reclaimed wooden table, large enough to sit ten people. A couple of white farm chairs lined the back wall on either side of a buffet hutch. Old pictures in black and white hung on the walls. One in particular was of an old barn, taken many decades ago. I'd passed by this barn on the walk in from the corn maze and it showed its age now. It was tipped heavily to the north, ready to crumble in a strong gust of wind. How long had the Lawtons had owned this piece of land, since nothing in my research yielded that information.

"So, Dearie, tell me more about your plan." Lynetta placed a cup of dark, steaming liquid in front of me.

The teacup was very quaint with red roses painted on it, and a gold rim above the vines. It resembled something you'd have at high tea with the Queen. A tray with a matching cream and sugar set, and a plate of fresh cookies with strawberry jam middles sat between us.

Meredith had provided the number, and I'd first contacted Mrs. Lawton earlier in the week. She seemed highly interested in meeting me in person to chat and work out the finer details. From the first moment I'd talked to her on the phone, she was easy to chat with. Being with her in person was even better. It was almost like I'd known her my entire life. She had a grandmother's warmth, and her soothing voice instantly put me at ease. I knew exactly where Meredith had got her gift. Apparently, it was a family gene.

"Well, Mrs. Lawton, I want to prove to your son that I can make a relationship work and how much I need to have him in my life." It filled my heart with joy to finally be able to share this and I could only imagine how my soul would sing when I told Chad the same thing.

"Hasn't he been already?"

My eyes fell to my tea, watching the cream swirl into the dark liquid. "He has, but only as far as I'd let him. It's hard to be…" I couldn't find the right word.

"Vulnerable?"

That was the word. "Yes," I said, softly.

"It's hard for everyone. I'm sure it was difficult for Chad to speak with you about his past."

"I suppose it was." I glanced in her direction.

The resemblance between them was remarkable – the same colour eyes, the shape of the top lip in how it curled into a smile. Her hair was as silver as a nickel, and yet, it suited her.

"Your son is very sweet."

"Yes, he is."

"You did a great job raising him."

A telltale flush spread over her cheeks and a sparkle danced on the edge of her lips. "Why thank you."

"I'm serious. He was so helpful in building the right deck for Michael, and I'm sure there were additional overages he did not make me aware of."

She nodded the same way Chad did. "I'm sure there were but that's my Chad. Don't you worry, Dearie. He has an endowment fund he pulls from thanks to Betsy, and he only ever wanted to use it on people who really needed it." A warm, soft hand wrapped around mine. "He must've seen something in you or your reasoning to dip into the money."

"Probably Michael."

"Probably you, and the way you cared for him." Her kind eyes turned downward. "I am deeply sorry for your loss."

My shoulders rolled inward and a heavy ached descended upon my chest. "Thank you."

"Chad shared with us about your powerful and unconditional love for your brother. He was taken in by it all; he's never seen the likes of it."

"But surely with all his siblings…"

"Of course, they would do anything for each other, and for that, I'm very proud, but to put aside everything for one person? Between you and me, I highly doubt it. They'd visit, but there would be a full-time nurse around, or two or three." She laughed. "You have a big heart."

"Thank you."

A soft hand wrapped around mine. "No wonder you and Chad connected. He feels the same way. Figured after Betsy, there'd never be another... But the way he talked about you. Well... a mother knows. A mother understands." She cocked her eyebrow and reached for a cookie, pushing the plate toward me. "Now let's hash out the details of your birthday surprise for my son because I can't wait to be a part of this."

Earlier in the week, when I'd first contacted her, she'd mentioned it was Chad's birthday. I didn't want to ruin anything and told her I'd find another night. My schedule was slowly changing; half my weekly shifts were nights as a waitress, the other half were days as a manager in training. But Mrs. Lawton refused, and figured the birthday celebration would be the most ideal time.

"I'll need a bit of help." I swallowed.

"Whatever you need, Dearie."

As I shared with her my extensive plans, she pointed out what couldn't work, and what I'd need to enlist in help from her other children, but otherwise she was totally onboard. Before she radioed over to her daughter Julia, she rose from the table and wrapped me in a comforting hug.

It was the nicest hug I'd had in a long time.

Chad's older sister, Julia, the one married to Batman, escorted me out to the maze to put it into motion. Peppy and bubbling with excitement, she reminded me of Rapunzel from Tangled, full of hope. She chattered the long walk down the winding driveway, while the picnic basket dangled from my arm, occasionally bumping into my hip when she got overly excited and misstepped.

Mrs. Lawton had generously allowed me to reheat the supper I'd made and tucked it into a heated pouch to keep it warm.

At my car, I grabbed a small blanket and threaded it through the handles. Double checking the bottle of bubbly was still nestled inside, I sighed. Our sunset meal was ready to go. My heart skipped a beat and nervous energy flooded through my veins, but I pushed it down. There was no doubt in my mind, this was what I wanted.

Julia snapped her fingers in front of me, a huge smile on her face. "Now, our last guest went through the gates about an hour ago, so there won't be any more guests coming through as we're closing early for Chad's birthday. Corbin and I will do a final walk through in thirty, so you'll hear chatter on the walkie talkies." The hand held crackled to life, and she dialled it to the right frequency, pushing it into my free hand. "Keep it on channel 2, that's the one you'll catch us on if the need arrives."

I followed her in through the main gate and took a sharp left into part two of the corn maze, matching her pace while she bustled through the rows of nine-foot tall dividers. Doing this nightly, she knew the place like the back of her hand.

"Almost there," she said, turning around a bend leading us back in the direction we came from.

It was hard to figure out where exactly in the maze I was. I kept up with her as she practically skipped along, making sure my focus stayed on not getting too far behind and actually getting lost. It was supposed to be a pretend lost, not the real deal.

"Voila, we've arrived."

And there was the bridge I first kissed him on; my heart knew then what my mind hadn't yet figured out.

"We'll send Chad around in about thirty minutes to help with the final walk through." She giggled as she spoke. We both knew it was a rouse to get him into this section. "I'll beep twice when he's nearby. Are you ready?"

I held the basket close. "A little nervous, to be honest."

"If you could sit with momma all afternoon and not cower,

this will be a walk in the park, sister." She pointed to the top of the bridge. "Up you go but stay low. If you get anxious, call me and I'll keep you company." She waved the walkie-talkie.

The fact she'd mentioned calling her twice and questioned my anxiety made me more nervous. Just how scary did the corn maze get at dusk? I wasn't sure I wanted to find out. However, I stepped up, my knuckles turning white as I wrapped them around the bannister.

On the second stair, I stopped climbing to admire the handiwork. It wasn't an overly ornate wooden bridge, but it was solid. Had Chad constructed it? My heart pounded within my chest as each thought turned to him. The bottom of the arch hovered just above the peaks of the corn rows; the last time I was here, there was still space under the bridge.

I can do this. I can be vulnerable. I want all my moments going forward to be with him.

"You'll be just fine," Julia said, once again waving the radio. "Just holler if you need me." She gave me a big hug and a gentle pat on the arm. "See you soon. Fireworks are at eight."

With a flash of her hand, she disappeared behind a towering corner of corn stalks.

And I was all alone, but in the physical sense only.

Glancing over the top of the bridge, the view was still remarkable. Golden shades of yellow and greens spanned the distance with the concession tent a long way away. The giddy sounds of children's laughter washed away in the breeze. The family house I'd hung out in the afternoon, appeared as a small square sitting on the edge of the horizon, all but lost if you didn't know where to look.

I set out the blanket and set up my idea of a romantic dinner and dessert, complete with two champagne flutes and plastic plates and cutlery. The food stayed in a thermal pouch, keeping it warm.

269

What's better than dining on spicy chicken and rice with the one you want to spend time with, all while watching the sun set? I checked on the bottle of bubbly. It was still cool. Confident the layout was as sweet and romantic as I could make it, I pulled out two jarred candles and set them in the middle. I dug through the basket, hunting for the lighter I was sure I'd tossed inside. It wasn't there. There would be no romantic candlelight dinner. *Damn.*

I sat on the stairs in frustration and waited. This moment was supposed to have been magical and full of hope, and I didn't even bring the most romantic part. How helpless was I now?

It was eerie sitting there, completely alone, in the middle of a corn field. Every few breaths, a slight breeze rustled over the maze and the hairs on the back of my neck stood at attention. Never mind what it did to the speed of my heart. I imagined how scary it would be in the dark, and how the Halloween Fright Night would be downright terrifying. It could be a lot of fun to visit it with Chad. I laughed at the crazy thought.

The crackle of the walkie-talkie by the picnic basket made me jump. Julia's voice rambled out co-ordinates that made zero sense to me. For all I understood, she was around the corner. However, the final walk through was in progress.

The sun inched its way to the horizon, changing the skies from golden to amber, the temperature cooling just enough to warrant a sweater which I slipped over my bare arms. My heart rhythm picked up speed with each passing moment, knowing Chad would've parked at the ranch house by now, helping his family close up shop so they could get the birthday festivities started. Apparently, each birthday was a big deal and the whole family got together for a full out BBQ and fireworks. From what Lynetta shared, it sounded really cool and something of a magnitude I couldn't comprehend.

Another crackle over the walkie-talkie, this time a man's

voice. "Alright, Chad's here. Time for a final walk through." I assumed it was Batman.

My heart skipped a beat, and my breath caught.

Showtime.

"Okay. We've got four walkers. Chad'll take six & seven, Corb's got one through three, Alex has four and five, and I'm bringing up the rear on eight through ten." Julia sounded exceptionally chipper.

I paced along the path in front of the bridge, making sure it stayed within visual range at all times. Nothing like getting lost in a maze, without a light, as dusk fell.

It didn't take long until voices radioed in announcing they were nearing the end of their double checking. Chad's voice echoed through, although he sounded very nearby without the radio. I climbed the stairs and sat cross legged on the bridge, the urge to jokingly yell out *help* squashed. It seemed like such a foolish thing to say. Besides my hands were shaking like a leaf and I wasn't sure I could speak.

My face basked in the final glow of the day and my ears stretched out into the distance. Telltale steps on the path announced his arrival before I saw him. My pulse accelerated to stratospheric levels as I turned to greet him.

Slowly he approached and radioed in. "Found someone. Give me a minute."

"Roger, he's got her," Batman said, a chuckle crackling through. "See you at the house, buddy."

He hooked the radio onto his belt buckle. "You're not supposed to be here," he said coolly, but a smile broke out across his face.

Damn he looked good; dark hair parted, skin golden. His button up shirt was loose at the top but tucked nicely into his jeans.

"Help?" I whispered, a laugh escaping me. "I've planned

this romantic dinner for an amazing guy, but my candle doesn't have a light which I'm afraid will ruin everything I'd had planned."

"All because of one unlit candle?"

"Two actually."

He pulled himself up onto the first step, a deep stare in my direction. After drinking me in, he gazed over my shoulder and checked out the layout I'd planned. He dug through his pocket, produced a lighter, and reached around me. With a quick flick, the candles began to glow inside the depths of the jar. "You did this all for a guy?"

I stood level with him. "I did. He's the best, and I was stupid before, and said some things in grief that I didn't mean. I wished I had a chance to tell him before I let him slip away."

Another crack in his façade spread across his face. "He's a lucky guy."

"If he'll take me back." A bubble formed at the back of my throat and my legs weakened. My words fell out before I had a chance to contain them. "You were right. It was a terrible way to live my life."

"That's not what I meant. I was upset and—"

"Shhh." I covered his kissable lips with my finger. "Let me finish."

I grabbed for the champagne. I needed do to something with my hands and unwrapped the wire but before it was completely free, the cork blasted off with a pop, falling into the corn maze a few feet away.

"Whoops," I said, my eyes getting bigger.

He stepped onto another stair, but his eyes didn't follow the champagne rocket. The muscles tightened in his neck and his shoulders tensed. "That's littering."

"I'll go find it." I pushed off from the bridge deck, my shirt ruffling in the breeze.

As he pulled himself up another step, he shook his head. "Don't bother. I'm sure there are worse things to find."

"Oh yeah?" I stood face to face with him, the distance between us still a disappointing arm's length.

"Yeah." A small smile played on his lips.

My eyes raked over him, and stared as the tension released from him, relaxing his shoulders. Maybe this would work out the way I'd hoped. I inhaled a slow, calculated breath. "I feel I should start with an apology."

"Okay," he said, but made no moves to stop me.

This was all on me. I set the bottle back down on the bridge deck.

"I'm sorry. For not believing in the possibility of us. For not listening to my heart." My chin tipped lower. "Michael's never coming back, I know that. I was living for him, and it's high time I start living for me. Besides, he'd be really pissed if I didn't do something more with my life."

"And now?" The hook of his finger tickled under my chin and brought it back up so we made eye contact.

"Now? I'm so ready to listen to whatever my heart tells me, because even if I didn't like what you said, underneath it all, you were right." My eyes scoured his, desperately searching for acceptance and hope. He was still like a statue, as if contemplating my words, so I carried on. "I'm ready to move on, be careless, and make as many moments with you as I can, starting with this..."

I tipped my head forward slightly and lifted my hands to cradle his face. The whiskers scratched against my palms, but oh they were so welcome. My lips parted, and I brushed them against his. When he didn't kiss me back, I pulled back and looked into his eyes.

"Are you sure that's what you really want?"

I was confused by his statement. Wasn't I standing here in

front of him declaring as much? My budding passion was slowly ebbing away. "I did a lot of work to get here. I had to enlist in your family to help make this as seamless as possible and–"

He looked over the horizon toward his parent's house. "So *that's* why Julia and Corbin insisted I do a walk through with them. I figured something was up, but I figured it was for something at the back of the house." He held my hand, his thumb caressing my knuckles.

The connection gave me hope. "Well, your mom helped me plan–"

"Wait… You've met my mom?" His eyes opened wide in surprise.

"Met her?" I laughed. "I've chatted with her on the phone and even had tea with her this afternoon. I've been out on the ranch since one. She's a lovely woman, and you're very lucky to have a kind and caring mother." I smiled broadly, proud of the effort I went through to prep for this. "She was totally on board and even gave us the small bottle of bubbly and flutes."

"Well, I'll be damned." He looked over my shoulder while giving my hand a squeeze. "You did this, for me?"

"I figured it would be a great way to end your birthday or start since I don't know what you've been up to all day. We could have a picnic dinner on this bridge, watch the sun set. Maybe afterwards, there could even be some kissing," I said with a wink. "Some heavy duty kissing with more moments thrown in for good measure."

"More moments," he whispered and brought his face closer to mine. "I'd like that. I'd like that a lot." With the softest touch, his lips sealed together with mine.

The kiss was the sweetest yet most passionate kiss I've ever had. It brought tingles to my toes, while making me feel lighter than air. When he wrapped his arms around my waist and pulled me close, I figured I was a goner. My heart belonged to Chad. It had from the moment I met him, it just took me a while to figure that out.

Epilogue

Seventeen months later

The fancy, cream-coloured envelope stood out like a sore thumb among a pile of liquor store flyers and catalogs. It sat on top, shimmering under the glow of the kitchen spotlights.

Chad waltzed over and gently placed his hands around my expanding belly. "What's with the wedding invite?"

It certainly looked the part, as it was too fancy to be tax forms though, which I was expecting, along with my separation papers.

"Not sure. It's from Westside."

It had been hard, after everything Westside did for me in the months following Michael's passing, but I gave notice of my last shift on New Year's Eve, just two months ago. Starting the new year off on a new foot, I started working at *Chad Lewandowski* as his business manager, having gained the experience after spending a solid fifteen months as Westside's manager. It just made sense for our surprising family expansion.

We only discovered the pregnancy when we were moving into our new house.

Chad and I both suspected my constant nausea was because

I was selling and moving out of the home I'd struggled to make perfect for Michael, and assumed I was having a hard time letting go, which I was. Even with an exact replica swing on our new front porch, I still had difficulty in moving on. Chad replaced the bird feeder and bird house, taking the originals and setting them up in eyesight from the swing, in an effort to make things better, but the nausea didn't improve.

After a quick visit to the doctor, a blood test had revealed the truth – I was five weeks along, and thanks to my wacky system, we never clued in until that moment.

The news freaked us out, more so Chad, who was hyper worried about everything. I wasn't allowed to stand on my feet for too long, and he made sure we went for daily walks, watched my nutrition, and monitored my stress levels.

But everything had been textbook. The baby was growing perfectly, no genetic anomalies either – not that we cared since I had plenty of experience with disabilities, we just wanted to be prepared.

Chad planted a quick kiss on my lips and led me over to the couch. "Let me rub your feet while you open the mail."

It was too hard to pass up a foot rub, so I plunked my butt into the sofa and popped my feet on his lap. I tore the envelope open and gave it a read.

"It's an invitation all right, but not too a wedding."

Chad found the sweet spot on the ball of my right foot, and pushed against it, releasing a wave of euphoria. I lost the will to speak with his touch.

"And?"

"Oh, sorry." I inhaled, feeling more relaxed with each knead. "Meghan is having a taste testing party for staff and former staff. She's opening another restaurant and is expanding the menu. She'd like to get everyone's opinion on the new dishes."

"That sounds interesting."

"Doesn't it?" I looked to the love of my life. "Should we go?"

Chad nodded. "I think it's best we do. It'll be fun."

"I wonder who will be there. Niall?"

"As if anyone would be able to keep him away." Chad chuckled.

But he was right. Even though Niall left, he was a frequent visitor to Westside, a VIP even. Yeah, he'd be there. My best friend wouldn't miss this event.

"We should get going."

"Aww, I was just getting started." Chad gave my foot another pass.

"Josephine is having us over for dinner. We should show up on time."

Josephine, or Joy as she was known around Westside, recently had a baby. Having zero experience with them, she figured it would be good practice to know how to hold them, but I think she was just thrilled with being a mom and having found the perfect guy for her.

"Let's go get some baby snuggles in." I rubbed my belly and my little one reciprocated with a kick. Under my breath I whispered, "That's my boy."

In a week we were going to find out the sex, although in my heart, I was pretty sure it was a boy. At least I hoped it was.

Sneak Peek of Serving Up Secrecy
—Chapter One

h, my throbbing head.

O The second I woke up with a killer headache, I knew I was in trouble. Big trouble. Plus, I was so hot. I lifted the blanket off me and welcomed the cool rush of air over my aching legs, and my body. Oh my god, why was I naked? Pushing myself up into a sitting position, I cradled my head between my hands and moaned. I'd deal with the nakedness in a moment.

"Are you okay?" An unrecognizable voice spoke from behind me on the bed.

Instantly I jumped off the mattress, panic filling me as I yanked the twisted sheet around me. "Who are you?"

"James, we met last night," the heavy, husky voice full of sleep said as he shuffled in bed.

I backed against the wall and fumbled my way through the dark, my hand rubbing against the rough wallpaper that had been touched by what? *Eww*... The thought of a recent undercover bust on the cleanliness of hotel rooms circulated in my brain as I managed my way. Rounding a corner, I kicked something soft in

279

the process. My hand patted along the wall for another corner where I remembered the bathroom was, and I inched my way in. locking the door.

What was going on?

The lights blinded me, and I groaned out in shock, shielding my eyes to drown out the intensity. At least I was in *my* hotel room, as my personal items were tucked neatly into my overnight case on the counter.

My head pounded, matching the speed of my racing heart and quick breaths. Again, I cradled it between my hands, the bedsheet puddling at my feet as my stomach soured and did a back flip. A second later, I buried my head into the toilet bowl, trying to expunge the toxins from my body.

Feeling perfectly drained, I braced my naked body against the cool bathroom counter, the terrible lighting doing zip to hide the ginormous bags under my eyes, ringed with dark, smudged mascara and eyeliner. My pale blonde hair which had looked magnificent when I left last night, now won the prize for the worst bed-head look. I shook my head in disgust and a bobby pin fell bouncing off the faux-marble counter top.

Grabbing one of the wrapped glasses, I cringed from the crackling as I pulled the plastic off. Even though it was protected, I still gave it a quick wash under the warm running water and filled it to the brim. It touched my lips, tasting stale and hotel-like, and laced with vomit. Yuck. I spit it into the sink, ensuring it rinsed down the drain.

A knock on the door. "Hey, Josephine, are you okay?"

No. I'm in a hotel room with a complete stranger.

But I took another swish of the clear liquid and spit again. "I'll be fine."

"You sure? You don't sound it?"

Did he hear me retching?

280

I searched the bathroom, looking for my phone but it wasn't there. I had no idea what time it was. It could be the middle of the night for all I knew.

"Hey," I called out, secretly hoping he still lingered on the other side of the door. "What time is it?"

A pause. "Eight forty-three."

"Okay, thanks."

I dug through my overnight bag and pulled out my toothbrush and paste. As the brush scraped and cleaned my teeth, I tried my best to recall how I got into this mess. My hangover was rank... just how much did I drink last night?

Last night. My cousin's wedding. The most beautiful bride ever married the man of her dreams. So regal and elegant, she had the entire ballroom in the palm of her hands. That's right – there was a ballroom involved. A big, royal production with fancy chandeliers and a live band. My cousin's fiancé—correction, husband—was partner in a prestigious law firm and could afford to have a lavish event.

Drinks were free, and very likely, my greatest undoing. The liquor flowed like a river, hard stuff too. At least that much I remembered. And the ballroom dance floor? I believe I was the one who was out there the most, dancing in my bare feet, the hem of my silver gown dusting the hardwood floors. Gawd, it was so fun.

Lights and music replayed like a film played in slo-mo. It was mesmerising. My arms wrapped around a handsome stranger's neck, his body moving in time with mine. Was that the same man in my hotel room? It was hard to tell in the dark of the room, but I sincerely hoped so.

A knock again. "Are you sure you're okay? You've been there a long time."

I hadn't booked a fancy hotel room as the standard room rate with the bare bones basics was all I could afford, which meant one bathroom. Perfect for just me. Maybe not the guy standing on the other side of the door though.

"Do you need in here?"

"I wouldn't mind."

"Gimme a sec." I re-wrapped the beige sheet around my body and yanked open the door.

Mr. Handsome covered his face with his free hand as the bright light washed over him. "Scuse me." He side-stepped me in the narrow space, a pair of tighty-whities hugging his fine form, leaving nothing to the imagination. A dark pair of pants hung off his toned arm.

Nice.

I averted my gaze when he spun around, his features shadowed from the Hollywood lighting in the bathroom.

"I'm meeting my buddies for breakfast in ten minutes in the restaurant downstairs. You're welcome to join us if you'd like," he said as he shut the bathroom door, plunging me back into darkness.

"I'm good, thanks."

It was bad enough to wake up next to a stranger. No way was I going to join him and his friends.

The light leaking out from under the door was all I needed to make myself a single cup of java in the tiny space. It reminded me of work with its little sink cut into a counter with barely enough space for the coffee machine. I ripped open the single serve packet, inhaling deeply. I needed the jolt to truly wake me up. Within a short minute, a steaming mugful of nasty coffee barely warmed my lips as I choked down the bitter flavour.

I shielded my eyes from the mess in the room, stepping on soft material I could only hope was clothing and kicking a glass container with my toes. The path to the window lasted forever.

Still dressed like the Statue of Liberty, I cracked open the dark, heavy curtains enough to let a stream of light wedge its way in. It was time to see what kind of disaster I created.

Scattered clothes, all mine as I looked around, accounted for the mess on the floor. My lace undies dangled from the corner of the tv and as I glanced at my ridiculous self, behind me I saw several used condom wrappers littered on the side table. Blonde hairs whipped me in the face as I spun around.

Several? Oh, dear God. Guess I really had a good time last night.

The bathroom door unlocked with a click.

"Mind if I make a cup of coffee?"

My eyes travelled over the mess in the room, spotting at least a half-dozen empty Heinekens and a couple of Palm Bays. I tightened my toga.

"Fill your boots. It doesn't taste very good." I wasn't about to face my indiscretion.

"Never is."

Curiosity about my guest winning any weak debate, I turned my head. He was out of sight, no doubt making the world's worst cup of coffee.

His voice smoldered as he spoke. "Sure you don't want to join me for breakfast?"

"Honestly, I'm good. My stomach is not so well." No sooner had I said it when it did another flip. Hiking up my makeshift night dress, I pushed past him into the bathroom, kicked the door closed and heaved again.

"Might make you feel better."

Exactly how much had I drank to feel this terrible? Wowsers.

"I feel bad leaving you like this. Maybe I should cancel."

"No, no, no" I said, the urgency in my voice. Last thing I needed was someone to take care of me. Especially someone I've known less than twelve hours. I spoke to the closed door. "I'll be fine, I think I've completely emptied it out now. Besides, I need to head home. I'm supposed to be at work by four."

Which gave me more than enough time to get home, it was an easy three-hour drive.

"You're sure?"

"Positive."

"Well, thanks for last night. I had a really good time."

I'll bet you did. Clearly, I must've too.

I'd let my inhibitions fly out the window and brought this man back to my room. But I stayed tight-lipped, leaning my wretched body against the counter.

"Can I call you?"

Why bother? It would never work.

"I don't live around here. I was just down for the weekend."

My home was three hours north in Edmonton, a place I'd lived all my life. I gave my pale face a rub, hoping it would perk up, and pinched some colour into my cheeks the way Grandma used to.

"I'll leave my number just in case." There was an edge of hopefulness in his tone. "Ciao for now, Josephine."

I nodded absently, knowing full well I wasn't going to make use of it. The less I knew of this guy the better. One-night stands were not my thing, so it was important to sweep this embarrassment under the rug. But I couldn't be rude about it.

"It was nice to have met you," I scrambled to remember his name. "James." I added when it hit me.

I pressed my ear to the door, listening. As soon as the main door latched shut, I tiptoed out of the bathroom. Relief covered me – I was alone.

Packing up my party dress and shoes, I tidied up the room to a decent standard, tossing the litter into a waste receptacle and stacking the used dishes by the sink. No hotel maid needed to know the shenanigans I was a part of, especially since the room was registered in my name.

I glanced quickly at the note he left on my pillow, seeing it as I remade the bed.

> *There once was a man named James*
> *Whose poetry jams were lames*
> *The girl he just met*
> *Was the cutest one yet*
> *So Cupid please take your aims.*
> *Last night was amazing.*
> *Feel better and call me.*
> *XOXO James*

I stared at the note, rereading it several times over. This James was a sweetie, but it wouldn't work. He lived here, I lived hours away. Besides, sleeping with a guy on the first night was not something I did. Last night was a drunken-fueled mistake and it was best to drop this from my memory like a bad dream. As I packed up my bag, the note called to me as if a neon arrow were pointing at it.

Bag in hand, I held it and debated. To keep it or not. My eyes scanned the words and without a final thought, I crumpled the note, and tossed it into the waste can.

Add SERVING UP SECRECY to your reading library today.

Dear Reader

I fell in love with Audrina and Michael, and loved the way the two interacted, and how seamlessly Chad wove himself into that. Their story was supposed to be a short one at a cap of 50K words, but they needed more of their story told. It's really a great love triangle, but not all points of it are of the romantic nature. I hope you enjoyed the second book of the Ladies of Westside – *Serving Up Devotion* as much as I enjoyed writing it. Now that you have read about Jade and Evanora, who are you excited to read more? Joy's? Meghan's?

As an author, it makes my day when someone shares their thoughts and gives me feedback on the characters you've invested your time with. It's because of early feedback on *Serving Up Innocence* that the rest of the stories came to be. My first beta readers wanted to know more about Evanora and Joy, and even Meghan, figuring because she's such a raging bitch, her story could be quite saucy. Share with me what you liked, what you loved, or even what you hated. I'd love to hear from you.

Contact me via email or via my website.

Finally, I need to ask you a favour. If you are so inclined, I'd love a review or a rating of *Serving Up Devotion*. It doesn't have to be long, even something as simple as "Loved it, looking forward to the next one" works. Reviews and ratings help me gain visibility and as I'm sure you can tell from my books, reviews are tough to come by. As a reader, you have the power to make or break a book, and your reviews are powerful to me. Thank you so much for spending time with me.

Yours,

H.M. Shander

Other Books by H.M. Shander

Duly Noted – book 1
That Summer – book 2
If You Say Yes – book 3
Serving Up Innocence
Serving Up Devotion
Serving Up Secrecy
Serving Up Hope
It All Began with a Note
It All Began with a Mai-Tai
It All Began with a Wedding
Whistler's Night
Noel
Dreamers in Cheshire Bay
Return to Cheshire Bay
Adrift in Cheshire Bay
Awake in Cheshire Bay
Christmas in Cheshire Bay
Journey to Cheshire Bay
Charmed in Cheshire Bay
Second Chances in Cheshire Bay
Unforgiven in Cheshire Bay
Flirty in Cheshire Bay
Messages & Mistletoe
Living La Vida Mocha

Acknowledgements

Gosh, it's hard to believe I am writing my seventh public thank you. Seventh! I'm in a perpetual state of shock. A million thanks to my family – Hubs, The Teen and Little Dude – and to my parents. Where would I be without your support and endless cheerleading? Thank you for the endless devotion you've given me to chase my dreams. For long walks when I needed to think, for seeing the beauty in the world around us when it doesn't feel like it and for always being who you are and standing up for what you believe in. Thank you for giving me time to sit and write while you played your games so I could make my daily word count. Thanks for all your help with signings (especially you my little PA – you are always out there smiling beside me and helping people pick out their swag.) Love you always.

To my wonderfully dedicated critique partner – Julie – Seriously, you are the sweetest. Every email from you is a gift and I know when I open it that I will have my work cut out for me, but in the best way possible. You are my writing rock and when the world beats on my literary world, you are there to point out the positives. I'm glad our relationship has evolved into one of strength and trust and most importantly of all – friendship. Thank you.

To my tribe of alpha and beta readers. Lacey, Emma, Jeannine, Mandy and Miranda and my five mystery readers at Indie Hub. Thank you from the bottom of my heart for all your comments and advice and wisdom and pointing out what didn't make sense and what needed to be expanded on. Thank you for falling in love with Audrina, Michael and Chad and seeing them through to the end.

To my cover designer Cassy – Great job! I had high hopes when we started on this journey and had a certain vision. You, with your brilliance and passion, captured it perfectly. I'm so thrilled we worked on this together, and I look forward to many more covers designed by you.

To my editor Irina – You had your work cut out for you. I appreciate your quick turnaround time and the back and forth with the comments, questions and suggestions. There was a lot of red, but the story is only better because of it.

If I missed you, it certainly wasn't intentional. I know I couldn't be where I am without the help of so many others. Thank you! And thank you for reading and making it all the way to the end. You all rock.

About the Author

H.M. Shander knows four languages—English, French, Sarcasm and ASL—and speaks two of them exceptionally well. Any guesses which two? She lives in the most beautiful city in Canada–Edmonton, AB, a big city with a small-town feel, where all her family live within a twenty-minute drive, although her parents are contemplating moving away. As much as she'd love the beach under a blanket of stars, this is her home.

A big time coffee addict, she prefers to start her day with a mug before attending to anything pressing, like driving the #momtaxi as she shuttles her kids off to school and various extracurricular activities. Secretly she loves it as when the vehicle is empty, it gives her time to think about what crazy things those characters will do next. She is a self-proclaimed nerd (and friends/family will back this up), revelling in all things science, however likes to be creative when there's time. Right brain, left brain? Both.

Did you know she once wanted to be a "Happy Clown" as she enjoys making people smile, but she's beyond terrified of scary clowns? How ever many different jobs she's worked, her favourite has been working as a birth doula and librarian, in addition to being a romance author. Because, let's be honest, who doesn't love falling in love?

No matter what happens in the day, there is beauty all around us. From the first light of sunrise to a rainbow in the sky or the chirp of a robin or the belly laugh of a child or the magical way the sun sets when the day is done.

You can follow her on Facebook, Twitter and Goodreads.

Thanks for reading– all the way to the very end.